The Seaforth Heiress

A NOVEL

Lady of the Last Prophecy

Inspired by the life of
Mary Elizabeth Frederica Mackenzie

Elizabeth Hutchison Bernard 11/2024

ELIZABETH HUTCHISON BERNARD

Black Rose Writing | Texas

The author grants the final approval for this literary material.

First printing

This is a work of fiction. Names, characters, businesses, places, events, and incidents are either the products of the author's imagination or used in a fictitious manner. Apart from well-known historical figures and events, any resemblance to actual persons, living or dead, or actual events is purely coincidental.

ISBN: 978-1-68513-476-1
LIBRARY OF CONGRESS CONTROL NUMBER: 2024934504
PUBLISHED BY BLACK ROSE WRITING
www.blackrosewriting.com

Printed in the United States of America
Suggested Retail Price (SRP) $22.95

The Seaforth Heiress is printed in Minion Pro

*As a planet-friendly publisher, Black Rose Writing does its best to eliminate unnecessary waste to reduce paper usage and energy costs, while never compromising the reading experience. As a result, the final word count vs. page count may not meet common expectations.

Cover design: Elizabeth C. Bernard
Cover images:
Illustration of Brahan Castle
© Courtesy of HES (Walter Severn Collection)

Photo of woman in a veil
nuevoimg © 123RF.com

To the Daughters of Scotia

Praise for *The Seaforth Heiress: Lady of the Last Prophecy*

"This second novel in Bernard's *Historic Women of the Highlands* series is rooted in historical sources (including the letters and diary of the real Mary Mackenzie) and brought to vivid life by the author's imagination and well paced prose. The poignant, highly dramatic family saga paints a detailed period portrait... A pleasantly engaging read for historical fiction fans." *–Kirkus Reviews*

"A gripping Regency adventure . . . [that] will resonate with readers of women's fiction and endear those who are fans of Penelope and Eloise in the *Bridgerton* series . . . If you're into historical fiction that immerses you in a very real past with captivating settings, make sure to add *The Seaforth Heiress* to your TBR pile." *–Independent Book Review*

"Mary Mackenzie's story is one of courage and determination in a time when women had few rights and no expectation of influencing their world. Ms. Bernard brings Clan Mackenzie's only female chief to full and intriguing life. Highly recommended!!" **–Linda Bennett Pennell, award-winning author of *The Last Dollar Princess* and *The American Countess* (*An American Heiress*, Books I & II)**

"The plot of this engaging and immersive historical work follows Mary Mackenzie, destined to be Clan Mackenzie's only female chief, as she grapples with her family's dark prophecy and her awakening conscience amidst colonial injustice and personal tragedy. Elizabeth Hutchison Bernard's vivid descriptive prose and meticulous research bring the historical setting to life in full living color, immersing readers in the complexities of [British] colonialism and [Highland] prophecy whilst delivering an authentic tale of empowerment. . . I would highly recommend to fans of historical dramas everywhere." **–K.C. Finn for *Readers' Favorite***

"The historical context, intertwined with the ancient prophecy of the Brahan Seer, creates a delicious tension . . . *The Seaforth Heiress* is an excellent work of historical fiction. It not only compels with romance and intrigue but also leaves a lingering impression about the consequences of choices, privilege, and the enduring human spirit." –**Rebecca Rosenberg, award-winning author of** *Champagne Widows* **and** *Madame Pommery*

"Mary Mackenzie, Clan Mackenzie's only female chief, must find the strength and courage to salvage her family's legacy against overwhelming odds. Inspired by true events, this novel is satisfying, rich, and memorable. Highly recommended!" –**Gail Ward Olmsted, best-selling author of** *Landscape of a Marriage: Central Park Was Only the Beginning* **and** *Katharine's Remarkable Road Trip*

"Bernard breathes life and spirit into Mary Mackenzie and the world she lived in. A sweeping and engaging tale of family, empire, and an ancient Scottish prophecy."–**Pamela Taylor, bestselling author of the** *Second Son Chronicles*

"Mary Mackenzie must outrun a deadly prophecy to become the Mackenzie Clan Chief. From Barbados to London to the Scottish Highlands, she fights for love, family, and independence. Historical readers will love this family saga tinged with Scottish lore." –**Kerry Chaput, award-winning author of the** *Defying the Crown* **series**

"An enchanting blend of historical fiction and adventure. Through sweeping legacies, Bernard transports the reader to different corners of the British Empire with detail, acumen and emotional tugs. Forevermore, Mary Mackenzie is heralded in her role as chieftain of her clan thanks to Bernard's masterful storytelling by delving into the complexities of human conscience and the inescapable ties of family history." –**Janis Robinson Daly, best-selling author of** *The Unlocked Path* **and** *The Path Beneath Her Feet* **(***The Path* **2-book series)**

"Finally, someone has produced a tale of one of the most fascinating characters in Clan Mackenzie lore, that of the heir to the line of Kintail, Lady Hood, Mary Mackenzie. Elizabeth Hutchison Bernard has accomplished this task in the most exceptional fashion. The reader is left wondering if in fact the Brahan Seer's prophecy was real after all." -**Jared Smart for the Clan Mackenzie Initiative (**<u>clanmackenzie.org</u>**) and host of The Clan Mackenzie Podcast**

The Seaforth Heiress

And thou, gentle Dame, who must bear, to thy grief, For thy clan and thy country the cares of a Chief, Whom brief rolling moons in six changes have left, Of thy husband, and father, and brethren, bereft; To thine ear of affection, how sad is the hail, That salutes thee the Heir of the line of Kintail!

From "Farewell to Mackenzie, High Chief of Kintail"
Walter Scott, 1815

PART I

CHAPTER ONE
BRITISH COLONY OF BARBADOS
JUNE 1803

Miss Mackenzie!"

I turned to see a young hooligan from the market running towards me, his grimy face streaked with sweat. It was another sweltering day on this hot, windy, and largely treeless island. I shielded my eyes from the sun's glare, watching as he approached. The lad looked familiar … Yes, he was the one I had seen only half an hour earlier, swiping tobacco from the cart of a plantation slave trying to better his lot with a bit of clandestine commerce. The boy, with his reddish hair and upturned nose, looked to be Irish. Probably descended from an early crop of indentured servants, now free and scattered amongst the meager white population of Barbados. Whatever the lad's name, I would have no reason to know it. But he recognized me, and not only because I was the British governor's daughter. To a believer in Celtic lore, I was a rare object of curiosity.

"I got somethin' fer ye, miss. Somethin' ye maybe want." Grinning, he held up a small white stone, smooth and round. His finger was strategically positioned over the center.

If he had thought to engage me in his foolish little prank, he would be sorely disappointed. Turning my back to him, I started up the hillside path that led to Pilgrim House, the sprawling three-story mansion provided by the Crown for its colonial governor and his family. It had never felt like home. I recalled how one of our neighbors back in Ross-shire had warned Father not to bring us here, calling Barbados "the white man's grave" with a climate ill-suited for Europeans and a host of exotic tropical diseases. It was two years since Mother, my five sisters, and I arrived, and all of us were still very much alive.

"Bet if ye look through this hole in the middle—"

I spun around, livid. The young scoundrel was taunting me! "There is not any such hole, and you know it well enough. Now off with you."

"But there is, miss. If ye just look … I can get me a shilling easy from anybody with a desire to see the future. But then … ye mightn't be wantin' to, eh?"

In a huff, I bent down and picked up a sharp rock, larger than the one in his hand. Throwing it as hard as I could, I watched with pleasure as it struck his kneecap, dead center. He cried out.

"Why'd ye do that?" he yelled, but I had already resumed my climb up the hillside. Mother would be furious if I was not ready for the arrival of our official guests from London. I would need time to change out of the simple loose frock I had worn to the marketplace and into something sufficiently elegant to create the impression that Barbados was a mecca for refined colonial living.

Reaching the crest of the long carriage lane in front of the house, I spared a moment to take in the property's privileged view. Pilgrim House sat atop one of the few elevations of any consequence on the tiny island, just over a mile from the pier in Bridgetown. As a busy port and seat of the British colonial government, the town had grown to a population of more than ten thousand and was always bustling. The reason Barbados was the brightest jewel in Britain's colonial crown, next to Jamaica, could be summed up in one word: sugarcane. Endless fields stretched across the three hundred square-mile island. Plantation owners, most of them English or Scots, made fortunes from it—and from the labor of many thousands of imported Africans, even while the British Parliament pretended to frown upon the slave trade. My father, as the Crown-appointed governor answering to the island Assembly, was uncomfortably caught in the middle.

"Mary, get yourself in here, child! Our company is expected in less than an hour."

Mother stood on the curved balcony above the front entrance to Pilgrim House. She wore a lovely high-waisted gown in a pastel floral pattern, a dress I had not seen before. But then, Mother was always ordering exquisite things from London—clothing, decorations for the house, culinary delicacies to impress political friends and enemies alike. Father, for his part, was a frequent importer of fine wines for his extensive collection, which required constant replenishment for occasions such as tonight's dinner. Even in this remote colonial outpost, high-ranking visitors from London expected all the amenities of the mother country. My parents considered it a matter of pride not to disappoint them.

"Where is your maid?" Mother's displeasure was apparent, even from where I stood below.

"She was tired halfway up and had to rest. I expect her in a minute." There was no way I could tell Mother that Sarah had lingered at the market, chatting with a young member of the island militia. She would be furious that I had been left on my own—as if I were not twenty and perfectly capable of walking home unaccompanied.

A few seconds later Sarah came running towards me, panting heavily, her face nearly as red as her flaming curls. I was relieved to see her, and that she had not made a liar of me, until I noticed her expression. Something was wrong. The first possibility that came to mind was that her new male acquaintance had made an improper advance. The island's militia were known as a rough and drunkenly lot, though the young man Sarah had befriended appeared rather more civilized.

Sarah was so out of breath she could hardly speak. "There's awful news. Another killing, even worse than the last."

A nauseous feeling toyed with my stomach. I glanced up at the balcony to see if Mother was still there, but she had gone inside. "Go on, tell me. What has happened?"

"Was one of the militia men that did it. From St. Michael's regiment."

"The militia!" I had already guessed that Sarah was about to relate the shocking details of yet another slave murder. We had heard of a gruesome one only the week before, a young African wounded and then buried alive. Such punishment, for disobedience or attempted escape, was usually meted out by the plantation owner or those who worked for him. Not the militia.

"Murdered a woman seven months with child and mother to six more. That fellow in the market, he saw it happen. No reason for it, he said. The militia man—name is Halls—was walking along and saw some Africans returning from their work in the fields. He called out, said he aimed to kill them. They thought it was all a joke and stepped aside to let him pass. But then"—she swiped at her eyes—"that beast, he took his bayonet and plunged it straight into the poor woman's belly. She dropped to the ground, died in an instant."

I stood silent. Before coming to Barbados, I had been oblivious to such horrors being committed by my own countrymen. I had known slavery existed in the colonies, but it was still something distant and unimaginable. Not any longer.

"My father must be told straight away." Such an act could not go unpunished, like all the other times. There must be a way to put a stop to such barbarity.

Yet hadn't Father been trying to do so since first setting foot in Barbados?

Hearing the roll and creak of wooden wheels on cobblestones, I turned to see Father's carriage, driven by our coachman Malcolm Ross, who was dressed in his finest livery. Perhaps the guests from London had arrived early. And me, in my plain white dress, my hair coming loose from its combs! I would have quickly disappeared into the house were I not preoccupied with matters more pressing than my appearance.

The carriage came to a halt. Ross jumped down from the box, opened the door, and Father stepped out. He was alone. His grim look made me think perhaps he already knew of the latest incident, but I could not yet ask him. Not unless he looked my way. My father was, for practical purposes, deaf, and had been since contracting scarlet fever at the age of twelve. Though he was adept at reading lips, family members usually employed hand signs to facilitate conversation with him. He would speak his reply, but given that his diction was somewhat slurred, those unaccustomed to it often found him difficult to understand.

I went to him and kissed his cheek, which elicited a distracted smile, before asking him whether he was aware of the unprovoked murder by a member of the island militia.

"I have dealt with it as best I can," Father said with a frown, shaking his head. "For the moment, the drunken scoundrel is confined. He ought to be hanged. But, of course, that is not the island law. The only penalty for murdering an African, for any reason or no reason, is a fine. A pittance."

"And you shall change that, Father. But, for now, something must be done to help her family. I was told she has six children."

"Mary, my dear Mary …" Father cupped my face in his hands. "Our neighbors are plantation owners, and they want no one meddling in their business. Especially the governor. You must know that by now. A bright girl like you."

I *did* know, but the truth was difficult to accept. Father had been at odds with the planters since the beginning of his appointment, and a large part of their animosity towards him had to do with his desire to hold white people accountable for the murders of Africans.

A distant thundering of hooves put me on alert. "Father, people are coming. Sounds like a great many of them."

He assumed an erect posture, smoothing his blue silk frock coat and straightening the high collar of his linen shirt. Father always looked impeccable, even under duress. "Go on inside," he said. "And tell your mother to stay there, too."

I looked around for Sarah. She had left, I assumed, to ready my toilette; I would require a good hour to prepare myself for company. But what if Father needed me? And besides, I wished to see what would happen next.

A dozen or so members of the island Assembly, all of them wealthy plantation owners, reined in their horses behind Father's carriage. At their head was Mr. Incer, the Assembly president, who sat atop a magnificent black stallion. He was a tall, well-built man, with steely grey eyes and a lean face weathered by sun and wind. From beneath his wide-brimmed hat, he barked at the others to remain in their saddles. Dismounting, he approached my father with long, determined strides, a horsewhip gripped in his leather-gloved hand.

"Lord Seaforth," he said curtly. He looked at me, standing beside my father, and nodded his acknowledgment. We had met several times before, at social events hosted by my parents for Assembly members and their families. "Miss Mackenzie, I have a message for your father. Tell him that we intend to release Mr. Halls from his confinement. There is no precedent in the law for him to be held."

Father, having read Mr. Incer's lips, had no need of a translation.

"I know all about precedents, Mr. Incer," said Father. "But under the circumstances—"

"Lord Seaforth, you are choosing to ignore the law. I suppose it should come as no surprise. You have made it your mission, from the day you arrived on our island, to usurp the authority of the Assembly and the militia's duly appointed colonels, and to ignore the legitimate concerns of those who create the wealth of this island for the benefit of the Crown you serve."

"You will have mayhem if the militia is not required to respect even the most basic principles of military conduct," Father retorted.

Mr. Incer sniffed contemptuously and pivoted to address me.

"If your father said what I think he said—"

I interrupted him mid-sentence. "Lord Seaforth has merely stated the obvious. Members of the militia have rules of conduct that must be upheld."

Mr. Incer turned back to Father. "The behavior of Mr. Halls is regrettable. But, while his actions apparently had no specific cause other than drunkenness and ill humor, there is no precedent in the law to detain him. Doing so can only call into question our established right to take whatever measures necessary for maintaining obedience and order among the slave population. I am aware, Governor, that you would like to turn any such action into a criminal offense. But let me assure you, sir, it will never come to pass on this island that a white man hangs for killing a Negro."

I felt Father's frustration as much as my own. And his humiliation. How dare Mr. Incer address the duly appointed governor, representative of the Crown, in such a manner! Neither did he show any respect for the fact that Father was, at least nominally, the militia commander. But titles are mere words. The Assembly had enacted legislation to maintain their control which, so far, my father had been unable to override.

Mr. Incer turned to his compatriots. "Anyone disagree with the sentiments I have conveyed to our honorable governor?"

The others muttered their assent with self-satisfied smiles.

"Very well, then. We will not take up any more of your valuable time, Lord Seaforth."

Turning on the heels of his polished riding boots, he sauntered back to his horse and was about to mount the impressive beast when I called out to him.

"Excuse me, sir, but how can you not care?"

He pivoted, regarding me with a look of astonishment. "I beg your pardon, Miss Mackenzie?"

"How can you not care that a senseless murder has been committed by one of your own? A man who shall receive no more than a slap on the wrist as punishment!"

His eyes narrowed. "What I care about, Miss Mackenzie, is neither yours to assume nor to judge."

"It is the right and obligation of every civilized person to condemn such acts in the strongest way possible. Common decency demands as much."

Mr. Incer's lip curled in a sneer. "Lord Seaforth, your daughter seems infected with the same misguided altruism as her father. I suggest you rein her in before she becomes an embarrassment."

Father placed a restraining hand on my arm. "We are done here," he said in a low voice. "Go on to the house, Mary."

I glared at Mr. Incer for a moment before obeying Father's tight-lipped order. By the time I reached the door, Mr. Incer and his band were heading down the lane towards Bridgetown.

·　　·　　·

I could always recognize Mother's tap on my door, gentle yet firm. Still in the middle of my toilette, I hoped she had not come to tell me our guests had arrived. But surely she would have sent one of the servants for such a simple purpose.

Without waiting for my reply, she entered the bedchamber. "I must speak with you, Mary. Privately," she added, glancing at Sarah. Though Mother was fond of Sarah, who had been a childhood playmate back in Ross-shire before entering our household service, she did not entirely approve of such familiarity as my lady's maid and I enjoyed.

"Of course, my lady." Sarah set down the curling tongs and hastily left the room, closing the door behind her. I remained sitting at my dressing table. In the mirror, I saw Mother's stern expression as she approached.

"Your father said that you remained outside when the men from the Assembly were here. And you spoke out of turn."

"I just thought that ..." Faltering, I tried to come up with an acceptable reason for my actions. But why must I? It irked me to think that if my two brothers were here, rather than at school in England, they would be encouraged to express their views despite a lack of knowledge or experience. I, on the other hand, must make excuses. "The men appeared so suddenly, there was no time for me to depart without appearing as though I were fleeing from them. Certainly that would have been impolite. And Mr. Incer's behavior towards Father was shameful. I had to say something."

Mother frowned. "It is not your place to be a party to official business between your father and the Assembly. You are too curious for your own good, as we have often discussed. If you continue to overstep the bounds of what is proper for a young lady in your position, I will have no choice but to place further restrictions on your comings and goings. Do you understand?"

"Yes, Mother."

It was simplest to agree, though Mother knew I would not be so easily tamed. When I was but ten, Father used to say that if I showed as much desire to behave like a good girl as I did to act like a big lad, he would be completely happy. But such a wish seemed not within my power to fulfill. I could no more change my temperament than Father could restore his lost hearing.

"Who are you entertaining tonight?" I asked, just to change the subject.

"Two representatives of the London Board of Customs, Mr. Joseph Clarke and Sir William Harrison. Oh yes—and Commodore Hood. If you promise to behave, you shall join us at the table."

Sir Samuel Hood, the naval commander stationed on the nearby Leeward Islands, had been a guest at our home twice before. The last time, I had felt his eyes upon me throughout the entire dinner.

"Thank you, Mother. But why are the customs officials visiting Barbados?"

"Your father has much business to discuss with them. He needs their support to enforce the restrictions he advocates on the island's trade with America. But, of course, that is not your concern," she added hastily. "Our job, darling daughter, is to be lovely and utterly charming." She smiled and patted my shoulder.

"And the commodore? Why was he invited?"

"He shares your father's desire to support the interests of our British merchants. And he is quite articulate."

I jumped to Father's defense. "If Father had full use of his hearing and speech, I am sure no one would be more persuasive than he."

"Certainly, Mary. You need not convince me. I have always believed in your father's abilities. He is a remarkable man and quite capable of managing the responsibilities of his position. But it is always nice to have helpers." She leaned forward to glimpse herself in the mirror. "You've said nothing about my new necklace."

Mother's gown had impressed me so greatly that I had failed to notice the dazzling sapphire necklace at her throat. I swiveled around to get a better look, suddenly recalling a conversation I had overheard just before we left Scotland for Barbados. It was between Father and our estate factor Mr. Fairbairn. Though I was not meant to know, Father had been persuaded to accept the governorship to help settle debts and avoid having to sell off parts of the family's Ross-shire estate. Judging from Mother's newly acquired jewels, the strategy must have proved successful.

"The necklace is stunning and goes perfectly with your new gown. You do look particularly well tonight, Mother."

"Looking well can be a challenge at this time of year," Mother replied with a wistful smile. "I keep hoping to adjust to the heat, but, apparently, I'm not meant for it. Thank goodness you have adapted so easily. I would almost think you've developed a fondness for the tropics."

"Not exactly." I was not one to complain but neither could I claim to be enamored of Barbados. When we first came here, I had been excited by the promise of a new adventure, but the intrigue wore off quickly. Whatever natural beauty there was on this remote colonial island had been devoured by commerce, and the stink of slavery hung over the land like a noxious fog. More and more, I longed for the brighter world I once knew. A world in which it was easier to convince myself of a power stronger than evil.

CHAPTER TWO

The ship bringing the London commissioners to Bridgetown did not arrive as expected. Consequently, our only guest for the evening was Sir Samuel Hood. After the distressing events of the afternoon, I wondered if Father might be relieved that the official visit was postponed and he could simply enjoy the company of Sir Samuel, whom he considered an ally—one of his very few since becoming governor of Barbados.

As the formal dining room was designed to accommodate much larger parties, tonight we were to eat in the family's private dining area. The table was set with Mother's gold dinner service that had been shipped from London along with her favorite cut-crystal glassware. With the sun's departure, a cooling sea breeze had found its way through the open French doors, which afforded a view into a lovely courtyard, its tropical garden bursting with blooms of red hibiscus, blue lotus, and yellow poppies.

Our butler, Cunningham, uncorked a bottle of Father's best claret and filled our glasses. My younger sisters Frances and Caroline occupied the seats previously intended for the commissioners.

"Our two London guests are unexpectedly absent," Father said, "but we shall have a merry time without them, shan't we?"

Whether the commodore understood precisely what Father had said, I couldn't tell; but he raised his glass with a smile. "Hear, hear."

Father was seated at the head of the table with Sir Samuel on his right, directly across from me. Despite what Mother had said earlier, there were times when she welcomed my ability to facilitate Father's conversations, especially when the gathering was large and the duties of a hostess demanded her full attention. Tonight was not such an occasion, though Mother seemed distracted nonetheless. I knew of no reason for it, unless she, too, was thinking of the afternoon's disturbing news. Mother did not often speak of her feelings about such matters, but she was a woman of great charity, and I did not doubt her compassion.

As the evening proceeded, my position at the table gave me ample opportunity to form a more studied opinion of Sir Samuel. He was quite tall, some might say ungainly, with a long face and sharply curved nose. He had wavy, reddish hair, and his eyebrows of the same color were highly arched, giving him a perpetually inquisitive look. The bright blue of his eyes seemed fitting for a man who had spent virtually his entire life at sea. A life in which, according to Father, Sir Samuel had earned an impressive array of honors for cunning and bravery in battle, as well as for his diplomatic skills.

Did I find him handsome? *Interesting* might be more accurate.

As I expected, it was not long before Father raised the subject of the militia, knowing he would find a sympathetic ear in the commodore. "I have never encountered a more useless bunch of misfits than this so-called island militia that answers to no one and goes about the countryside wreaking havoc. On numerous occasions I have warned that unless the governor is granted the power to appoint militia officers and enforce discipline, we leave ourselves vulnerable. Especially now, with hints that the French and Spanish may soon be threatening our shores, we must be prepared with a tightly coordinated defense."

Sir Samuel tossed me a questioning look from across the table. Father's usual slur suffered further from his love of wine.

"Lord Seaforth has long advocated for a more centralized command of all the forces on the island," I said by way of explanation. "Especially now, with rumors of an imminent attack by our enemies."

"Ah, yes." Sir Samuel turned to Father, nodding his agreement. "There is no question that the installation of royal forces on the Leeward Islands has increased the chances of an attack on Barbados. If that were to happen, it might be best to isolate the militia in a remote area of the island, just to keep them out of the way."

"But is it not preferable to have the largest possible force to defend us?" I countered, ignoring that Sir Samuel's dialogue was with Father, not me.

"That would be preferable if it were possible," Sir Samuel replied, looking directly at me. "But island politics is working against it. And against Lord Seaforth, who is correct in his assessment of the problem."

"Let us forget about problems for an hour or two, may we?" Mother said, lifting her wineglass. "We have much to be thankful for. Above all, our health. Many on this island have not been so fortunate this season."

"You are right, Lady Seaforth. I hear that yellow fever has taken a heavy toll." Sir Samuel touched his glass to Father's. "Let us drink to the health of those dearest to us. And to the safety and prosperity of Barbados."

"Will we be taken as prisoners if the French attack?" Frances asked in a small, frightened voice. Only a year younger than I, my sister's quiet, reserved nature made her far less comfortable with company.

"Of course not, Frances," I said. "We would be protected."

"But how? What would prevent them from capturing us?"

"You need not be afraid," said Sir Samuel. "The British Royal Navy is prepared to defend your island, and there is no better fleet in the entire world."

"God would protect us," seventeen-year-old Caroline added softly. Naturally she would say that—and believe it, too. Sometimes I envied her unquestioning faith. Mine was a bit shakier. I preferred to rely more upon the resilience of my own nature.

"The rules of war dictate that enemies are forbidden from harming diplomats and their families," I said. "Isn't that correct, Sir Samuel?"

"Yes, Miss Mackenzie. A very good point."

I was rather proud of myself—though I sensed a certain hesitance in the commodore's response, as if there were something more he could have said. Or should have.

"Then, too, the French—rascals that they are—regard Sir Samuel with a certain measure of fondness," Mother added amiably. "Isn't that so, Commodore?"

"I would not characterize their attitude as *fondness*."

"But you know what I mean," Mother insisted. "Sir Samuel is too modest to mention his extraordinary gallantry in returning a shipload of wounded French sailors to their commanders in Martinique, after having utterly vanquished their fleet in battle. Such acts of civility are not common in a time of war."

I offered the commodore an approving smile. "How heroic of you."

"Did you say *hero*?" Father was struggling to keep up with the conversation. "Why, there is a bona fide one sitting right here at our table!"

"Please, might we find another topic?" Sir Samuel said with a bashful chuckle.

"Not only that," Father continued, either failing to notice or choosing to ignore the commodore's suggestion, "but Sir Samuel is an expert navigator, astronomer, shipbuilder, and mechanic—*and*," he added, lifting a finger to the air, "fluent in three languages. I can think of no one who better exemplifies the qualities of a Renaissance man."

I wondered if there was a reason my father was so eager to sing Sir Samuel's praises. Undoubtedly our guest was deserving, but Father seemed to be directing his comments mostly towards me. Thankfully, Mother obliged Sir Samuel by taking control of the conversation for the duration of dinner. There was no more talk of war or the militia or Father's political foes, nor of Sir Samuel's virtues, of which I assumed there must be many more. At various times, no matter who might be speaking, I noticed his calm, reflective gaze upon my face. Once, just to see what would happen, I dared meet his eyes.

He quickly looked away, and I was sorry.

• • •

The following morning, I was up at dawn. The rest of the house was quiet. Father and Sir Samuel had stayed up late, drinking spirits and smoking cigars on the veranda. As far as I knew, the commissioners from London had yet to arrive.

I loved this time just after sunrise, when everyone else was asleep and I could wander about the house and gardens as I pleased. Often I would take my drawing pad outside to capture the views from our hilltop or wander into the courtyard garden to sketch the intricacies of some exotic bloom. But my early morning wanderings were not always so innocent. Occasionally I would venture into Father's office to shuffle through the official papers on his desk, telling myself it was for his sake that I wished to better understand the complexities of his position.

I was concerned that Father was sinking beneath the weight of his vast responsibilities. Lately his countenance bore signs of fatigue, and the slump of his shoulders—when he thought no one watched him— was further evidence of his mental and physical exhaustion. Yet he was too proud to ask for help.

I wondered how much of his frustration Father had confided to Sir Samuel. They seemed to enjoy a certain camaraderie. My father's naval experience could hardly be compared to Sir Samuel's, yet they shared a love of the high seas and both had been tested in battle. I imagined if my brothers were here, they might have been invited to listen in on Sir Samuel's accounts of his wartime adventures. No one would think to make me such an offer. But I was not the sort to stifle my curiosity. What I was not meant to know held the most fascination for me.

As I had done on quite a few mornings like this one, I approached Father's office, tapped on the closed door just to be certain the room was unoccupied, and entered. This was my father's hideaway, a private space where he could immerse himself in the pursuits he cherished. The chamber was paneled in teak, an entire wall taken up by books he had brought here from Scotland. Father was well known as an accomplished amateur scientist, having spent a great deal of time and money on expeditions to gather specimens for his impressive botanical and herbarium collections. Though most of his organized compilations were housed at Brahan Castle, he had brought with him some splendid examples of minerals and a few rare fossils of plants and marine life preserved in sedimentary rocks, some of which were displayed on an open shelf next to the window.

I meandered over to his desk. As usual, it was strewn with loose papers. I selected one randomly. It was a letter from a Custom House officer in London. The writer referred to a previous conversation in which Father had strongly advocated preference for British merchants in British ships as the sole suppliers of goods to the island. As governor, he wished to ban virtually all trade with our former colony, America. I surmised he had been reviewing the letter in preparation for a meeting with the guests who had not yet landed.

I set it aside and flipped through a few more pages. Discovering a letter from a London solicitor, I quickly scanned the contents. While the initial greeting was scrupulously cordial, the tone of the second paragraph was less so. "On the third of January 1800, you engaged in a game of chance, the result of which was a gambling debt of eight thousand pounds, twelve shillings. My client, being aware of your esteemed position in society, assumes this matter has simply escaped your attention. He does, however, respectfully request its immediate resolution."

Perhaps I should not have been surprised. I knew of Father's propensity for gambling, but, given the dignity of his position as governor, there was little opportunity to indulge it here in Barbados. I looked again at the date mentioned. The debt to which the letter referred must have been incurred just before he left London to assume his new post. Had he merely forgotten to pay it, as the solicitor suggested? Or did Father not have the money to settle it? I had noticed no recent changes in our style of living. If anything, since Father had become governor, my parents spent more lavishly than ever. How would that be possible if funds were in short supply?

With a sigh, I stuck the letter beneath several others. Almost reluctantly, I reached for another, thinking it would be the last, and started reading. The letter was from a Mr. Fraser, who reported a recent boom in cotton manufacturing in Scotland. "A timely opportunity for you, Lord Seaforth," he wrote. "The cotton from your new plantation in Berbice will surely be welcomed at home, and you should find your investment quite profitable. I anticipate it will not be terribly long before you recoup your initial expenditures for reclamation and your recent purchase of two hundred slaves."

My mouth went dry. Had I misread the letter? Was this Mr. Fraser trying to convince Father to buy a plantation in the Berbice region of Guiana? I reread the damning paragraph, hoping my initial impression had been wrong. This was the first I'd heard of a plantation in Guiana, and never a word had been spoken about Father purchasing even one African slave, let alone two hundred.

No, it was impossible that my father, who time and again had portrayed himself as a humanitarian, was in fact a slave owner! But, indeed, the letter seemed to suggest he was. I tossed it onto the desktop like some vile, filthy thing. Was Mother aware of this? Perhaps I ought to ask her if she knew, but then I would be forced to admit I had been snooping amongst Father's private correspondence. Did I dare say something to him myself? Perhaps there was a good explanation, though I could not imagine one good enough.

"Mary! What are you doing in here?" Father stood in the doorway, dressed in his white cotton nightshirt and cap.

"I was just—" I stopped, then started again, signing as I spoke. "I wondered if the view from this window might make an interesting sketch."

Father frowned. "And does it?"

"Yes, it's quite lovely."

He came towards me. "Let me have a look at your drawing."

I realized suddenly that I had left my sketchbook in my room. "I have yet to draw anything. I just wanted to refresh my memory."

He nodded, seeming satisfied enough with my answer. "Then if you are done here, please run along."

I turned to leave, but changed my mind. How could I pretend that nothing was wrong when everything I thought I knew about my father was suddenly in question? I swung around, struggling to put aside my disappointment and confusion. There was no reason I should jump to conclusions. "I must ask you something."

He had already begun searching through his papers and did not realize I was speaking. I tapped him on the shoulder.

"Yes?" he said, looking up.

Finding the words, whether spoken or signed, was going to be difficult. "Do you own a plantation in Guiana?"

He stared at me a moment before pulling out his desk chair and easing himself down, slowly, carefully—as he often did of late.

"I never meant to pry into your affairs, Father, but now that I have … would you please explain to me how it is possible that you would have purchased two hundred slaves?"

He appeared more embarrassed than angry over my intrusion into his business. For a moment I felt guilty for ambushing him with such vitriol, which even my hand movements conveyed. But I could not hide what I felt.

"You must understand, when I inherited our family estates—the year that you were born—the lands were already heavily in debt. I tried my best to make them profitable, but my efforts have not been enough."

"But a slave plantation! How *could* you?"

"Sometimes we must do things we regret in order to achieve a greater good. These plantations will be our salvation, Mary. Otherwise, we were in danger of losing our family estates in Ross-shire, which would be tantamount to forfeiting our Mackenzie heritage."

"There must be another way."

"Another way? Let me tell you what the estate factors wanted me to do: clear our Highland properties and open them up for raising sheep. Throw our countrymen and clansmen off the land their families have worked for generations. Is that what you would have me do?"

"You refused?"

"Must you even ask? Of course I did!"

At least there was something for which I could look up to him. But I could not let rest the matter of slaves. "Are there no free men willing to tend cotton for a fair wage?"

His patience snapped. "Daughter, you understand nothing of commerce. And I haven't the time to educate you in subjects for which you have no use."

"So I am not worth educating simply because I am a daughter, not a son? Well, thankfully I have eavesdropped enough to gather a few crumbs of your privileged wisdom." Young women do not address their fathers in such a way! But despite his stern look, I was undeterred from further argument. "Does it not strike you as hypocrisy? You have stood before the Barbados Assembly and *condemned* the murder and torture of slaves."

"That is another issue entirely. I assure you, Mary, the Africans on my plantations will never be mistreated. I have banned all corporal punishment. Their living conditions are quite humane."

"How can slavery in any form be humane? You cannot say one thing and do another. If you continue, no one will believe in your leadership."

It was an awful thing for me to say, and I was immediately sorry. Father had struggled all his life to be respected. I admired his tenacity. And there was never a man who cared more for his family—and the clan that recognized him as its chief. As Cabarfeidh, he would sooner have died than ignore the responsibilities conferred by that ancient title.

"Let us not speak any further about this. Someday, Parliament will put an end to slavery in the colonies, and I will rejoice. But until then, I will do what I must." Father reached for my hand, which I could not deny him. "I'm sorry if you are disappointed in your father, Mary. If I have made mistakes, as I surely have, I hope you can find it in your heart to forgive me."

He appeared like a broken old man. I had never seen him quite like this, and it frightened me. Throwing my arms around his neck, I rested my cheek against the soft cotton of his nightcap. "Don't worry, Father. Please … don't worry."

But in the days and weeks that followed my discovery of the Berbice plantation, I found it difficult to do what he had asked of me. I could not bring myself to forgive him. Until the day he took to his bed and had not the strength to rise.

Then, all that mattered was how to take away the pain.

CHAPTER THREE

For a few years my father had been subject to attacks of gout, which had lately grown worse. As much as possible, he tried to keep it from my sisters and me, but Mother could not. Many mornings she would warn us not to disturb him and, upon questioning, admit that he had slept little the night before. Typically, he would wake a couple of hours after retiring for the night, aware of a mild pain in his calf, or sometimes his toe, heel, or ankle. Soon after, he would be seized by a terrible chill and set to shivering beneath his quilt; a fever would follow, the pain in his extremities becoming more severe until it was so excruciating that he could barely tolerate the weight of his dressing gown. If anyone approached his bed, the subtle vibration of the floor beneath their feet caused him great agony. Though the condition would eventually subside, it always returned.

The British medics on the island had, on numerous occasions, administered treatments attempting to relieve his symptoms. Their success was unremarkable, and the resulting effects on his general constitution intolerable. One day, Father announced he had decided to consult a doctor in London. He joked that perhaps time away from the island, and its innumerable problems, was enough to effect a cure.

I dreaded Father's leaving. Not that we were unaccustomed to his absence. When he served as a Member of Parliament, he would spend nearly half the year in London. Though our family sometimes joined him there, more often we stayed at Brahan Castle or Seaforth Lodge on the Isle of Lewis. We understood that his official duties were a source of great pride for my father, and the diligence with which he attended to them was beyond reproach. One could say the same for his performance as governor. Except here in Barbados, his every move was subject to criticism. Father's absence from his post, regardless of the reason, would go neither unnoticed nor unexploited. His adversaries would seek to gain whatever advantage they could while he was away. The constant tug-of-war with the island Assembly was taking a huge toll on Father's health and encouraging a persistent melancholy that, despite his fighting spirit, threatened to overwhelm him. Which was why, a week before his scheduled departure for London, I went to see the Obeah-woman.

This decision was not made lightly. If anyone were to find out, it would be not only embarrassing for my father but cause for the planters to further question his loyalties. They were highly suspicious of the African practitioners of Obeah, calling them sorcerers and fearing their power at the same time they dismissed it as illusionary. Worse, they believed the Obeah-men and -women were instigators of discontent; the possibility of a slave revolt as had occurred on the neighboring island of Grenada was enough to cause them nightmares.

I did not believe in Obeah magic—or any sort of magic. In that, I was different from most people back home in Ross-shire. For them, Highland magic was everywhere. Standing stones were gateways into other realms; magic wells and springs healed what medicines could not; fairies inhabited the hills and glens and forests; and the power to harm or protect or divine the future belonged to those known as *seers*. Were it not for the prophecy propagated by one such seer, long before I was born, I might have been a believer in visions and spells. But I had shut my mind to all that. I would fight it to my last breath.

I was not in search of a magical cure for Father's illness, only an effective one. The Obeah-woman was a doctor, not a sorceress. Well, some might argue she was both; they were entitled to their superstitions. All I wanted from the Obeah-woman was to help my father. The notion that she might succeed where others had failed was not as preposterous as one might think. I had overheard an island merchant telling Father of a secret contest between one of our European-trained surgeons and the Obeah-woman known as Lovely. On the plantation where she worked, many of the slaves were suffering from a skin disease called yaws, which causes painful lumps and ulcers. The plantation owner, Mr. Hedgeford, asked the surgeon to treat half of the afflicted Africans, and placed the other half in the Obeah-woman's care. Those treated by the Obeah-woman were cured within a fortnight, while the surgeon failed to cure any of his patients. The widely circulated account was one that medics in Barbados sought to deny, but I was intrigued. Might there be some as-yet unheralded approach to treating the symptoms of Father's gout? Or even addressing its cause?

Though it was Sunday, I begged off attending church with the complaint of a stomachache. Mother did not question my claim. Asking me to keep an eye on Father, who had remained in bed, she left for Sunday services with my five sisters in tow. Once I was certain she had gone and would not double back for some forgotten item, as she often did, I saddled my beloved white stallion, Cloudy, and began the trek to the African village on the western edge of Mr. Hedgeford's property, a large plantation not terribly far from Pilgrim House. To avoid calling attention to myself, I had borrowed one of Sarah's plain dresses, pulling the brim of her simple bonnet low to hide my face.

I started out riding through the outskirts of town, where most of the wealthier British had built fine wooden houses of two or three stories— in sharp contrast to the narrow brick houses that lined the streets at the commercial center of Bridgetown. And then there were places like Roebuck Street, inhabited by the poorest of the white population, free people of color, and the few slaves permitted to live away from the plantations where they worked. Rows and rows of miserable hovels patched together with whatever might keep out the rain, and a cockfight in progress almost any night of the week.

I soon reached the southernmost border of Mr. Hedgeford's plantation. Before me stretched field after field of sugarcane, almost ready for harvest. The stalks must have been fifteen feet high. At this time of year their narrow, grass-like leaves—usually a vibrant green—were tinged with yellow. I steered Cloudy down one of the narrow aisles between the planted rows, the rustling of stalks in the wind creating their own sort of music. Sugarcane ruled Barbados. Its demands had raped the land and enslaved thousands of Africans. Now, engulfed by these giant, leafy canes, I felt their aliveness with an intensity that was unnerving. I clicked my tongue, and Cloudy shifted from a walk to a canter.

We passed through several more fields until I saw, a short distance ahead, the wattle and daub houses of the plantation's African community. Realizing that a horse like Cloudy was bound to attract admiring eyes, I steered him to a small grove of plantain trees and tied him to a trunk, then covered the remaining ground on foot.

The slave yard was comprised of maybe fifty dwellings arranged in clusters. In my time in Barbados, I had visited enough plantations to have a good idea of how planters organized their African communities. Typically, four or five slaves would live in each little house; they might be of the same family but often were not. Today being Sunday, most laborers were relieved of their usual tasks. Some were outside, working small plots of land allocated to grow food for their own households. Others were tending to goats, pigs, and chickens, which many planters permitted them to raise for personal use or commerce. Close to the slave yard were the sugar mill, stables, and other work buildings, while the master's grand, white-pillared house looked down on the entire scene from its remote hilltop perch.

Despite my efforts to blend in, it was impossible for a young white woman to travel through the yard unnoticed. And I would need to ask someone for help. All the tiny houses looked the same; there was none identifiable as the dwelling of the Obeah-woman. I could only hope that word of my inquiry did not reach the house on the hill.

I chose to approach a young African woman, thin as a rake, wearing a shabby cotton dress that hung loose to the ground. She leaned in the doorway of a dilapidated shack, cradling a baby in her arms and staring dreamily at the distant hills of what was called the Scottish district, a rugged land area that had been last to be consumed by the sugar plantations and, even now, remained partially wooded.

"Pardon me, but I'm looking for the Obeah-doctor called Lovely. Can you tell me where to find her?"

She straightened up, giving me a look both suspicious and curious. "You wan' de Obi-woman?"

"Yes. Which house is hers?"

She chewed her lower lip, thinking. "Ain't no Obi-woman here," she finally said.

Maybe the rule was that no one spoke of Obeah to strangers. Especially white strangers. "I need her help—for someone I love."

"You wan' love potion, eh?"

"No—not love potion. Medicine."

She frowned. "No Obi-woman here."

"Her name is Lovely." I pulled out a half crown from the small reticule I was carrying and held it out to her. "Please, it's very important that I find her."

The baby began to wail. She shifted it higher, pressing the infant's face against her chest to muffle its cries before freeing a hand with which to snatch the coin from me. "Dat way," she said, inclining her head to the right. "Go five down, and dat's de one. But anybody ask, you ain't got it from me."

"Yes, of course. I won't say a word."

As she was clearly anxious to be rid of me, I thanked her and hurried off, keeping my head down so the sides of my bonnet covered my face. I doubted there was anyone around who would recognize me. Nevertheless, the last thing I would want circulating was talk of the governor's daughter visiting a local sorceress, which was surely how Father's detractors would wish to portray the Obeah-woman called Lovely.

My first knock upon the door produced nothing, so I knocked again. After my third try, I decided it was useless. But just as I was turning away, the door opened. Standing before me was a tiny woman, her skin deeply wrinkled and ink-black. She wore a white scarf wrapped around her head like a turban and several strings of colored beads around her neck. Her plain white dress was spotlessly clean but no less ragged than that of the young woman with the baby.

She looked at me with dark, piercing eyes.

"I hope I'm not interrupting," I said, my heart pounding, "but are you the woman they call Lovely?"

"Who wan' to know?"

"I have come alone to ask for your help—for healing."

She studied me a moment longer and then stepped aside, motioning to come in. A good start, but I was still uncertain as to what her reaction might be; most likely, young women such as myself did not often appear on her doorstep. Perhaps she would have no interest in helping me. Why should she? My kind had done nothing but create misery for her people. And though doctors are ethically obliged to treat the sick no matter the patient's circumstances, such rules might not apply to Obeah.

I quickly scanned the dim interior. The house was a single room with just one window, over which a black cloth was hung to block the light from outside; or perhaps more importantly, to keep others from looking in. The floor was dirt, the furnishings scant: a woven grass mat for sleeping, a rudimentary hearth for cooking, open shelves for storing a few pots and utensils, and four cane chairs around a square wooden table, to which Lovely steered me now.

"Sit," she said, pointing to one of the chairs.

I did as she commanded, Lovely taking the chair opposite mine. She folded her hands and rested them on the table, staring at me with those impenetrable eyes. I suddenly wondered how I could have been foolish enough to come here, knowing nothing of this woman—her motives or her methods. But I had made it this far; I would complete my mission.

"My father is very ill. He has what the European doctors call gout. Are you familiar with the disease?"

She raised her eyebrows. "You wan' de cure fuh yuh faddah?"

"Yes, that's right."

"And why you come here?"

"The doctors my father has seen haven't been able to help him. He seems only to get worse. Today, he is too ill to leave his bed." I had seldom been so nervous as I felt at that moment. "I have heard of your success in curing yaws and hope you might have a medicine for gout."

"Yuh faddah know you come see me?"

I dropped my gaze. "No, I am afraid he might not approve. I was hoping whatever medicine you have could be administered by way of food or tea—that is, without his being aware of it." She frowned, and I quickly added, "But if not, I will certainly tell him the truth. He has little to lose by trying something new."

"Lady, you know nothin' 'bout Obeah." She shook her head disapprovingly, and I worried that I'd offended her. "Some kinds o' sickness," she said, lowering her voice almost to a whisper, "come from de outside world, an' fuh dem, de cure is easier. But sickness what start from de mind need de head to cure it."

"I don't understand. Are you saying that my father's gout is all in his mind?"

"What yuh faddah fear de most?"

I hesitated. "What he fears most is being unable to fulfill his duties," I said, careful not to define what those duties were. My identity, and my father's, must remain hidden.

Lovely closed her eyes. Touching the beads around her neck, she said, "You an' yuh faddah share de same pain."

"Oh—no, not at all. He has gout. I have nothing of the kind."

She rubbed several beads between her thumb and index finger, gently rocking forward and back. "Not de *gout*."

She opened her eyes. "Lotta time, people die 'cause dey believe dey *must* die. Dey believe evil be strong and dey got nothin' to fight it wid."

I understood too well what she meant. For as long as I could remember, my entire family had known of the legend of Coinneach Odhar and the curse laid upon the Seaforth line more than a century ago. Thinking of it now, I shuddered. But this woman, Lovely, was wrong to say that my father and I shared the same fear. I was uncertain how he felt, but I did not believe in the curse. I refused to.

"Perhaps, as you say, my father fears what he doesn't understand," I conceded, "but his more immediate problem is gout. If you have a remedy for him to try, I would be very grateful."

She reached beneath the table, dragging out a large round basket in which were all manner of odds and ends—rags and rope, skulls of small animals, along with assorted bones and beaks and feathers, broken bottles, eggshells, and what looked like human hair. Among these raw implements of her trade were numerous stoppered vials containing liquid of a murky brown color. They all appeared identical. If they were different, and meant to treat specific diseases, how did she tell them apart?

Lovely chose one of the vials and handed it to me. "Five drops wid hot tea, four times a day. Taste bad, an' de body ain't gonna like it none in de beginning. But after a while, he be better. Tell him dat, eh?"

I nodded. "But what's in it?"

"You don't never ask Obi doctor what's de cure. It's not for you to know."

"Of course. Forgive me." I slipped the vial into my reticule. "What do I owe you?"

She held up one finger. I withdrew a pound note and laid it on the table in front of her. She nodded but made no move to pick it up.

"If I need more medicine, may I come back?"

"You won't."

Whether she meant a single vial would be sufficient, or I would not return in any event, I couldn't tell. I stood, eager to leave. Besides wanting to be home before Mother returned, I had the uncomfortable feeling that nothing was hidden from Lovely's wise eyes—including my growing doubts about whether, after all, I should try out her cure on my unsuspecting father. But I could decide that later.

She walked ahead of me to the door and opened it. The noonday sun flooded her dark little hovel, and I felt a rush of relief. The world outside was just the same as before.

"Thank you for your help. You've been very kind."

I was surprised when she took my hand, pressing something slightly sharp into my palm. "Fuh when de evil come," she whispered.

CHAPTER FOUR

O nly when I had left the slave yard did I dare look at what Lovely had given me. Opening my hand, I found six tiny bones, naturally fused, each about a quarter-inch across and shaped somewhat like a star. I had seen enough bones and fossils in my father's collections to recognize them as snake vertebrae. Lovely had gifted me a charm to ward off evil. But why? What did she know?

My first instinct was to toss it away; instead, I dropped it into my reticule. There would be no time to waste if I was to be back at Pilgrim House before Mother and my sisters. Hurrying towards the stand of plantain trees where I had tied Cloudy, I strained for a glimpse of him. I remembered the exact location of the tree where I had tied him. The knot had been well secured. But where was he now?

I broke into a run, my heart pounding. How could he have got loose? And if he had, how far had he roamed? What if he had gone all the way back to Pilgrim House? When given the opportunity, a horse will often head for his stable. In that case, I had a long walk ahead of me. It was not the distance that worried me, only the time.

But another possibility concerned me even more. What if someone had stolen my horse?

I spent the next half hour searching for Cloudy, berating my stupidity for having left him unattended. What had I been thinking? Theft was rampant on the island, and a horse like mine would bring a large bounty for some enterprising African or poor white, or perhaps even someone without need of stealing but unable to resist the temptation. As my search continued without any sign of him, I could no longer hold back my tears. I loved that horse, and I might never know what had become of him—who had taken him and whether he would be treated well or carelessly. Barbados was a place where cruelty was so ubiquitous that many had become inured to it.

I could not help the thought that this might be punishment for my having sought help from the Obeah-woman. Or maybe she had somehow spirited away my horse, leaving me stranded. Perhaps she had only pretended to help me when, in fact, her intention was to harm me. And my father.

I started to walk, the sun beating down upon me with relentless spite. How I hated the heat and dust and the sense of weariness that hung over this island prison. I often thought of Barbados that way, for it truly was a prison to many thousands of unfortunate souls who never asked to be brought here, and certainly not in chains.

I was making my way down one of the long aisles between the sugarcane when I heard the approach of horses. Turning, I saw three militia men among the tall stalks, trotting towards me. I could only hope they were sober.

"Where are you heading, miss?" The first in line reined in his horse just behind me.

Dressed as I was, they would assume me to be a servant, which suited my situation fine. "I was out on an errand for my mistress, Lady Seaforth, and my horse ran off. I'm sure to be in trouble. That horse is the favorite of Lord and Lady Seaforth's daughter, and she don't like me much as it is."

"Got away from you, eh?" The young militia man swiveled in his saddle to address his two companions, who had lined their horses behind him. "This young lady works at the governor's house," he said. "Says she lost her horse. Guess the least we can do is offer her a ride. Help her up here, would you?"

Grunting his assent, one of the men dismounted and came over to hoist me onto the saddle behind their leader.

There was no attempt at conversation, for which I was grateful, and we passed through Bridgetown without incident. All the while, I was searching the landscape for a flash of white. When we reached the base of the private lane leading up to Pilgrim House, I tapped my escort's shoulder.

"You had better leave me here," I said.

"No trouble taking you all the way."

"Please, better if you don't. I'm hoping my lady's horse might've come back to the stables himself, and nobody can know what happened."

He stopped at the bottom of the cobblestone drive. "If you say so." He called back to the fellow who had assisted me earlier. "Help her down, man."

Again, I felt the pressure of his hands around my waist, but this time I held my breath in order to avoid smelling his, which reeked of whiskey and stale tobacco.

"By the way, what does that horse look like—in case we spot him somewhere?"

"He's a white stallion. Name's Cloudy."

"Cloudy," he repeated. "All right then."

Thanking the three of them, I quickly took my leave, scurrying up the hillside as fast as I could get away. There was still a chance that Mother was not back. And a chance—though I feared not much of one—that Cloudy would be in his stable, oblivious to what his wanderlust had put me through.

But my bad luck seemed bound to continue. When I had almost reached the house, our carriage came ambling up the hill. Though Mother did not order Ross to stop, she would soon be demanding to know where I had been—and what about my difficult stomach? Wishing to delay the confrontation, I diverted my path and headed directly to the stables. As I had feared, Cloudy was not there.

Dejected and again on the verge of tears, I entered the house through a back door and tiptoed up the stairs to my bedchamber. Mother had arrived there ahead of me.

"What is the meaning of all this?" She looked me up and down, realizing, of course, that I was dressed in servant's clothing. "Why are you wearing *that*?"

I sank onto the ottoman at the foot of my bed, uncertain how to answer her. I did not enjoy lying to my mother, but there were times—more than there used to be—when it became necessary.

"I thought some air would do me good, and ..." I faltered. What possible reason could I have for dressing as a servant? "I was playing a little game with Sarah. Pretending I was her maid and she my mistress."

Mother sniffed. "You are long past the age of playing dress-up, Mary. I want to know what is going on. You said you felt ill. Obviously, that was untrue. And now this ridiculous story about trading gowns with your maid ... Really, do you think me utterly stupid?"

I should have known better. Still, telling her my true mission was out of the question. As devoutly Christian as Mother was, visiting an Obeah-woman would be akin to paying homage to the devil.

"Excuse me, my lady." One of our footmen stood just outside my open door. "I am asked to tell you that a member of the island militia has returned one of the horses, which apparently ran off. The white one—I believe it belongs to you, Miss Mary?"

My relief was such that I jumped up from the ottoman with an exclamation of joy. Looking at Mother's face, however, quickly sobered me.

"Please thank him, Barclay," Mother said, eyeing me with disdain.

"Yes, my lady." I listened to his footsteps receding until all was perfectly still. Too still. Mother's stare was burning a hole through me, and my choices had dwindled to almost nothing. I could try to come up with a more plausible lie, or I could tell her the truth and hope she might understand that my intentions were only the best.

"I am terribly worried about Father."

"Do not try to change the subject, Mary. Your behavior requires an explanation."

"I am coming to that." I reached for the reticule that was sitting on the ottoman. Opening it, I removed the bottle of medicine. The liquid looked disgusting, both the color and the unidentifiable particles floating in it. The thought of my father ingesting such a concoction was revolting—and my actions entirely indefensible. Still, my father was desperate, and so had I been, on his behalf. "Father says he is leaving for London, seeking a cure for the gout, but he is too unwell for such a journey. Besides, none of the European doctors have yet found anything to relieve his misery, and this new doctor in London, whoever he is, shall be no different."

"Get to the point, Mary. And what is that in your hand?"

I swallowed hard, raising the bottle for her to see. "I went to see an Obeah-doctor."

"You *what*?" Clutching her bosom, Mother plopped down on the edge of my bed.

"The Obeah-doctor who cured Mr. Hedgeford's slaves of the yaws. His British plantation doctor is still scratching his head over it, but the Obeah cure worked. No one can deny that it did."

"Who knows what ungodly methods that witch doctor used! How could you possibly put your faith in an African who bewitches people into believing they will die unless they do as he says? Because that is what these Obeah-men do: They have been known to inflict the most awful and painful deaths on their victims, causing them to suffer for days, weeks, or even years. And you would entrust one of them with your father's life? Mary, you shock me with your ignorance. I know you are impulsive and too daring for your own good, but this ..." She shook her head in disbelief. "This is beyond anything I could have imagined you would do."

"I didn't go to an Obeah-man," I said weakly. "This was a woman."

"A man, a woman—what difference does it make? How do you know she didn't give you some sort of poison for your father? What a feather in her cap to take vengeance on the governor himself!"

"She didn't know who my father is. And, anyway, she wasn't like that." I felt I should defend Lovely. She had been kind to me. But Mother was right. What did I really know of her? The ones she had cured of yaws had all been Africans, like her. Perhaps she hated white people. I had considered this before, but wanted to think of her as a doctor. A healer. I did not wish to think about evil.

Mother stood up. "Give me that bottle and promise me that you will say nothing of this to anyone else. Do you realize how the members of the Assembly would react to finding out Lord Seaforth's daughter was consulting with an Obeah-woman? You know the planters consider them agitators, wanting to prove their power by encouraging their slaves to revolt." Mother sighed. "You know very well that I am a compassionate person, and I share your father's concern that the Africans be treated with greater respect for their safety. But a slave revolt is in no one's interests."

"Yes, Mother." I was too weary to argue, too ashamed. I suddenly saw myself as just another hypocrite, like everyone else. I had trusted Lovely enough to ask for her help but was unwilling to stand by my original assessment of her. A few words of condemnation from my mother had been enough to destroy my confidence.

And my courage.

CHAPTER FIVE

ather left for London on the twenty-fifth of June. He informed us that he had invited Samuel Hood to drop by from time to time, just to make sure all was well. He expected us to extend our most gracious hospitality, something that Mother certainly would have done in any event.

I was not unhappy at the prospect of company. With Father away, our day-to-day life at Pilgrim House was sure to be even duller than usual. Sketching and reading, playing the piano, and taking tea with the wives and daughters of various island officials could be no substitute for the life I'd once had in the Highlands or, less often, at our townhouse in Grosvenor Square, one of the most fashionable addresses in London. My coming-out ball at Pilgrim House was more lavish than anything Barbados had ever seen, but it was hardly the same as being presented to London society and partaking in a whirlwind of social events for an entire season. As for meeting eligible marriage partners, there was little opportunity for that here. Surprisingly, neither Mother or Father seemed terribly concerned about my lack of prospects, even if the rule of thumb was that a young woman had better be engaged within two years of coming out or risk spinsterhood.

Sir Samuel's first visit came only three weeks after Father's departure. Though his duties as a naval commander protecting British interests often required liaising with government officials, only recently had he become a visitor to Pilgrim House. As was proper, I had never been in his company without Mother and Father present. But that first evening, following a late supper, Mother claimed a nasty headache for which she apologized and excused herself. I expected that Sir Samuel, who was to stay the night before leaving on an extended voyage, would announce he was retiring early as well. But just as I was about to call Cunningham to see our guest to his room, the commodore turned to me with an eager smile.

"I don't wish to keep you up if you are tired. But I would very much enjoy a glass of your father's excellent Madeira. Might you join me?"

"Why … of course." In truth, I rather liked the idea of entertaining Sir Samuel on my own. The absence of a chaperone was no fault of mine.

Soon Sir Samuel and I were sipping Madeira on the terrace off the drawing room, as we looked out upon the port of Bridgetown. The moon was full, casting its brilliant light on the calm water and a dozen or more ships anchored there, masts lowered. The scene would have made a lovely drawing.

"Last time you were here, as I recall, Father was expecting commerce officials from London," I said, anxious to fill the silence that had enveloped us.

"Yes, I believe you're correct."

"They never came. He learned later that some sort of important business had detained them in London. Of course, in his mind nothing could be more important than the affairs of Barbados."

"Lord Seaforth is a man of extraordinary dedication. And unafraid to make his views known—even when they are unpopular," Sir Samuel added with a chuckle.

I welcomed an opening to talk of island politics. "I often wonder if Father realized what he was getting himself into when he accepted his position as governor. The planters seem determined to reject the Crown's authority."

"Until they need its protection."

"Indeed. It's funny … Barbados is a British colony, yet I sometimes feel as though I'm living not just in a foreign land but on another planet. People here have a strange way of looking at things."

"Strange?"

"What I mean is, many of them seem lacking in basic humanity. I suppose I expected too much. I thought Britain aimed to share the best of what has made it great, not give free rein to the worst."

Sir Samuel turned his gaze from the moon to me. "I take it you miss your home. Certainly, no one could blame you. Barbados is a very different environment—one that, for a variety of reasons, many find intolerable. Even the climate, though relatively mild, is anathema to Europeans."

"I've heard it said the European constitution is not suited for it. Perhaps that's why Father is suffering so." I realized my indiscretion too late. Father wished for his malady, and his reason for traveling to London, to be kept confidential. My comment might make Sir Samuel curious. I hoped he would not ask me to explain.

"And you, Miss Mackenzie? How has Barbados affected you personally?"

It might have been the Madeira, to which I was unaccustomed, but I found myself eager to speak honestly, and perhaps more openly than I should. "Living here has reminded me that evil is very much alive in the world. And difficult to defeat."

"Difficult? Or impossible?"

"Here in Barbados, perhaps it *is* impossible. But only because people call evil by other names to avoid acknowledging it in themselves. I see no difference between cruelty and evil. Whether one actively engages in it or simply tolerates it matters little. Either way, they are guilty."

"Hmm." Sir Samuel sipped his wine while I fretted over what he might be thinking. Perhaps that I hadn't the worldly experience to justify such outspokenness? My own father had accused me of ignorance on more than one occasion, though only when I disagreed with him.

"You sound very impassioned. Like your father."

"I suppose we are similar in some respects. We both want to believe that justice shall prevail. I should say, we *do* believe. Because we must. Father's success as governor depends upon it. And my …" I hesitated. "My faith that the future is what we make of it gives me strength."

I could hear the pounding of my heart and a tiny voice in my head warning *Watch what you say*.

"As a military man, I often come face-to-face with injustice. Even when the cause is righteous, the actions of men can be shockingly depraved. War is an abomination, no matter how you look at it. But I have come to accept it as a fact of life. Men fight to survive, just like everything in nature. Such is the world we live in. And yet, I wish this world could be a place where *you* would always feel safe, Miss Mackenzie. If I could, I would make it that way."

I was about to thank him for his kind sentiment when a hair-raising shriek pierced the night. Startled, I dropped the crystal glass in my hand; it shattered into a multitude of tiny diamonds on the stone floor. "My goodness, Mother will have my head! But never mind. That scream came from inside the house. I'd better see what is going on."

Sir Samuel laid his hand on my wrist. "No, you stay right where you are. I will investigate."

"I'm coming with you."

"Miss Mackenzie, please—"

Ignoring him, I darted from the terrace, dashing through the drawing room towards the entrance hall. When I arrived, I saw that Cunningham was already halfway up the curved staircase.

"Where are you off to?" I called out.

"Lady Seaforth's bedchamber." Cunningham was so short of breath that he could barely shout out his reply. Given his age and girth, I worried he might collapse before reaching the top of the stairs.

Sir Samuel had quickly overtaken me and started up, taking the steps two at a time. The last to arrive at Mother's chamber, I found her and four of my sisters huddled around the bed. Lying on top of the satin coverlet was four-year-old Helen. I stood behind the footboard, next to

Sir Samuel, looking down at her. There was no blood, no evidence of injury—or none that I could see. Her eyes were open, and she was crying.

"Cunningham," Mother said in a strained voice, "send Ross to fetch the doctor. You go with him and tell him it's an emergency. Possibly a poisoning."

Cunningham gave a quick nod and hurried out the door.

"A poisoning?" I had to raise my voice to be heard over Helen's screams.

Mother cast me a sharp look before scooping up something from the night table, holding it so I could clearly see. My legs began to shake.

"How did she get it?"

"If you want me to say it was my fault, then yes—it was. I should have disposed of it immediately, but I was in a hurry and I couldn't decide what exactly to do with it. So I tossed it into the drawer of my dressing table and promptly forgot about it. And that ridiculous excuse for a nanny—she knows not to let Helen out of her sight, even if the child seems to be asleep."

My heart was pumping so hard I feared I would faint. Mother was being inordinately generous. The fault was mine, and we both knew it. I was the one who brought Obeah medicine into the house. Or I had thought it was medicine. Now at least half of it was gone. Helen was holding her stomach and shrieking in pain.

Sir Samuel seemed the only calm one among us. "Lady Seaforth, what makes you think there was poison in that bottle?"

Mother looked again at me, this time with a helpless quivering of her lips that rendered her speechless.

"I got it from an Obeah-woman," I replied in a choked whisper. "I—I asked her for medicine to cure Father's gout, and she gave me that."

Sir Samuel's shock was apparent. "And has your father taken this medicine before?"

"No, Mother and I—" I swallowed what I had been about to say; it would not be fair to exonerate myself in any way. "Mother had the good sense to confiscate it."

"And you don't know what the medicine is? Let us assume, for the moment, it is not poison. Did the Obeah-woman mention any herbs or other ingredients?"

I shook my head. "No, I asked, but she wouldn't tell me."

"All right." Sir Samuel stepped away from the bed. "You and I are going to find this Obeah-woman and get her to tell us what was in that bottle. I take it you know where she lives?"

"Mr. Hedgeford's plantation."

"We will find her. Come with me."

I glanced at Mother, who nodded her assent. "You'll have to go on horseback. The carriage is gone. And—" She shook her head, covering her mouth with trembling hands.

"Don't worry, Mother," I said, though she had every reason to worry. So did I. "We'll make certain no one sees us."

The fire returned to Mother's eyes. "At this point, I don't care who knows the foolish thing you did, Mary. Helen's life is more important. If you need Mr. Hedgeford's help, you go to his house and get him. Just be quick about it."

●　　●　　●

Sir Samuel insisted it would be best to take a single horse. I clung to him with an unaccustomed feeling of helplessness. We were fortunate the moon was full and, even when we were past the town, our path remained well lit. We did not attempt to speak during the ride. I imagined Sir Samuel was too disgusted to want anything to do with me, and I couldn't blame him. What if the Obeah-woman *did* give me poison? It appeared Helen had consumed half the bottle. It must have tasted awful, but the thrill of stealing something from Mother's dressing table was all the enticement she needed.

Still, I resisted the idea that Lovely might wish harm to my father. Hadn't she shown unexpected kindness in giving me a charm meant to protect me? Even if I had no use for such hocus-pocus, the gesture had been generous. I believed she bore no resentment towards me.

But what if I was wrong?

Sir Samuel knew the island and was familiar with the location of Mr. Hedgeford's property. Near the end of our ride, I directed him to the exact spot where we should enter the African yard, close to the Obeah-woman's tiny house. The sound of rhythmic music could be heard in the distance, a gathering of some sort, but there was no one close by to notice us. We tied our horse to a post and approached Lovely's door. It was impossible to tell if there was light inside; the sole window was covered with a piece of cloth, as it had been when I was here before.

Sir Samuel knocked and we waited. "She took a while to answer last time," I said, my fear mounting. Every minute that passed could be crucial to Helen's recovery.

Sir Samuel turned to me with a determined look. "We need to find Hedgeford. Right away."

I had hoped we could handle this on our own, but that was not to be. Returning to our horse, we set off for the grand house atop the hill overlooking the yard. When we arrived in front, we were met by a man in rugged trousers and jacket, a pistol and short cutlass hanging from his leather belt.

"Help you folks?"

"We need to see Mr. Hedgeford," Sir Samuel replied.

"Sailed off to England three weeks ago. Left me in charge. Name's Jake Holmquist."

Though I was familiar with many of the large plantation managers, I had never seen him before. Something in the way he carried himself, perhaps with a bit too much swagger, made me think he might be new to the job.

"Fine, Mr. Holmquist. You have an Obeah-woman here, lives on the edge of the African yard. She is not at her house, and we need to find her immediately. The situation is urgent."

"Her name is Lovely," I added.

Mr. Holmquist narrowed his eyes, regarding us now with a touch of suspicion. "What you want with her?"

"She must tell us what was in a medicine she prepared for this young lady," Sir Samuel replied. "A child drank from the bottle and appears quite ill. We need to advise the doctor treating her as to what he is dealing with—what kind of concoction it is."

The man gave me a look that seemed both disbelieving and hostile. "What you doing going to an Obi-woman, anyway? You tryin' to stir up trouble?" Taking a step closer, he peered at me in the moonlight. "Hey, you're the governor's daughter, ain't you?"

Before I could answer, Sir Samuel spoke up. "I'm afraid you're mistaken, sir. This is my wife."

"And you are …?"

"Sir Samuel Hood, naval commander of the West Indies British fleet. Now are you going to help us, or do I need to speak with someone else?"

His title, and perhaps the tone of authority in his voice, effected a marked change. "Sure, I know where she probably is. There's some sort of celebration goin' on across the yard, behind the stables. You don't hear the drums?"

"You'll come with us then and point her out, in case the young lady has trouble recognizing her."

Mr. Holmquist nodded. "My horse is over there. You can follow me."

It took only a couple of minutes to reach the stables. After our horses were tied, he led us around the back where a large group of Africans, maybe as many as fifty, were having a party. The merriment stopped abruptly the moment Mr. Holmquist strutted into the crowd's midst.

"Lookin' for Lovely. She here?"

Everyone was silent, eyes to the ground. After a few seconds, Lovely stepped from behind a group of four or five women in raggedy cotton shifts. Lovely's dress was the same as theirs, but her white turban and colored beads gave her an air of distinction.

"You're comin' with me," Mr. Holmquist said sharply.

I could feel a wave of fear ripple through the crowd. "We just want to talk with you, Lovely," I said. "It will only take a minute."

As she approached us, Lovely's eyes locked with mine, but her expression was unreadable. Was she thinking I had betrayed her? That I had reported her for selling her services? Fearing all forms of Obeah, many slave owners forbade such commerce. Whether Mr. Hedgeford was among them, I didn't know. But he must have been impressed by her remarkable achievement in curing the yaws.

Mr. Holmquist grabbed Lovely by the arm. "You all go on with your dancin'," he said to the onlookers, none of whom dared say a word.

He led Lovely around the corner of the stables, the commodore and I falling into step behind them. Once we were entirely out of sight, he shoved Lovely against the stable wall.

"What you give this woman, Lovely? What kinda medicine? I want to know exactly what was in it, you hear? And if you lie, I swear I'll cut out your tongue before you know what hit you."

"Mr. Holmquist, please. Give her a chance to speak," I said, disgusted by his bullying. "There's no need to threaten her. I'm sure she will tell us what we need to know." I turned to Lovely. "I'm so sorry, I don't mean to cause you trouble. But please, a little girl got hold of the vial you gave me, and she drank some of it. Was there anything in the medicine that would harm her?"

"Maybe give her some hurt in her stomach, maybe de runs, but ain't gonna kill her." I saw no trace of subterfuge in her razor-sharp stare. Nor any fear.

"Tell 'em what's in the medicine, Lovely," Mr. Holmquist prodded, giving her shoulder a push. "Everything. And don't you try to keep no secrets."

"Ain't nothin' secret in what I give her. Just ground-up grapple plant. She say her faddah got gout. I never say de cure is fuh no baby." She looked at me again. "How old?"

"Four years."

"Ach!" She dismissed me with a wave of her hand. "She be sick a day or two, but dat's all."

"You sure there's nothing else in there?" Mr. Holmquist stuck a malicious finger in her face. "Mushrooms? Bugs? I know what you Obi people put in them brews, and it ain't pretty."

Lovely shrugged. "Bit o' hog fat and deer dung. Dat's all."

He took a step back and looked at us. "You satisfied? Got what you need?" he asked Sir Samuel. I was glad he didn't address me; at that moment I felt like I might be sick. Deer dung! No wonder Helen was in a fit.

Sir Samuel directed his reply to Lovely. "Yes. Thank you, ma'am." He placed his hand at the small of my back, and we turned to leave. The next second, I heard the sound of a hard slap. I whirled around to see Lovely up against the building.

"What are you doing?" I shouted. "Leave her alone!"

"She got no business givin' her potions to white folks. She want to treat the other slaves, that's fine. Long as she don't make 'em sicker or put no hexes on 'em. But she starts thinkin' she's a doctor to white folks, and that's nothin' but trouble."

"I came to her. She didn't invite me nor did she offer me anything I didn't ask for. If you insist on taking out your anger on someone, it ought to be me."

"She knows the rules—and what's in store for somebody who gets it in their head to break 'em. She shoulda had the sense to turn you away, ma'am. You see what happened. Your little baby got hurt." He turned back to Lovely, giving her a hard poke in the ribs. "Ain't that right, Lovely? You know what you done."

"Mr. Holmquist, please." I tried one last persuasion. "Mr. Hedgeford will be terribly angry if he finds out you've been rough with her. She cured his slaves of the yaws, when every one of the European doctors failed. Maybe you don't know about that."

The manager's sadistic grin abruptly faded. "Anyway, I'm finished with her this time." He gave Lovely a half-hearted push. "Go on now, and get yourself a dancin' partner."

I watched her leave, admiring the dignity with which she carried herself. She did not run. She did not even walk quickly. She sauntered.

As Sir Samuel and I rode off, I regretted that we couldn't have stayed a little longer, just to be certain Lovely suffered no further harassment from Mr. Holmquist. But my concern for Helen took precedence. We must get back and tell the doctor what we had learned.

When we returned to Pilgrim House, he was already there. We told him what was in the brownish-yellow brew, and though he blanched at the mention of deer dung, he mostly seemed relieved. Still, he warned there was likely more that the African woman hadn't revealed.

"They're very secretive, those Obeah-doctors. Sometimes you can bribe them; you never know if you're getting the whole truth. But I doubt there was poison or, by now, this little girl would be a good deal worse off than she appears. I've given her a purgative to cleanse her bowels. I expect she will be better tomorrow."

Helen had quietened down. Mother remained perched on the edge of the bed, smoothing and resmoothing Helen's fine, tawny hair. Poor Mother. She must be exhausted. And with the purgative doing its work, this night was bound to be a long and unpleasant one.

"I'll take her to my room, Mother. She can sleep with me."

She looked up at me, her face still etched with worry. "All right, if the doctor has no objection. I don't trust Nanny to watch her. I'm going to have to get rid of that woman. Send her back to Scotland just as soon as I can."

I turned to Sir Samuel. "Thank you for your help tonight. It seems everything is under control now, as much as it can be. Cunningham will see you to your room, if you like. You must be tired."

"I've prepared the same room you had last time," Mother said. "You found it comfortable, as I recall."

"I did." He smiled at her and then me—though I hardly deserved it. "No need to call for Cunningham. I know which room it is. I believe just above yours, Miss Mackenzie?"

He surely meant it as a reassurance, in case I needed assistance with Helen during the night. But, for a second, I imagined something else.

CHAPTER SIX

December was the end of the rainy season in Barbados. It had been a long and dangerous one, with the incidence of yellow fever the highest since we had arrived here nearly three years ago. Thankfully, all of us escaped the disease, but a record number of the island's British had perished.

Father was expected back from London any day when we received word that the wife and two young sons of Mr. Bennett, one of the British colonial administrators, had come down with the fever. The Bennetts occupied a large house at the base of our hill and were our nearest neighbors.

"What about Catherine?" I asked Mother, as we sat down to breakfast after hearing the news.

Catherine, nineteen, was my closest friend and confidante on the entire island. When she had her coming-out ball last year, the two of us plotted together how she would ensnare the most eligible marriage prospect. One candidate was the obvious choice: His name was George Jameson, and he was the son of the wealthiest merchant in Barbados. Now, Catherine was set to marry him next spring.

"Catherine is fine, and, so far, her younger sisters are as well." Mother hesitated, appearing somewhat conflicted. "I've decided the three girls should come here. Perhaps there is a risk in having them, but

I cannot in good conscience allow them to remain in a home with yellow fever."

I understood the risk. We could not know to what extent they might have been exposed to the disease. No one was certain how the fever spreads, but close contact with the infected was thought to be dangerous. Still, Mother was right. If we could do nothing for those already afflicted, at least we could try to save others from becoming ill.

I was especially glad to have Catherine coming to us, not only for her own safety but for the company she would provide. Though I was close to my sisters, being the eldest was sometimes a burden. I must always be on guard to set a good example. With Catherine, I could simply be myself.

The Bennett sisters arrived that evening, along with Dr. Williams, the physician treating their mother and brothers. He introduced himself as new to the island, having come at the recent invitation of the head of the British Hospital. He appeared rather young; I could only hope that his experience equipped him to properly care for our ailing neighbors. But if good looks could cure, he most certainly had an advantage over the island's other doctors.

The girls went upstairs to get settled in their rooms, while Mother invited Dr. Williams to take tea with us, including Frances and Caroline. Both were old enough to appreciate Dr. Williams's extraordinary gifts—his wavy black hair and quiet hazel eyes, and the broad shoulders and strong physique that his somber black waistcoat could not disguise. It was odd, but for the first time I felt a twinge of competitiveness with my sisters. To my eye, Caroline was the most striking among us, with her golden hair and soft blue eyes. Frances was a bit of a wallflower, but some men find that charming. As for me, I was the liveliest—and the one most prone to recklessness.

"I wanted to assure you, Lady Seaforth, that I have carefully examined the Bennett sisters and find no evidence that any of them are infected with yellow fever," Dr. Williams said, accepting a steaming cup from Mother. "If anything should develop, however, please send word to me immediately, and I will arrange for their care elsewhere."

"Certainly. But how is their mother doing?" Mrs. Bennett was one of Mother's favorites among the British wives.

"It is too early to say, I'm afraid. I have halted the bloodletting; it seemed not to be effective and was only making her weaker. There is hope that the calomel may prove beneficial. Our focus now is to keep her hydrated and as comfortable as possible."

"I see." Mother stared into her teacup, clearly distressed by the doctor's report. "And the two boys?"

"So far, they appear somewhat more resilient. We shall see."

"Why do you think none of us has it?" Frances asked shyly.

Dr. Williams smiled. "It's difficult to say. Maybe because you have had the good fortune not to be in close contact with anyone carrying the disease. Or you may have been blessed with a constitution that somehow protects you from this kind of infection. At any rate, whatever you have been doing, keep on with it."

"Perhaps God is protecting us so that we can help the Bennetts," Caroline offered.

It was Mother's turn to smile. "No doubt our family is among the most fortunate, my dear. We must never forget that, nor take it for granted."

I couldn't help thinking that Father might take exception to Mother's assessment of our family's fortunes—or at least his. Though he was always stoic, sometimes I could see that the weight of his afflictions bore down on him to the breaking point. Father constantly felt the need to prove himself, as if no accomplishment was ever enough. I was proud of him but still found it difficult to look him in the eyes, knowing what I did about his plantation in Berbice. The subject had not come up again between us, though I entertained a hope that he might have got rid of it. But what would he do about the two hundred African slaves? There could be no moral choice other than to free them.

"If you don't mind, Lady Seaforth, I would like to drop by every couple of days to look in on the girls. Just to see that there is no change. And, of course, to let them know how the rest of their family is faring. I trust that would not be an imposition?"

"Not at all," I blurted out. The prospect of seeing Dr. Williams again was a welcome distraction. "Your visit will help to put all our minds at ease."

"It is my hope that Mr. Bennett does not return from London until the worst of this is over. There is nothing he can do here except to expose himself to disease. For the sake of the children, it's best that he remains healthy."

"That makes perfect sense," Mother said, "though I am certain he would wish to be near his ailing wife."

"Being near her is exactly what he must avoid, for now."

Mother nodded, but I knew she was thinking how our father would feel if any of us were to perish from yellow fever and he had not been here to share our last moments.

"These tropical diseases are among the greatest challenges a physician can face. We doctors are sometimes at a loss." Dr. Williams stroked his smooth chin with a thoughtful frown. "Perhaps we could learn a few things from the Africans, if there were not so much mistrust. But, of course, it is understandable why there is, on both sides."

"Are you speaking of the Obeah-doctors?" I asked, avoiding Mother's stern look.

"Yes, I am. There have been a few interesting studies of Obeah medicine. No one has all the answers, but the Africans have substantial experience with tropical diseases. It's possible they could help us, but too many European physicians are unwilling to give it a try."

His words felt like a partial exoneration for my failed attempt at finding a cure for Father's gout. Even though gout is no more a tropical disease than the rheumatic fever that stole my father's hearing. But I liked Dr. Williams. He seemed more open-minded than most. Maybe it was his youth. I liked that, too.

He left half an hour later, with the promise to return in two days. I made a note of it, already planning what I would wear.

•　　　•　　　•

"Oh, Mary, you can't imagine what it's like."

Catherine and I sat on a bench beneath the silk-cotton tree behind Pilgrim House, its enormous canopy of heart-shaped leaves providing enough shade from the mid-afternoon sun that we had set aside our parasols.

"But how did it happen? Was it just ...well, spontaneous?"

"Somewhat. George had hinted at it a few times and, naturally, I had given him no encouragement whatsoever. But our wedding is only five months away ... and I know how to be careful."

"You do? How?"

My eyes must have been popping out of my head because Catherine started to laugh. "How do I know, or how can one be careful?"

I sighed in exasperation. Obviously I wanted to know the method she had used. Not that I needed the information. My interest was only curiosity. "What precautions did you take?"

"A cloth soaked in vinegar. You put it inside, as far as you can. It doesn't hurt."

I crinkled my nose. "Sounds disgusting."

"Believe me, you forget about it quickly." She laughed again, that gloriously musical laugh of hers, like chimes in the wind. Catherine was something special. If anyone were to ask me who was the most beautiful, brilliant person I knew, not only in Barbados but anywhere, I would have said Catherine Bennett. The best word to describe Catherine—with her thick, toffee-colored curls, her sultry grey eyes, and perfect arched brows—was *alluring*. And she was clever. Catherine had a knack for numbers and could calculate them in her head. She had read more novels than I knew existed and remembered every detail of each one. If I had not adored her so, I would have been shamefully jealous.

"So ..." I hesitated, not sure how far I should go. Some things were clearly not my business to know. But it couldn't hurt to ask. "What is George like? I mean ..."

"You mean, is he a good lover?"

"Well, if you want to tell me."

"Remember, it only happened once. Afterwards, I asked George if he'd ever been with a woman before, because—well, he seemed very adept. He blushed a bit, but then insisted he had not. So I don't really know for certain. But if he's only just begun to learn, I'd say he has a very promising future."

"Do you care if he's been with someone else?"

"I hope I'm *not* his first. That way, he'll less likely be curious about other women in the future."

"I suppose you're right." I didn't know how I would feel, but then I didn't have a fiancé. When I thought about the possibility of having one, the only gentleman who came to mind was Dr. Williams. Or maybe Sir Samuel, though I doubted a man of the world such as he would find me sufficiently interesting. But I'd probably be more tolerant of Sir Samuel having had affairs with women, since he was in his forties. It would be unusual for a man to remain virginal that long— and not especially desirable. After all, what is the appeal of an older man if not his superior experience?

"All I can say, Mary, is that you should not put off marriage too much longer. You'll be missing out and, besides, what about children? They say it's best to have as many as you can while you're still young."

"I plan to be young for a very long time." I pinched her cheek playfully. "Don't you worry about me. As soon as I get off this island, my life will be a dream. I promise, you will be the one envious of me!"

"It sounds like you have grand plans. What are they?"

She had caught me. I hadn't any plans. I didn't even know where I would live if Father was no longer governor. Brahan Castle or Seaforth Lodge on the Isle of Lewis, or maybe London. Wherever I might end up, I would have no young man waiting for me, dying to take me into his bed and show me all the pleasures to which Catherine had alluded. I had always said that I wanted adventure, but right now it would be enough just to leave Barbados. I recalled how, in the beginning, I had been excited to come here. But the reality was far different from the dream. Might the rest of life be like that, too—all that we so eagerly anticipate failing to meet our expectations? Turning out, in fact, to be the opposite of what we had hoped?

"Perhaps I'll sail the high seas and fall in love with a pirate," I said, gazing towards the docks of Bridgetown. "Would that be enough to impress you?"

"Maybe." She glanced towards the sun. "It must be about time for Dr. Williams. He's very punctual, have you noticed?"

"Punctual? Yes, I suppose. But that's not what I've noticed most about him."

Catherine gave me a sly smile. "He is rather handsome, isn't he? If I weren't already engaged, I might be interested—even if he has no money. But there's nothing stopping you, Mary."

"I'm afraid he barely notices me. All he seems interested in is making sure you and your sisters are healthy."

Catherine's eyes suddenly lost their sparkle. "It's good of him—but, Mary, I'm so worried about Mother and the boys. Dr. Williams hasn't told me much about their condition, whether it's improving or not, which could be a bad sign. Well, I suppose he did say my brothers were showing themselves to be strong young boys, whatever that means. But all he has said about Mother is that we must take it day by day."

I reached for Catherine's hand. "They are receiving the best of care. You must keep up your spirits."

She nodded with a wistful smile. "Speaking of keeping up my spirits—after Dr. Williams leaves this afternoon, I'm meeting George down by the swamp."

I gave her a tiny poke in the ribs. "Naughty girl! So that's where the two of you go to be alone!"

"George knows all the most secluded places. The only problem is the mosquitoes. We try to stay under a blanket, but it's so awfully hot."

"What do you suppose your mother would say if she knew you'd not saved yourself for marriage?"

A momentary flash of guilt passed over Catherine's face. "Need you ask? But, Mary, we're not in London now, and the old rules don't apply.

I feel so much freer here. That's the best thing about Barbados, don't you agree?"

"I used to think so, but it's not really so different after all. The British are always trying to pretend they're still in England. They don't want to admit that nothing is the same here and never will be."

"Well, I don't care. George will be rich, just like his father, and we'll have lots of children and a beautiful life."

I threw my arms around her and hugged her tight against me. "I'm so glad you're happy."

• • •

Dr. Williams arrived with his medical bag in one hand and two large bouquets in the other. It was more than a coincidence that I happened to be in the hall when Cunningham admitted him.

"Good afternoon, Doctor. What lovely flowers!"

"A strong dose of cheer is always the best antidote to troubled times," he replied, handing one of the bouquets to me. "Please tell your mother that I greatly appreciate her indulgence in allowing me to check in with my patients."

"Oh …" So, the gift was meant for Mother. I hoped he didn't sense my disappointment. But there was still one more bouquet … "She will love them. Thank you."

"My pleasure. May I go upstairs to look in on the Bennett sisters? Then I must head over to check on Mrs. Bennett. I tried a new herbal remedy for her last evening and am anxious to see if it reduced her fever."

"I do hope it works. I believe Catherine is expecting you." I hesitated, knowing I should say nothing but unable to resist, on the chance he might simply have forgotten the other bouquet—and it was intended for me. "I'm sure she will be touched by your thoughtfulness," I said, eyeing the flowers.

"Oh yes—these." I held my breath. "I believe part of what a doctor should do for his patients is help to raise their spirits."

He seemed so earnest that I forgave him, almost, for passing over me in favor of my friend. I doubted that he knew Catherine was engaged. There would have been no reason for her to tell him. In fact, knowing Catherine, she would enjoy a touch of forbidden flirtation.

"If you don't mind my asking, have the sisters confined themselves to the house and the gardens, as I asked them to?"

"Oh yes, completely." My reply was the absolute truth, though I knew Catherine had other plans for later. Still, I could not violate her trust by telling Dr. Williams where she was going—and why. "Do you mind seeing yourself upstairs? As I said, the sisters are expecting you."

Ordinarily, I would have escorted Dr. Williams myself, or at least summoned Cunningham, but at that moment I was not in the politest of moods. Perhaps it was petty of me. But, the more I thought about it, I rather resented the fact it had never once occurred to him that I might be worthy of his attentions. Perhaps a flower or two.

As I watched Dr. Williams ascend to the upper floor, I resolved not to waste another moment of my time wondering what he thought or believed or wanted. Even if I were madly in love with him, and he with me, he was not a suitor that Father would particularly welcome. Presumably he held no titles or estates or any prospects of note.

I sighed and turned towards the drawing room, thinking I would play the piano for a while to occupy my mind. Entering the room, I was surprised to see Mother sitting alone, her expression morose.

"What is it, Mother? You look awfully glum."

"I heard Dr. Williams in the hall, but I simply could not bring myself to go out and speak with him."

"Why not? Is something wrong?"

"He didn't tell you? Well … perhaps he doesn't know yet. I heard it just minutes ago from Cunningham, who was informed by the Bennetts' butler." Mother bowed her head. "God has seen fit to take Mrs. Bennett from our midst. She succumbed early this afternoon to yellow fever."

"Oh no!" I thought of Catherine upstairs with Dr. Williams, neither of them knowing, and I wondered if I should go and tell them. But the doctor would find out soon enough, and as for Catherine—let her have a few moments of happiness this afternoon with George before her world collapsed. Death could wait its turn.

"I'm so sorry, Mother. She was a lovely woman, and I know you cared for her."

"She was a woman of principle, with a kind heart. That combination is rare these days." Mother took a long, deep breath. "It's difficult to understand God's purpose in such a tragedy, but surely He has one."

I sat down next to her on the sofa and drew her into my arms. Though I knew her feelings ran deep, she seldom allowed herself tears.

"You will need to be there for Catherine, dear. Such an awful blow. And only five months from her wedding day."

"I'll help her, Mother. Don't worry."

"I suppose we should go upstairs and break the news. But let us compose ourselves first."

I eased myself away from our embrace. "Wouldn't it be best if Dr. Williams were the one to tell Catherine? Besides, all we have is second-hand information. What if there's been a mistake? A miscommunication of some sort. How awful to put the girls through this if there is even one tiny possibility that Cunningham's source was wrong. Dr. Williams told me that he is planning to see Mrs. Bennett after he leaves here. He will know soon enough, and then he can tell the girls. There should be only a short delay."

Mother appeared to be weighing my advice. "Very well," she said finally, "we will leave it to Dr. Williams to determine his patient's condition and inform the daughters."

I was relieved. Not only did I want to spare Catherine from the news a bit longer, but I believed what I had said was true. It was not our place to intervene. Thinking again of Dr. Williams, I could imagine how devastated he would be to discover his new remedy had failed and he had lost his patient. He might even wonder if the medicine, untried as he had intimated it was, could be responsible for the suddenness of her departure. But then, it wasn't really sudden at all. She had been ill for over a week. Yellow fever often took its victims in a matter of days.

"I thank God every day for having spared our family," Mother said, giving my hand a gentle squeeze. "Whatever his purpose in doing so."

A thought sprang to my mind, and I struggled to blot it out, but it was too late. The voice of Coinneach Odhar, the Brahan Seer, whispered in my ear: *A different fate awaits yer kin, a destiny to unfold in its ain way and its ain time.*

CHAPTER SEVEN

That night, Mother and I were the only ones at the dinner table who knew of Mrs. Bennett's passing, and the chatter of her daughters was as lively as ever. With Christmas drawing near, there was talk of holiday decorations and hoped-for gifts, as if this year would be like any other. But yellow fever had reached epidemic proportions and, for many on the island, Christmas would be a somber affair, a time to feel their losses even more acutely. Mother and I exchanged glances many times over dinner, which tonight seemed to last longer than usual. She surely was as uncomfortable as I was, hiding the truth from the girls. Especially Catherine who, being the eldest, must now take over a mother's role.

The moment Cunningham announced that Dr. Williams was in the entrance hall, Mother lifted the napkin from her lap, folded it and laid it on the table with an attitude of finality. "Show him in."

A minute later, Dr. Williams appeared in the doorway. The look on his face was not difficult to interpret, but, of course, I knew what was on his mind. The task that no doctor relishes but one as much a part of his duty as attempting the cure he now must pronounce a failure.

"I'm terribly sorry to interrupt your dinner, Lady Seaforth. Young ladies …" His gaze swept the table, lingering the longest on Catherine.

"Is there news?" she asked. "Good news, I hope."

"Let us allow Dr. Williams to sit down," Mother said. "He must be exhausted after a long day of caring for the sick."

"I am tired, yes," he said, taking the chair that Cunningham pulled out for him, "but that is the least of what I feel tonight." His eyes again found Catherine. "Miss Bennett, you and your sisters have been exceedingly brave throughout your family's ordeal, but I fear you now must summon your greatest strength and rely upon each other for solace. Your—" His voice broke. "Your dear mother was unable to overcome her illness. She left us this afternoon, after a long and valiant struggle. I am so terribly sorry."

A long, pitiful wail came from Catherine's youngest sister, Hannah. Catherine pressed a dinner napkin to her mouth, muffling the sobs that rose from her throat. I jumped from my seat and circled the table, falling to my knees next to her.

"My darling Catherine!" I threw my arms around her waist, pressing my head against her stomach. All I could think to do was hold on to her, silently, feeling the pain of every breath she took.

After a minute, Dr. Williams spoke again. "Your mother would have been relieved to know that her two sons are doing much better now. I am guardedly optimistic that they will make a full recovery."

"Thank God," Mother said, dabbing at her eyes with a handkerchief. "And thanks to our Lord that the girls are safe. And their father," she added, remembering that Mr. Bennett had been mercifully spared to care for his family in their time of greatest need.

"Did she ..." Catherine's voice trembled as she spoke. "Did she pass peacefully?"

"Yes, she did," Dr. Williams said. It seemed unlikely that he spoke the truth, but, under the circumstances, who would blame him?

The three sisters were crying, as were the rest of us. All except Dr. Williams. Through my tears, I noticed he kept glancing at Catherine—perhaps wishing that he, instead of me, could be the one to comfort her.

"Dr. Williams," Mother said quietly, "I think the girls need to be alone with each other, upstairs. Or wherever they would like to be. But the rest of us must give them some privacy."

60 THE SEAFORTH HEIRESS

Dr. Williams stood, appearing somewhat relieved to be dismissed. Yet I sensed his reluctance as well. "My day is not yet over, even though night has fallen. This disease does not sleep, and neither can I."

"Come along, Catherine," I said gently, standing and helping her up from her chair. "Is it all right if I stay with you? Just for a little while?"

She nodded. Then, taking each of her sisters by the hand, she silently led them towards the hallway. I trailed behind, hearing Dr. Williams say to Mother, "If it would not be an imposition, I would like to stop by tomorrow afternoon to check on the girls. Mostly to see how they are dealing with their loss."

He was certainly no ordinary doctor, I thought. Or was his solicitousness not simply a matter of duty but an overpowering infatuation? Either way, I admired his sensitivity; in my limited experience, such a quality was rare in a man. I had certainly seen no evidence of it in the behavior of Catherine's fiancé, George. In the midst of a yellow fever epidemic, with my friend's mother and brothers fighting for their lives, it hardly seemed the best timing for her first intimate experience. But apparently George had insisted.

I would never agree to such a thing, unless I had thought of it first.

The next morning, Catherine refused the breakfast tray that had been brought to her room. Her door was still closed when I went to check on her at noon. Pressing my ear to the wood, I heard no stirring from within. Worried, I sought out her sister Hannah, who was painting with watercolors in the back drawing room.

"Have you seen Catherine this morning?"

Hannah looked up from her work. The rims of her eyes were red from crying. "I don't think she's got out of bed."

I checked the longcase clock. Dr. Williams was due to arrive at two. Catherine would not want him to find her still in her nightdress. Deciding to alert her to his planned visit, I returned to her bedchamber. Again, I listened through the door but heard nothing.

"Catherine, are you up?"

I heard a low groan.

"May I come in?"

When she didn't answer, I opened the door. As I expected, she was lying in bed. "I thought you would want to know that Dr. Williams plans to pay you a visit soon."

Catherine rolled over on her side, pulling up the covers so they hid the lower half of her face. "Send him away," she murmured, so softly I could barely hear.

"You should at least talk to him. Thank him for coming. I'm sure he'll have more news of your brothers. What he told us yesterday was very encouraging. They should make a full recovery, he said. That's something to be grateful for."

I waited for her to reply, but she remained silent.

"Catherine, I know you must be exhausted, but you'll feel better once you're up and about. I'll send Sarah to help you dress."

"I have it, Mary. I have the fever."

Panic gripped my heart. "Don't be daft, Catherine. You're feeling poorly because of all you've been through. It's only natural."

"You must stay away. Everyone must."

"Listen to me. You do *not* have yellow fever." I had to make her believe. She mustn't give in to the fear. "Dr. Williams will be here soon. He will tell you the same as I'm saying."

"Warn him to put on his coat and mask, like he did with Mother. And let George know. I was to meet him this afternoon, down by the swamp. God, I hope he doesn't have it, too."

"George won't be expecting you to come. He must have heard about your mother by now."

"Just tell him I will do my best not to die."

"Catherine, stop it!" I was terrified, but I kept on. "After Dr. Williams has pronounced you free of yellow fever, we can sit outside again, under the silk-cotton tree. You can tell me more about what it's like—you know …" I thought to cheer her, but my words sounded hollow, even to me. The exciting future that yesterday beckoned us to follow, today seemed forever beyond our reach.

CHAPTER EIGHT

After the diagnosis of yellow fever had been made, I was adamant that Catherine must remain with us, and Mother did not object. My friend was confined to her room, and Dr. Williams was the only one allowed to see her. He came every day. But it was to no avail. Six days after falling ill, Catherine died.

I took to sitting on the veranda, hour after hour, staring out to sea as though the answers I sought might be found there. It wasn't fair. It wasn't right. Catherine did not deserve to die. But my tearful protests went unacknowledged. Unheard. And the belief I had clung to for so long—that one can circumvent misfortune through superior strength—was shaken. Perhaps none among us possesses strength enough to ward off evil once we are in its grip. But what is the turning point? When is it too late to alter destiny?

Catherine's fiancé George had so far not contracted yellow fever. If contact with an infected person was indeed the way the fever spreads, why should he have been spared? I thought of telling Dr. Williams about the twosome's trysts, thinking it might be useful to his research, but to do so surely would diminish Catherine in the good doctor's eyes. Whether for her sake or his, I did not wish for that to happen. I wanted him to remember Catherine as I would remember her. A beautiful soul. A joy to all who knew her.

Catherine and her mother were laid to rest in what was now designated the Bennett family plot. Mother, Frances, Caroline, Augusta, and I accompanied the two surviving Bennett sisters to the burial. The only others present were Dr. Williams and several of the Bennett family's servants. The young sons were not yet well enough to attend, and Mr. Bennett was aboard a ship, on his way back to the island. There should have been more in attendance, but the fear of becoming yellow fever's next victim kept them away.

That afternoon, a light rain was falling. Already pools of water were collecting at the bottom of the graves into which the coffins would soon be lowered. I only half listened as the preacher droned on, insisting that the deaths of my dearest friend and her mother were the will of God and not to be questioned. Though I acted like one of the faithful, in my mind the same troubling questions kept resurfacing, over and over. Perhaps George had led Catherine into sin, but had she not followed him in innocence? Who, or what, decides when and how we die? Catherine did not deserve her fate; if God were to ask me, I would tell Him so and rail at the injustice. But God does not ask, nor does He care if we approve. And, somehow, that seems to be all right with His believers.

"Let us cherish the memories of those we lay to rest today, knowing that their lives were not without purpose and that God has fulfilled their destiny according to His plan," the preacher said in a booming voice, louder than necessary considering the small group of mourners. "As mortals, we can never fully understand God's ways, but remember this: Belief in His eternal wisdom is our only salvation, our only chance for redemption. So, as we say a final goodbye to our loved ones, let us pray that the grace of Lord Jesus Christ will be with them and the light of God shine upon them, now and forevermore."

He led us in the Lord's Prayer, which I recited along with the others. The coffin containing the remains of Catherine's mother was first to be lowered into the ground. Though I was deeply sorry for her death, it was not until Catherine's coffin had settled into the open grave assigned to her that I released my pent-up tears. The day Catherine's lifeless body was carried from Pilgrim House to await burial, I could not bear to look at her. Later, I begged to see her one last time, but Mother forbade it. Today's service had not offered the sense of closure for which I had hoped. It had only served to open the wound again.

I tossed my small bouquet onto her coffin. Next was Dr. Williams. I stole a glance at him as the flowers slipped from his fingers, falling into the dark abyss from which Catherine would never rise. I wondered if he blamed himself for her death. I hoped not. He had tried his best to save her—not only as her doctor but, I felt certain, as a man who would have loved her deeply if given the chance.

We watched as shovelfuls of dirt, dumped in rapid succession, covered over our final tributes.

"Lady Seaforth ... ladies." Dr. Williams acknowledged Mother and all of us with a single sober nod. "This dreary day suits the occasion, does it not? Even the sky mourns."

"Yes, our hearts are heavy," Mother replied, "but there is joy in knowing our departed ones have met the Lord."

Dr. Williams looked down at the freshly covered graves. "Dust to dust," he murmured.

There was a long silence before Mother asked, "Would you care to join us for tea? Perhaps we can cheer each other a bit."

"Very kind of you, Lady Seaforth, but I'm afraid I have patients who need my attention."

"Of course, I understand. This dread disease is still with us and seems to have no intention of abating. Even the young and healthy fall prey to it. Is there nothing we can do?"

"I assure you, Lady Seaforth, we are doing everything possible to contain its spread."

"Why can't you cure it?" Augusta said with her usual naïve bluntness.

"It would help if we knew what causes it. More and better research is sorely needed."

"Perhaps we must look beyond science for the cause," said Caroline. "Might it be that God is sending us a message—that those of us still here must serve Him better?"

My dear Caroline was so like our mother! I would not change her for the world. Still, it worried me that she was too eager to substitute faith for reason.

"I do not profess to have the answer to your question, Miss Caroline. My role as a doctor is to explore the science of disease."

"What if we keep dying until there is no one left?" Augusta cried.

"We *will* find the cause of yellow fever—and the cure. And remember, not everyone who contracts the sickness dies from it. Many are able to fight it off. Someday we will understand what makes certain people more susceptible than others."

"Catherine should have been one who lived."

Dr. Williams swallowed hard. "Yes, she should have been."

I decided to put an end to the conversation, which was not helping anyone to deal with our shared tragedy. "We must let Dr. Williams be on his way. As he said, there are people counting on him whose need is greater than ours."

"Thank you, Miss Mackenzie." He hastily said his goodbyes and hurried off to wherever he had tethered his horse. It must have been some distance from the graveyard, because he was still on foot when his black frock coat and top hat faded from view.

"Come along, Ross is waiting," Mother said, motioning for us to follow her across the cemetery to the gravel drive where the carriage was waiting. She had taken no more than a dozen steps when she suddenly clutched my arm.

"Are you all right, Mother?" She seemed to be struggling for breath. "Mother?"

"Yes, yes. I need a moment."

Seeing that we had stopped, Caroline rushed over to us, taking Mother's left arm while I supported her on the right. "There is a bench in front of that tall monument, not far," she said. "Shall we sit there for a minute?"

"I don't want to sit." Mother's tone was sharp. She hated to be fussed over.

Frances came up beside us. "Is Mother ill?"

"I'm perfectly fine," Mother said, freeing herself from our grasp. "Now let us continue to the carriage, please."

When we reached the driveway, Ross jumped down from the box to help us into the carriage. Mother was first. I observed how heavily she dropped onto the velvet seat. She appeared utterly exhausted.

No one said anything on the ride home. Mother closed her eyes, leaning her head against the seatback. I couldn't tell if she was asleep or just resting, but she did not look well. My first thought was yellow fever, but I dared not touch her forehead now. She would have my head.

As soon as we arrived at Pilgrim House, Mother retired to her bedchamber, saying that the burial of our friends had affected her deeply. It had, of course, but there seemed more to her fatigue. Perhaps it was normal for a woman of fifty; I didn't know.

Our mother had been late to marry, late to have her ten children, of which all but two sons had survived infancy. I only hoped she would be late to meet her end as well. Our family was exceptionally close, and it was Mother who held us together. But as much as her children loved and needed her, Father depended on her most. I had always been touched by the way he began every letter he wrote to her: not with *Dear Mira*, but *Dear Life*.

Mother did not come down for dinner that night, leaving us to wonder if she might indeed be in a fever. It was decided that Caroline and I should be the ones to check on her. Caroline because of her natural instinct for nurturing, so much like our mother, and me because I was the eldest and therefore the one who must assume the major responsibility if Mother were to be seriously ill.

Caroline and I tiptoed up the stairs and down the landing towards Mother's apartment. Why we felt the need for stealth was unspoken; both of us knew that Mother, if given the opportunity, would try to hide her distress. The element of surprise was essential to evaluating her condition. Out of courtesy, however, I gave the door a light tap, waiting only a second before opening it.

But Mother was not in bed. The room was empty. We crossed over to her dressing room, peeking around the corner to see if she might be composing a letter at her desk. She was not there.

"Perhaps you should ask McAlister where Mother is." Mother scarcely made a move without her maid knowing about it.

"All right. I'll go." Caroline hurried off while I continued to ponder where our mother might have gone. Perhaps to the library in search of a book to take her mind off the day's heart-wrenching events? That would, of course, be an excellent sign that whatever ailed her at the cemetery had passed.

My idea proved wrong; she was not in the library. I continued down the hall and had arrived at Father's study when I heard a noise from within, like a drawer slamming shut. To my knowledge, Mother was not one to rummage through Father's desk. But then, she would never suspect me of having the gall to snoop through his papers either—or, on second thought, perhaps she wouldn't be surprised.

The door was slightly ajar so that I could see only a slice of the room from the hallway. I pushed it open a little more. Mother was sitting in Father's chair, her elbows on the desktop, her face buried in her hands. Was she crying?

"Mother!"

Startled, she raised her head. On her face I saw no evidence of tears, only the pall of worry.

"Caroline and I have been looking all over for you," I said. "Are you feeling better?"

Mother sighed. "Yes and no."

"Do you have a fever?

"Fever? Heavens, no. Is that what you're concerned about?"

"Isn't it on all our minds these days?"

Mother picked up a sheet of paper from the desk and waved it in the air. "This is what's making me ill, if you must know. I would not burden you with it, except—well, perhaps it's best that you understand. Someday you will marry, and your husband's problems will become yours. Just as your father's are mine. And, my dear, he has many problems indeed. Not only the obvious ones." She leaned back in Father's chair. "You know how proud I am of your father, Mary. Though he can become terribly discouraged by the obstacles he faces, he always picks himself up, determined to overcome them. But this …" She tossed the paper in her hand onto the desktop with an air of futility. "Your grandmother is certainly within her rights, but she is not helping her son by such rantings as are in this letter."

"Rantings about what?" My grandmother, who lived in London, was known for her outspokenness, harsh at times, but I was not aware of it being directed towards Father.

"Ah, the same old thing. But now she is threatening *disagreeable consequences*. Can you imagine? Bringing legal proceedings against her own son?"

"Mother, you are not being clear. Proceedings concerning what?"

"Payment of her annuity. It is late again, which is unfortunate, but she should understand that her lifestyle in London is an untenable drain on the estate. Still, she continues to reject any suggestion of moving elsewhere—except perhaps France, given her affection for French republicanism." Mother's tone was caustic. My grandmother's politics were unpopular with most of her family. "The sensible thing would be for her to establish residence at Brahan Castle, but she insists that is out of the question."

"Does Father know what she is threatening to do?"

"Not yet. When he returns from London, even if his health has improved, this news will surely set him back. I have been trying to think of what to do, but I simply can't come up with a solution. Perhaps your father will have conducted some sort of favorable business while he was away. I can only hope so."

I had never told Mother that I was aware of Father's debts, his gambling losses, the pressure he was under to sell off the family's Highland properties, or his purchase of the Berbice plantation and two hundred slaves. In fact, I was uncertain whether Mother herself knew such details. I was not going to be the one to tell her.

"When did the letter arrive?"

"A couple of days ago. I must have read and reread it a hundred times, for all the good that does."

"You are right, it does no good for you to worry yourself sick over such matters. Father will deal with the situation when he returns from London. Might he have taken the opportunity while being there to see Grannie? A personal visit might help to smooth things over with her."

"Let us hope that is the case. But, Mary—you must not speak of this to your sisters. Not to anyone. Your father is a very private person and does not like his affairs out in the open. You do understand, don't you?"

"You can trust me."

She gave me a weary smile. "I know, dear. There have been times when I doubted your judgment—not long ago, in fact," she said, and I knew she was referring to the incident of the Obeah-doctor. "But, in general, you are a level-headed girl." She chuckled. "Well, not such a girl anymore. I often wonder when your father and I shall lose you to a husband. I'm surprised that we haven't already, but being here in Barbados has put you at a distinct disadvantage. I am sorry for that, Mary."

"No need to be sorry," I said, though the senselessness of Catherine's death had made me recognize, more than ever, that I despised almost everything about Barbados.

CHAPTER NINE

U pon Father's return in February his health seemed somewhat better. Perhaps having a break from the political tensions in Barbados had indeed been a good tonic. But, with my burgeoning talent for sleuthing, I discovered that Father had made use of his time in London to revisit his habit of gambling at cards. Perhaps he really believed that, by luck, he might pull himself out of debt. But, apparently, Father was as unlucky as ever.

Compounding the financial strain of his gambling losses and his delinquency in paying Grannie's annuity was the impending ball at Pilgrim House to mark Frances's official coming out. No expense had been spared in my parents' efforts to provide the local gentry with a memorable evening, and it was certain that my sister's coming out would proceed with all the splendor that had attended mine two years earlier.

On the night of the ball, I readied myself early so I could join Frances in her dressing room and offer much-needed moral support. She had always lacked self-confidence, for no reason I could fathom. Though Frances might have been somewhat plainer in appearance than I, she was far more talented. I was good at drawing; she was masterful. My piano playing was adequate; hers was worthy of the concert hall. Yet she hated playing for anyone beyond our immediate family, avoiding it whenever she could. She and Mother had quarreled over whether she must perform at her coming out, which was often done but by no means mandatory. My sister was grateful when I interceded on her behalf, saying that she was entitled to enjoy rather than dread the ball in her honor. Besides, there would be an orchestra for dancing and a theatrical display featuring two operatic singers—enough musical entertainment to satisfy everyone. Mother finally agreed, perhaps recognizing that Frances would find it difficult enough simply being the center of attention.

I arrived just as the maid was nestling a delicate pearl and diamond comb into her upswept hair. Sitting at her dressing table, Frances studied her reflection in the trifold mirror with a critical eye.

"Should I wear the diamond earrings or the pearls?" she asked, nervously fingering the soft curls framing her face.

"We already decided you would wear the diamonds, remember?"

"Yes, I know. But now I'm not sure."

"When you are fully dressed, you'll see that the diamonds best complement your outfit. Especially with the necklace you've chosen."

"I'm so afraid of making a mistake. Everyone will be looking for something to criticize about me."

Asking the maid to step aside, I stood behind Frances, resting my hands on her shoulders. "My darling sister, forget about making mistakes. All you must do is to be yourself—well, perhaps a slightly more outgoing version of yourself, if you can. Just smile and make people feel you're interested in them, even if they bore you to tears. Remember, none of them really care about anybody but themselves. Even on your special night. They are here to eat and drink and show off their jewels, perhaps kick up their heels a bit on the dance floor. Wishing you well, or even noticing you at all, is more of an afterthought."

"But they will remember your coming out and how beautiful you were." Frances turned to look up at me with her soulful brown eyes. "I'm sorry ... I don't mean to sound jealous. It's just that they can't help but compare me to you, and I won't ever win that contest."

"Listen to me, darling: There will be no one lovelier than you, I promise. Look at yourself—see how you glow? You are absolutely stunning!"

Frances reached up and squeezed my hand. "Thank you, Mary."

"One more thing: I don't expect you'll meet the man of your dreams tonight. Not unless some handsome vagabond prince happens to find his way to our doorstep within the next few hours. But you can at least have some fun. Try not to take it all so seriously."

She gave me a tremulous smile. "I'll try."

"All right, I'm going to leave you now. But don't dilly-dally. The first guests should be arriving soon."

Tonight, the ballroom in Pilgrim House was dazzling to behold. Crystal chandeliers shimmered gold with candlelight, their brilliance amplified tenfold by the tall, gilt-framed mirrors positioned at intervals along the walls. Tropical blooms of bright red, yellow, and pink burst from enormous vases atop marble stands, or were woven into gigantic arrangements hung from the high ceiling. The dance floor had been polished with care. At ten-thirty, it still awaited the first dance, while guests chatted in small groups on the surrounding carpeted areas. An orchestra in the far corner warmed up with a few quiet selections as a small army of footmen bustled about, serving wine, spirits, and hors d'oeuvres of imported delicacies.

With my reception duties over, I was free to mingle. But my main concern was to observe Frances and make certain she did not falter in her role as debutante. She appeared to be handling it well enough, though I had yet to see her talking with any of the young men present.

"You look very lovely tonight, Miss Mackenzie."

I'd been so intent on watching Frances that I had not noticed the approach of Dr. Williams, dashing in his black evening suit and starched white collar. I was aware that Mother had invited him, though he was not part of the preferred social set. He had exhibited such devotion to the care of our dear friends, she said, and the guest list was in need of a few more handsome young men.

"How lovely to see you, Dr. Williams," I said, extending my hand. "We used to look forward to your visits—of course, not the reason for them," I added hastily. I had not, by any measure, recovered from the loss of my dear Catherine, nor did I think Dr. Williams had. "Thank goodness the epidemic is behind us."

"Let us hope so. Yellow fever has taken a terrible toll on this island, especially among the African population. The only bright spot is that several of the planters have pledged their monetary support for my research into the cause and cure."

"I must say that I'm surprised. Barbados planters are not known for their generosity."

"I'm afraid it is not generosity motivating them, but the opposite. For every slave they lose, another must be bought. That's how they look at it. But I must accept support from wherever I can find it. In the long run, such research benefits everyone."

"I wish you luck." Again, I thought of telling him about Catherine—how George had failed to contract yellow fever despite their intimate contact. But, as before, I chose not to say a word. "How is your approach to be different from what others have tried?"

"I am still designing my study. But one thing it will include that many others have overlooked is a sampling of African medicine. There are many plant cures known to the Africans which might possibly prove useful in treating yellow fever. We don't know—and we can't know unless we investigate. Unfortunately, some of my fellow Europeans want to dismiss Obeah medicine as witchcraft, when there is a great deal more to it than that."

"I do not believe in witchcraft. Or sorcery." It felt good to announce my rejection of evil magic's power.

"Nor do I. But I do acknowledge, in some instances, the power of the mind over the body."

The orchestra had stopped playing. As Dr. Williams and I watched the first group of dancers assemble for the opening country-dance, I was dismayed to see Frances being led onto the floor by Catherine's former beau, George.

"Oh no," I murmured.

"Is something wrong?"

"Not really. Just that there are other young men who would be a better match for my sister."

"Well, it's only a dance."

We observed as the two of them informed the master of ceremonies of the chosen tune and figure for the first set.

"Is she a skilled dancer?"

I glanced at him. Might he have an interest in Frances? And still none at all in me?

"Why don't you dance with her and find out?" My tone was slightly chilly, for which I was immediately ashamed. This was Frances's night, and a dance with Dr. Williams might be just the encouragement she needed.

"An excellent idea," he said. "And perhaps you might do me the honor as well?"

I smiled and was about to reply that I would be delighted when I spied Sir Samuel across the room. Though he stood with several other men, my father among them, he was looking straight at me. Our eyes met. His gaze did not flinch. But there was an unsettled look about him. I felt as if he wanted to tell me something; I had no inkling what it might be.

"Yes, we will have a dance this evening, certainly," I said, turning back to Dr. Williams. "But, right now, I must ask you to excuse me. I believe I'm needed elsewhere."

I made my way across the ballroom, pausing here and there to greet friends and acquaintances for the sake of cordiality, but acutely aware of Sir Samuel's eyes still upon me. As I drew near, he stepped away from the men with whom he'd been conversing to greet me.

"Miss Mackenzie, your beauty puts to shame every other woman here tonight."

"Thank you, but I prefer for my sister Frances to take that honor. Doesn't she look lovely? And Caroline, too. Another year and it will be her turn to break young men's hearts."

"You must have broken many in the last couple of years."

"Not really. To break a heart, you must first encourage it to hope."

"And the gentleman you were speaking with just now? A young doctor, I believe. He looked rather hopeful."

"I doubt it very much." Could that be why Sir Samuel had been watching me so intently? "Mother invited Dr. Williams in gratitude for his devoted care of our dear friends, the Bennetts, when they fell ill with yellow fever."

"Hmm." He did not sound convinced. "At any rate, I need to warn you about something. Mr. Hedgeford's plantation manager, that crude American fellow, is here tonight. I was surprised to see him, but apparently Mr. Hedgeford is away again on business. Having no sons to stand in for her husband, Mrs. Hedgeford insisted on their manager, whatever his name is, serving as a perfunctory escort. I don't know where he is at the moment, but I thought you should be prepared. As you'll recall, when we went on our secret mission to the Hedgeford plantation, I introduced you as my wife."

The twinkle in his lively blue eyes hinted that he would not mind continuing our little charade. It might in fact be necessary should I run into that most disagreeable character. My foray into the world of Obeah must not become common knowledge.

"I shall try to remember to conduct myself as you would have your wife behave," I said coyly. "Though I may not be capable."

"No question in my mind that you are. But I hope this doesn't mean I shall be denied a dance with you. Unless someone else has already filled your card."

He clearly was alluding to Dr. Williams. "You know, of course, that etiquette demands a husband and wife shall not be partners in the dance," I replied with a flutter of my feathered fan.

"True, but I'm quite certain our American friend has no idea of etiquette, and he is the only one who considers us married."

"Very well, then your name shall be at the top of my dance card, Sir Samuel," I conceded.

"How extraordinarily lucky! Shall we take our places now?"

Many couples were already claiming their positions down the line. Sir Samuel and I found ourselves situated near the bottom of the longways set. At my earlier suggestion, my sister had chosen "La Belle Catherine" to begin the evening's dancing. The orchestra played it through once to familiarize the dancers with the tempo, after which George bowed to Frances, and she returned his acknowledgment with a slight curtsy. Inwardly, I cringed.

"Do you imagine I'm the oldest gentleman on the dance floor?" Sir Samuel said with a wink.

"No, but the tallest."

"I must warn you that gracefulness is not my forte. But to dance with you is worth whatever humiliation I am forced to suffer."

His self-effacing manner was endearing given that he was probably the most famous person in the room, and the most admired. I had come to realize, from listening to Father, that Sir Samuel's brilliance as a commander had made him a living legend.

"Frances and I have been practicing some of the elegant new steps, but I won't be surprised if she chooses the simplest. I trust you shall have no trouble with a step-hop step."

The line was long, and the commodore and I waited some time for our turn. But when it came, we moved through the figures with gay simplicity, our steps easy and the corresponding motion of our arms as smooth as any of the couples preceding us. Throughout, our eyes were locked, as is proper for partners in the country-dance. For fun, I tried imagining that I actually was Lady Hood. The sensation I derived from this improbable fantasy was not unpleasant.

"You dance beautifully," he said, once we had completed our journey down the line and resumed our stationary positions. "But I'm sure all your partners tell you that."

"I've had few opportunities for partners, other than Frances. The epidemic put a halt to most of our social gatherings last winter."

"It's a shame for a lovely young woman to be hidden away on a tropical island, rather than enjoying the culture and social life of London. A shame for you and a loss for London society."

"I'm quite sure London society does not notice my absence. I was never really part of it anyway. I was too young."

We both fell silent, waiting for the set to end. The rule is that standing couples pay polite attention to the dancers, but more often our eyes were upon each other, and I cared not a bit for what anyone might think. That sense of intimacy in the middle of a crowded dance floor, and with a hundred curious spectators, was something new and thrilling.

I had debated with myself, on several occasions, whether Sir Samuel was attractive; now I wondered how I could ever have doubted it. His long face and aquiline nose gave him an air of distinction, but it was his probing blue eyes that sent a shiver through me. Those eyes had seen the world—as an adventurer, a leader. A hero. Samuel Hood was not a boy, not a young man with unrealistic dreams. He knew the reality of life, and he was afraid of nothing.

Sir Samuel had just led me off the dance floor when Dr. Williams appeared out of nowhere. "If you're not too tired, I would be honored to have the next dance," he said, looking expectantly at the card dangling from my wrist.

I glanced at the commodore, whose lips had tightened, almost imperceptibly but enough for me to notice. "I don't suppose you gentlemen are acquainted. Sir Samuel, this is Dr. Williams. He attended to the Bennett family during the epidemic and cared for the daughters here at Pilgrim House. Dr. Williams, Sir Samuel Hood is commander of the British naval forces in the West Indies."

"A pleasure." Sir Samuel offered an acknowledging nod. "I don't envy you doctors having to deal with this most recent yellow fever outbreak. They say it's been the worst in memory."

"Hard to know for certain. But yes, it was a difficult time for everyone."

"Dr. Williams is doing research on the disease," I said, thinking to myself that I wouldn't mind at all adding Dr. Williams's name to my dance card.

"So you'll be staying on the island for some time?" asked Sir Samuel.

"That's my plan, yes."

"I see. Well, the rest of us are grateful for your dedication, Doctor." He turned to me. "I will leave the two of you to your dance. Do remember what I told you—about our American friend. Perhaps we can discuss the situation further when you are *finished* with Dr. Williams?"

The emphasis on *finished* made his meaning clear. Commodore Hood had designs on me—and wanted no interference. At least for tonight.

As Sir Samuel was about to move on, Jake Holmquist, manager of the Hedgeford plantation, sidled up to the three of us, wearing a lopsided grin and holding a glass of sherry in each hand. Even in a formal evening suit he appeared rough around the edges—and more than a little intoxicated. "Well, well. Sir Samuel Hood and the lovely Lady Hood! I don't suppose you two remember me?"

I glanced at Sir Samuel, who was unruffled by the ambush. Dr. Williams was the one who appeared taken aback, not by the awkward intrusion but by hearing me addressed as Lady Hood.

"Forgive me—I can't recall your name," the commodore said with a vague smile.

"Jake Holmquist."

Sir Samuel turned to Dr. Williams. "Ah yes. Mr. Holmquist manages the Hedgeford plantation."

"Guess Sir Samuel and his Lady have a thing for doctors, of one sort or another," Mr. Holmquist said with a snide chuckle.

Dr. Williams looked more than a bit confused. "Yes .... well, if you all will excuse me, I'd best hurry if I hope to be added to the debutante's dance card."

"By all means. My dear, didn't you say that you wished for a breath of air? Remember what the doctor advised. You mustn't overdo the dancing. Not in your condition."

"You're right, of course," I replied, enjoying our little game. "Forgive us, Mr. Holmquist, but if I don't get out of this stuffy room, I'm afraid I shall faint right on the spot."

"Please, ma'am. Go with your husband, and God be with you and … and the little ones."

I maintained my composure as Sir Samuel propelled me towards the balcony. But once we were outside, seeing no one within earshot, we roared with laughter.

"Thank goodness we got away from that horrid fellow," I said, wiping tears from my eyes. "But poor Dr. Williams. He must be wondering how I managed to be both married and expecting within the last twenty minutes."

"Undoubtedly he's disappointed."

"Dr. Williams would have no reason to be disappointed. But did you really have to lead Mr. Holmquist to believe I'm expecting a baby?" I said, scolding him lightly. "Now the news will be all over Barbados."

"The news about whom? Lady Hood?" He smiled devilishly. "That poor fellow isn't bright enough to question whether two and two makes five. Nor does he care. His main concern is where to rustle up another shot of whiskey."

"He was drinking sherry," I said playfully.

"Apparently you didn't notice the distinctive aroma of his breath. A unique blend of whiskey and horse dung."

"Thankfully I wasn't in the line of fire."

"And if he had asked to be added to your dance card?"

I laughed. "You are wicked, Sir Samuel. Truly wicked."

"I am only hoping you might appreciate me more."

I thought back to our dance together and how perfectly in step we were. And his eyes … "I have no need to compare you with anyone else."

"Because I am in a class of my own, or I have failed to qualify for the competition?"

I felt myself blush, but I didn't mind so terribly. "There is no competition. At least none that I know of."

"Come now, no eligible bachelor on this island would pass up a chance to be in your favor. But then, you know that very well."

I did, but had never seriously considered any of them. My focus had been on men quite a bit younger than Sir Samuel. And not nearly as interesting.

He looked up, his eyes scanning the night sky. "Soon I will be gazing at these same stars from the stone frigate of Diamond Rock."

I cocked my head, puzzled. "I thought a frigate was a ship. Isn't Diamond Rock an island?"

"So it is. An uninhabited island. A giant stone rising out of the sea. On a sunny day, when the light hits it just right, it appears like a glistening diamond, hence the name."

"But why did you call it a frigate?"

"It's become a sort of joke in the Royal Navy. To circumvent the prohibitions against our exercising authority over land, I came up with the idea of commissioning Diamond Rock as a frigate, complete with cannons and a crew of one hundred and twenty sailors."

"For what purpose?"

"A strategic one. The island is situated in an important position relative to the port of French-occupied Martinique. We aim to make life difficult for French ships seeking safe harbor."

What he meant suddenly sank in. "You'll be engaged in combat?"

"War is a nasty business. But, my dear Miss Mackenzie," he said, reaching for my gloved hand, "I would be most heartened if I felt you were looking forward to my safe return."

I was flustered by his unexpected declaration. "We all will—Father especially. He has come to value your friendship greatly." It was not what he had wanted to hear, and his look of disappointment made that very clear. I could have kicked myself. My feelings were not at all what my words conveyed.

Impetuously, I raised myself up on my toes, and, with a swift motion, kissed his cheek. "I have been wanting to do that all night, you know."

"I wasn't aware."

"Well, you are now. And when you come back from Diamond Rock, I might kiss the other cheek as well."

"You *might*? Then you're unwilling to promise?"

I hesitated. Was I ready for this? But what was I promising, really. Only a kiss.

"Very well, I promise. Provided no other young lady's lips have preceded mine."

Sir Samuel smiled. "I can assure you of that. And I'll do my best to discourage my sailors as well."

CHAPTER TEN

By August, I had spent several months dreaming of Sir Samuel's return. And fretting that something might happen to prevent it. I distracted myself by questioning Father on every detail of the commodore's distinguished naval career. Though I claimed it was only curiosity, I did not fool him.

Father told me that Sir Samuel had been in the Royal Navy nearly thirty years, since the start of the American War of Independence. He achieved fame during the Napoleonic Wars for his blockade command in the Battle of the Nile, isolating Napoleon's forces in Egypt and ultimately giving the British control of the Mediterranean. For restoring British dominance in the West Indies, he was knighted. Now he was on another dangerous mission.

The risks and responsibilities of his position could not help but inspire my respect. And cause me to wonder what such an extraordinary man could find admirable, or even interesting, about me. Unless it had been only the magic of a single night, a dance by candlelight, and the sort of recklessness that imbibing spirits can so easily induce. Feelings that soon fade and then are forgotten entirely.

But I did not forget. I was constantly asking Father if there was any news from Diamond Rock; the answer was always no. Until one evening when word reached us of an accident on the island. A captured French vessel had exploded, killing nearly the entire crew.

"The French crew?" I asked breathlessly.

With a somber face, Father shook his head. "No, the vessel was acting as a British tender. The crew was ours."

"Oh …" To think of Sir Samuel, dead … It would be devastating. Not only for Britain.

"We don't know yet if any officers were onboard," he said, reading my mind.

"When will we know?"

"I assume it is Sir Samuel you wish to know about."

There was no reason to deny my feelings. They had become obvious to everyone. Even my sisters prodded me occasionally. Especially Caroline, always observant and sensitive to the emotions of others. Only a few days after Frances's ball, she had inquired whether Sir Samuel and I would be making our announcement soon.

"Announcement? Whatever do you mean?" I had said, feigning bewilderment.

"Everyone was talking about what a handsome couple you made, dancing together as though you had done it a thousand times before."

"Don't be silly. Granted, Sir Samuel is a better dancer than one might expect. But people will jump at any opportunity for gossip, don't you know?"

"I like him," Caroline said. "He seems quite the gentleman."

"I shan't disagree with you."

"And Father is inordinately fond of him." She grabbed my hand, nearly bursting with curiosity. "Oh, Mary! For heaven's sake, you can tell *me*. I'm your favorite sister, am I not?"

Though she had spoken jokingly, we both knew it was true. I loved all my sisters, and Frances was the closest to me in age. But Caroline, almost three years younger, had come at a time when my heart was ripe for capture. I could remember patiently rocking her cradle until she fell asleep, delighting in her smiles and gurgling baby sounds. I was even eager for the task of changing her soiled napkins. I liked to pretend she was *my* baby. I suppose it was only a matter of timing that the sisters and brothers who came after her did not hold quite the same fascination.

Then, too, Caroline's nature was such that no one could help loving her. Sometimes I envied the extraordinary kindness of her spirit, mine being far less so. Perhaps *envied* is not the right word, for I could never begrudge Caroline anything. If she was indeed more beloved than I, it was because she deserved to be.

"There's nothing to tell," I had insisted, still unsure of what to call these new, rather frightening emotions, so different from anything I had known before.

"All right, if you want to be like that, go ahead. But when I last gazed into my crystal ball, I saw a wedding in your future. And the groom looked suspiciously like Sir Samuel Hood."

"I happen to know you don't have a crystal ball, thank goodness, so I can only surmise you are allowing your colorful imagination to run wild."

"But wouldn't it be nice if Sir Samuel were to whisk you away to London, and you could leave Barbados behind forever?"

What she described was not far from the thoughts that had been keeping me awake at night. Might I be courting Sir Samuel's affections, if in fact I was, simply to escape my life in Barbados?

"That's not a good enough reason for marriage," I said, almost firmly enough to convince myself of it.

"I never meant to imply that it was. But if you truly love him …" Her voice trailed off, her eyes searching mine for confirmation.

"I think that I might."

Caroline smiled. "By the time he returns, perhaps you'll know for certain."

It seemed that Caroline had been right. But what I didn't know was whether Sir Samuel would return. Even Father could not tell me; he'd heard nothing more about the accident at Diamond Rock or the fate of one of the Royal Navy's most decorated heroes.

CHAPTER ELEVEN

My two youngest sisters, Charlotte and Helen, were of an age when they thought nothing of wandering off, causing panic amongst servants and family alike. Helen, just turned five, could hardly be blamed for following Charlotte who, at eight, should know better than to leave the safety of Pilgrim House unaccompanied.

Nanny was first to raise the alarm; of course, she should have been the one to prevent such a thing from happening at all. She burst into the drawing room just as Mother was about to serve tea. Two ladies from our church, wives of British officials, had called on us, and Mother had persuaded Caroline and me to partake in the late afternoon ritual.

"Pardon me, Lady Seaforth, but I'm looking for Charlotte and Helen. Searched the entire house, I have. Might the wee ones be in here?"

Mother set down the teapot, casting a stern look upon the young woman, who had always been prone to laxity in her duties. "They are not here. Have you tried the courtyard?"

"I sent two others from the kitchen to look outside, my lady. They didn't see them anywhere."

"May I ask what you were doing when you were supposed to be watching them?" Mother's tone was harsh. Once Charlotte and Helen were found, she would for the hundredth time threaten to send Nanny back to Scotland.

There was likely nothing to worry about, and the girls would be discovered within shouting distance. But it was a good excuse to extricate myself from the exceedingly boring conversation of these churchgoing wives and mothers with whom I shared little in common. "If you ladies will excuse me, I shall join the hunt. My little sisters cannot have gone far."

"Excellent, Mary," Mother said, resuming her tea service.

I left with Nanny and, outside in the hallway, conferred with her as to what ground had already been covered.

"You're certain they're not hiding somewhere in the house?" I asked, recalling the last time they disappeared, only to be found curled up asleep beneath Mother's bed.

"Can't swear to it, miss, but we searched every nook and cranny. And if they're on the property outside, they must have heard us calling."

I tried to put myself in their place. Inside their innocent little minds. What held the most fascination for them? Yesterday, when Caroline and I took them down to the beach for a picnic, Charlotte had begged to wade in the sea. We told her it was too dangerous. Even in shallow water there could be currents and unexpected drop-offs, creatures that sting, and sharp coral to injure bare feet. Spoiling what should have been a pleasant afternoon, Charlotte had thrown a tantrum for which she was roundly scolded. I wondered whether, intent on having her way, she might have gone back. It would not be unlike Charlotte. Of all my sisters, she was the most apt to disobey.

"You continue looking around the house," I said to Nanny. "I'm going to check down at the beach."

"The beach! Oh no, you don't think they could have gone so far as that?"

"It's not the distance I'm worried about as much as what they might do when they get there. Charlotte is fascinated with the sea, and she has no idea of the danger."

"But shouldn't I go along with you? Lady Seaforth doesn't approve of us being out and about alone. Women and girls, that is. Surely her own daughters, most of all."

"I shall be fine."

I hurried to the stables, had the groom saddle Cloudy, and then took off down the hill towards the sea. Adjacent to the port of Bridgetown was a sandy beach, away from the major commotion, where one could walk or sit. If Charlotte had headed for the sea, I assumed she would return to a familiar spot, where we had been just the day before.

I tried to keep my anxiety in check as I made my way along the path towards the harbor. From a distance the water's surface appeared placid, smooth blue beneath a sky so clear it seemed a mirror image of the sea. But I knew what lay hidden below. It made my skin crawl to think Charlotte and Helen might innocently venture into that unknown world of swirling currents and venomous sea creatures.

I gently prodded Cloudy and kept my eyes on the small patch of beach. From this distance, it appeared there was no one there. Rather than a comfort, however, their absence seemed more cause for apprehension. Perhaps they already had been swept out to sea.

There were, of course, a thousand other places they could have gone. Looking for them here was probably a waste of time. Still, my fear kept growing as I drew closer to the beach. When I arrived, I coaxed Cloudy to the water's edge, looking for footprints. I only hoped they would not disappear into the blue.

But there was no sign of them, no footprints in the sand, nothing to indicate they had been here. Both relieved and frustrated, I started back to Pilgrim House, until it occurred to me that I should ride by the ship landing. It was not unthinkable that the girls might be wandering about, closer to the dock. Since I had come this far, there was no reason not to look.

The port's wharves and piers teamed with sailors and dock workers busily loading and unloading cargo. Their whistles and shouts were interspersed with the heavy thud of enormous wooden boxes being lowered to the docks, then hoisted onto horse-drawn wagons to be transported to nearby warehouses. I stopped on the fringes, fascinated by the commotion. The volume of goods going to and from this tiny Caribbean outpost was astounding. Barren and primitive as it sometimes seemed, Barbados was Britain's second most important colony, its revenues vital to the Crown's push for industrialization. For a moment, my pride swelled to think of my father at the helm of such an enterprise. Then, as always, I remembered the dark side of Barbados. None of this would exist but for the scourge of slavery.

My eyes scoured the docks and surrounding areas until I was convinced that my sisters were not here. There was nothing to do now except return home.

"Miss Mackenzie!"

A man's voice rang out from behind me. I twisted in the saddle but saw no one calling to me. Deciding I must have been mistaken, I nudged Cloudy with my heels, and he started forward.

"Miss Mackenzie! Wait!"

A coach drew up beside me. It stopped, and the door opened from within. A single leg in cream-colored breeches and a tall black boot appeared first, followed by the lean figure of Sir Samuel Hood. He stood taller than I remembered, a broad smile lighting his long, angular face.

It took me a moment to be certain it was really him, after which my stomach was quickly overrun with butterflies. "Sir Samuel! How wonderful to see you!"

He came up beside my horse. "How did you know I was arriving today?"

"Would you believe that I read it in the stars?" I laughed. "I hadn't the slightest idea you were expected in Bridgetown. Does my father know?"

"No, my visit is rather a last-minute detour. And I'm afraid you are to blame. I've thought a great deal about you since I left for Diamond Rock."

His words were beyond anything I'd expected, though they were only words. "I heard about the explosion, and I—I'm glad to see you alive and well."

"I was away from the island when it occurred. Still not sure about the cause, but we suspect sabotage."

"The French?"

"Who else?" He shook his head. "An awful tragedy. I can't help but feel responsible for those boys who gave their lives."

"But, otherwise, the mission is going well?" I asked, sorry to have brought up a subject so obviously painful.

"For the most part, the blockade is holding."

"Where are you off to now?" I hesitated to invite him to the house for dinner. Perhaps he had only meant to say hello and had other plans for the evening.

"Actually, I was hoping I might spend the night at Pilgrim House, if it's not an imposition. I must be on my way early tomorrow morning."

"An imposition?" I said, trying not to sound overly eager. "Not at all. Father will be delighted with your company. And Mother always enjoys the opportunity for some lively conversation at dinner."

"And you?"

"I would welcome it, naturally."

"Very well. Perhaps you should go ahead of me to warn the household of an uninvited guest."

"I will warn them, but I shan't announce you in quite that fashion."

· · ·

I was beside myself with excitement as Cloudy trotted up the lane leading to Pilgrim House. It would have been enough simply to know Sir Samuel was safe, but to hear that seeing me was the reason for postponing his official mission was almost too much.

In the several months since Frances's ball, I had tried to picture myself and Sir Samuel together. The possibility seemed more fantasy than real. But could his intentions towards me indeed be serious? What if he were to propose marriage? Tonight. Would I have an answer for him? Was I ready?

I was jolted from my self-absorption by the sudden recollection that I still didn't know what had become of Charlotte and Helen. In fact, I had forgotten they were missing! Urging Cloudy on a bit faster, I chastised myself for the time spent chatting with Sir Samuel, precious time that could mean the difference between my sisters' safe return and some disastrous event from which they might never recover.

Arriving at Pilgrim House, I handed Cloudy's reins to the groom and ran to the house. In the hall, I encountered one of the housemaids mopping the floor.

"Have Charlotte and Helen been found?" I asked, breathless.

"Found?" The young woman appeared puzzled. "Oh! Yes, miss," she said, her face relaxing in a smile. "Some time ago. The wee ones are fine, thank God."

I sighed in relief. "Where were they?"

"There's an old barrel by the stables. The little imps climbed in and got stuck. Can you imagine? Said they wanted to know what it felt like for the Seer," she added, oblivious to the effect her words would have upon me.

I hated being reminded of Coinneach Odhar. But I, like every Scot, was well familiar with the details of his death. Accused by the third Lady Seaforth of being a sorcerer, he was burned in a spiked barrel filled with hot tar. I knew every word of the curse he laid upon the Seaforth line— at least the version put to paper by the Seer's present-day followers. At times, those words would circle my mind like a tired old song one tries to forget but cannot.

I see into the far future, and I read the doom of the race of my oppressor. The long-descended line of Seaforth will, ere many generations have passed, end in extinction and in sorrow. I see a chief, the last of his house, both deaf and dumb. He will be the father of four fair sons, all of whom he will follow to the tomb. He will live careworn and die mourning, knowing that the honors of his line are to be extinguished forever, and that no future chief of the Mackenzies shall bear rule at Brahan or in Kintail.

After lamenting over the last and most promising of his sons, he himself shall sink into the grave, and the remnant of his possessions shall be inherited by a white-hooded lassie from the East, and she is to kill her sister. And as a sign by which it may be known—

"Miss? Are ye all right?"

I pulled myself back from the brink of that great abyss. "What you just said—about the Seer—do not speak of this again. It is not to be talked about in this house, do you understand?"

The poor girl's face flushed scarlet. "So sorry, miss. I would never mean to upset ye. I ought to have known better than to speak a word of such nonsense. And the wee ones, they must have nothin' of the kind troublin' their sweet, innocent minds."

"Where is my mother?" I asked abruptly, remembering that Sir Samuel was on his way.

"Last I saw her, miss, she was in the library."

Casting off those bitter promises of doom, I hastened to the east wing to impart the news that Sir Samuel was alive. Mother was not alone in the library. My father sat in the armchair opposite hers, immersed in one of his enormous volumes on botanical science.

"Guess who I saw down at the docks?"

Mother glanced up from her book. "Your hair is a mess, Mary! I hope you've not been out and about looking like that."

"If you recall, I was searching for Helen and Charlotte," I replied, slightly piqued. Could Mother not thank me for my efforts rather than criticizing how I looked?

"Ah, they were here all the time," she said, with a wave of her hand.

Father, his back to the door, had not realized I was there until he noticed Mother's gesture. Turning to me, he smiled. "Suppose you've heard what your little sisters were up to?"

I nodded, not wishing to revisit their disturbing adventure in the barrel. "But I have other news. Sir Samuel is here in Barbados! I have invited him for dinner and to stay the night at Pilgrim House. I knew you both would wish to extend your hospitality."

Mother jumped from her chair as if I'd announced the house was on fire. "What time did you tell him to come?"

"He should be here any minute."

"Any minute!" Mother gave me a swift look of reproach. "You should know better."

Father closed his book and placed it back on the shelf. "Wonderful news. We were worried about his safety, weren't we?" he said, eyeing me keenly.

I stared at the floor, considering whether I should prepare them for what had transpired between Sir Samuel and me. Perhaps it was better not to, in case I was mistaken. To my knowledge, Samuel Hood had never been married, but how many times had he come close to it, only to change his mind?

"Francis, come along. We must change into something suitable. I will leave it to you, Mary, to inform the kitchen that we have a guest for dinner. Make sure everything is in order and the menu is appropriate."

"I'll see to it, Mother."

"Tell Cunningham to apologize to Sir Samuel and see to his comfort until we can join him in the drawing room. And for goodness' sake, Mary, don't let him see you looking like *that*!"

Taking Mother's advice, I made a quick stop at my dressing room to fix my hair, tucking the windblown strands back into my bun as best I could. A change of clothes would have to wait. Fortunately, I'd been dressed for tea when I went off in search of my sisters and, though my gown had gathered a bit of road dust, the outfit was quite becoming.

I dispatched my orders to the kitchen and alerted Cunningham to expect our guest shortly. Needing to calm my jitters, I went into the drawing room and sat down at the piano. I had played but a few bars of Beethoven when Cunningham appeared in the doorway, announcing Sir Samuel's arrival.

"See him in," I said, pretending it was nothing out of the ordinary for me to entertain a man alone. "And Cunningham—bring us a bottle of Father's best pale sherry."

"How many glasses, miss?" he asked, one eyebrow slightly raised.

"Just two."

A minute later, he ushered Sir Samuel into the room. Apparently, the commodore had stopped somewhere along the way, because now he wore his Royal Navy dress uniform, a dark-blue, double-breasted coat with gold embroidery and fringed epaulets, along with white breeches, waistcoat, and cravat.

"You'll have to excuse the way I look," I said, rising from the piano, "but I didn't want you to arrive with no one to welcome you. Mother and Father apologize for their absence. They are dressing and should be joining us shortly."

"No apologies necessary. I am the one out of order, calling on you so unexpectedly."

I nodded to Cunningham to uncork the sherry. "I thought you might enjoy some refreshment. Please, make yourself comfortable." I perched on the edge of the sofa, waiting to see where Sir Samuel would choose to sit: next to me or in the adjacent chair. He selected the latter.

Cunningham served us our drinks, after which he stood at attention. I considered whether I should have him stay but quickly decided otherwise, dismissing him with a curt *That will be all.*

"We were terribly worried when we heard about the explosion on Diamond Rock."

"I lost some very good men. They won't soon be forgotten." He took a sip of sherry. "But if you don't mind, may we save that discussion for another time? I would rather hear about you."

"Oh—oh, of course," I stuttered. Already I had blundered, forgetting my earlier resolve not to bring up the unfortunate incident. "But I'm afraid there isn't much to say, not about me. I've been busy with more of the same—helping Mother with her social and charitable obligations. Keeping up with my reading and drawing. Music lessons." It was embarrassing to realize how boring my life must sound.

"Biding your time?"

"I suppose, in a way. Though I'm not sure what I'm waiting for."

"Could I venture a guess?" He leaned towards me with an intense look in his eyes. I had not noticed before the gold flecks mixed in with the blue. "You have been here in Barbados long enough. It's time for a change. Time for the life *you* want to live, not the life others have chosen for you. A dutiful young woman does what her parents ask of her—as you have done, with the utmost grace—but, by a certain age, she has the right to decide for herself. What will it be? More of the same? Or something different?"

"My parents have never asked much of me, though I've always felt they needed me."

"But what about now? Your sister Frances has entered society, and Caroline is not far behind. Your duties as the eldest surely have become less."

How could I explain to him that I was worried about my father's gout, his political enemies, his debts and gambling? And island life was taking its toll on Mother's health as well. She said nothing, but the weary look in her eyes told me more than words.

"Sometimes, in order to become who we truly are," he said, "we must let go of the person we were. I believe I could help you to do that."

"You, Sir Samuel?" I hated that my voice sounded small and childish, when I so wanted to be the woman he imagined me. But how sure was I of him? He was worldly and brave, and he danced far better than I'd expected. But could we make each other happy?

He reached for my hand and, rather timidly, I allowed him to take it. "I think I understand what you want. A different kind of freedom than your life here has afforded you. A fashionable townhouse in London. Dinners with friends, outings to concerts and the theater." He paused, and I cared for nothing but what he would say next. "A gentleman who adores you."

He still hadn't spoken of *marriage*. I was beginning to wonder if, as a long-time bachelor, the idea of matrimony was anathema to him.

"Sir Samuel, what a lovely surprise!" Mother swept into the room in a cloud of perfume, Father tight on her heels. Sir Samuel and I hastily unlocked our hands.

"Awfully kind of you to offer food and shelter to a poor traveler at such short notice," he said, rising to greet them with a bow to each.

"Our pleasure, of course. I trust that our eldest has been keeping you properly entertained," Father said, casting an inquisitive look my way.

"I attempted to trick Sir Samuel into revealing his secret military strategies, but to no avail," I said, rising from the sofa. "Now that everyone is here, you must excuse me while I go upstairs to dress for dinner. I shan't be long."

Sir Samuel's lingering gaze made it clear he wished for my quick return. But I could not dine dressed as I was, and, even more important, I needed time to think.

Sarah already was in my room, bustling about to make sure everything I needed for my toilette was in order, readying my underthings, my gown, jewelry, slippers. As she helped me dress, I said not a word, my mind spinning with a thousand thoughts. The picture Sir Samuel had painted of a future life in London, amidst the city's sophisticated culture and social life, was enchanting. I realized now how much I longed for these things, more than I had been willing to admit. But no amount of luxury or stimulating society was enough to justify marrying a man for whom I did not care deeply. It was true that women in my position, or their families, often chose marriage partners on the basis of wealth and social standing. Wouldn't I prefer a choice based upon love and mutual respect? Yet it was possible Sir Samuel satisfied all those requirements, and more.

I thought again of my parents, my sisters. Was it true what Sir Samuel had said? Did they need me less than I imagined?

"Is everything all right, miss?" Sarah asked, addressing my reflection in the dressing table mirror.

I was reluctant to tell her what I pictured might happen this evening. Wouldn't I feel foolish if, in fact, there was no proposal? "I was just thinking about this afternoon, about Charlotte and Helen and how worried we all were."

"Aye, I've not often seen Lady Seaforth so beside herself."

"Really? I thought she seemed surprisingly calm when I left to search for them."

"Oh no. Soon as her company was gone, her ladyship took to her bed."

"She was reading in the library when I came back from the docks and seemed fine."

"I suppose by then she was back to herself." Sarah arranged the curls framing my face. "But it seems these days it doesn't take much to knock the wind out of her. Not that she ever complains. That woman would sooner suffer in silence than trouble anybody about herself, especially her children."

The timing of Sarah's observations could not have been worse. How could I leave my ailing parents on this inhospitable, disease-infested island to go romping off to London with Sir Samuel?

But if I once said no to Sir Samuel, it was unlikely he would make the offer again.

CHAPTER TWELVE

The rituals necessary in dressing for the evening had taken nearly an hour, but I was rewarded for my efforts with Sir Samuel's obvious admiration. His steady blue eyes were upon me throughout the lengthy dinner, and, despite my inner conflict, I found myself unable to resist a bit of demure flirtation.

I could not help wondering what sort of conversation had ensued after my departure from the drawing room. If Sir Samuel had serious intentions of proposing tonight, might he have taken the opportunity to ask Father for his blessing? By rights, he should approach me first, and perhaps he would have had we not been interrupted. But if such a conversation with Father had indeed taken place, I sensed no hint of it.

Again, I questioned whether I might have misread Sir Samuel. Were the comments he made to me over a glass of sherry simply musings, without motive?

Dinner seemed to drag on and on, with the usual talk of island politics, the latest debates in Parliament, gossip about the Crown. The only conversation engaging my interest was when Sir Samuel spoke of his mission on Diamond Rock, which he had declined to discuss when we were alone.

"My assignment to blockade the bays at Fort Royal and Saint Pierre has gone swimmingly," he said, aiming his speech towards Father. "But, of course, you heard of the mishap with the captured schooner, *Ma*

Sophie, out of Guadeloupe. When we took her, after a chase of some twenty-four leagues, she had a crew of forty-five and was equipped with eight guns. Put her to good use for a while. But this recent loss of our sailors was an unforgivable affront. One that cannot go unanswered."

"Damn French!" Father muttered. "Well, you've earned your bed tonight, my friend. No doubt it's good to get away for a while from that blasted rock."

In the months since he had left for Diamond Rock, I had tried to picture what Sir Samuel's daily life must be like, but I simply could not conceive of it. "Your living conditions must be very difficult. May I ask, where do you sleep? And what is there to eat?"

"The men sleep in caves. We officers, deserving or not, have the luxury of tents. Food has been a challenge, but now we have some goats and chickens that are surviving well enough. We've even set up a hospital for the sick and injured in a cave at the rock's base."

"How many times have you been attacked?" Augusta, with the curiosity of an eleven-year-old, seemed eager for a harrowing story; I was not.

"The French have made several attempts to retake the rock. None successful," Sir Samuel replied with an indulgent smile. He turned again to Father. "Probably the most serious threat was their plan to install a mortar battery on Martinique that could have been used to shell the rock. Fortunately, we learned of the scheme from an African slave who made it to the rock one night, under cover of darkness, and told us what he had observed on the plantation where he worked. After that, our landing of twenty-three men was able to capture the engineer and seventeen French soldiers."

"What happened to the spy?" I asked, fearing for the retribution he would face should his actions be discovered.

"I'm pleased to report he is alive and well. Quite happy, too. I granted him protection, and he now serves in the Royal Navy as a free man."

"Are you going to stay on Diamond Rock forever?" Augusta asked. This time, I was glad for my sister's forthright questioning. The length of Sir Samuel's commission had never been discussed.

"Not too much longer, I hope," he said with a sideways glance at me.

After dessert, my sisters headed upstairs. Mother asked to be excused as well, which was odd. But when Father said he would accompany her, I began to suspect that my parents' early withdrawal had been prearranged.

With a confident smile, Sir Samuel pushed back his chair from the table. "Shall we have a look at the stars, Miss Mackenzie? See if they are any brighter than last time I was here?"

Sir Samuel intended to propose. My mother and father knew and apparently approved. I had dreamed of this for months, yet now it seemed everything was moving too fast.

"It's a lovely night." Mother rose from her chair, smiling.

"Yes indeed," agreed Father.

"A bit cloudy though," I murmured, fidgeting with my pearls.

"Mira!"

Startled by Father's sudden cry of alarm, I turned to see Mother, who had stepped away from the table, spiraling to the floor in an apparent swoon. Before I could move, Sir Samuel leaped from his seat, rushing over to her and dropping to his knees. She was fully conscious, seeming more concerned about the disarray of her dress than anything else.

"Stay as you are for a moment, Lady Seaforth," Sir Samuel said calmly. "Catch your breath."

Father was hovering over them with a look of horror. "Mira, my love. Stop fussing and do as Sir Samuel tells you."

Mother, in her usual manner, was not eager to follow orders. "I'm fine. Get up, Sir Samuel, and the two of you lend me a hand. And don't step on my gown, Francis."

Sir Samuel jumped to his feet with the agility of a man half his age. Then he and Father positioned themselves on either side of her and gently lifted. She struggled to find her balance but, as soon as she was steady, demanded they let go of her.

"Enough, enough," she said, smoothing the folds of her skirt. "Next time, I shall watch where I'm going."

But it was clear to me that Mother had not bumped into anything, nor had she tripped. "Were you dizzy? Is that why you fell?"

"Please, don't interrogate me, Mary."

"But, Mother—"

"I'll help your mother upstairs to bed." Father took her arm, which she allowed without protest. Watching the two of them, I was reminded of the expression *the blind leading the blind.*

After they had gone, Sir Samuel and I stood together in silence. Part of me felt that I should be upstairs with Mother. But the other part …

"I was thinking we might go out on the veranda off the ballroom," said Sir Samuel. "As we did the last time you and I were together."

I smiled, recalling that evening as I had done so often. The night of Frances's ball, when I first considered the possibility that I could fall in love with Sir Samuel Hood, as incongruous a pair as some might find us—he with his gangly arms and legs and a leathery face weathered by decades of sea and sun, and I, a rosy-cheeked Scottish lass, slender but sturdily built, and young enough to be his daughter.

We entered the ballroom, and he took my hand. "I would ask you to dance except we have no music. But perhaps that needn't stop us." He gave me a sly smile. "Have you ever tried the waltz?"

"The waltz!" No one I knew danced the waltz, which was considered too risqué for English society.

"When I was in Vienna, I learned the steps. Just to be sociable, mind you."

That Sir Samuel knew how to waltz was certainly surprising. I couldn't help wondering with whom he had danced it.

He placed his left hand at the small of my back. "Put your hand on my shoulder," he said, "like so. Now, we clasp our right hands together." We were so close that I could feel the softness of his breath on my face. It was sweet, like Madeira. "Start with your feet together, like this. Step forward with your left foot, now to the side with your right. Excellent." He smiled encouragingly. "Close your left foot to your right, step back, to the side. Now close your right foot to your left."

It took all my concentration to follow him, but I did a fairly decent job of it. After practicing a few more times, we began to glide across the floor, falling into a smooth rhythm that felt almost effortless. I could see how the waltz had gained its reputation. There was no need for conversation; the message passing between our eyes was communication enough.

Suddenly he stopped. "I don't wish for you to tire yourself. Not tonight of all nights."

I felt a fluttering in my stomach. "Perhaps it's enough for now. But I should like to try it again sometime."

"We shall. I promise."

In a sort of trance, I let him guide me through the French doors and onto the veranda. We stood beside the iron railing, the moon golden, serenaded by the mating calls of crickets.

Sir Samuel swept both my hands into his. "I imagine you know what is on my mind. I hope you do, and that you welcome my affections."

My knees began to wobble beneath my gown. Was this what love felt like? Or was it anxiety? Uncertainty?

"I spoke with your father tonight and told him of my feelings for you. I asked for his blessing for our marriage—that is, should I be so fortunate as to win your heart."

"Sir Samuel—" My voice faltered. I pictured my mother lying on the dining room floor, my father's helpless look as Sir Samuel rushed to her aid. "I have never been in love before. Still, I believe I can recognize it. And I believe, too, that you would make a fine husband. But—"

"But?"

By the close of dinner, I had decided what I would say when this moment came. I would accept Sir Samuel's proposal, leave my family to become his wife. But now, I wasn't sure.

"You saw what happened tonight. My parents—"

"Stop." He pressed a finger to my lips. "I've heard everything I need to hear. You believe in us. You want me. There can be nothing else of importance."

I stepped back, needing space to breathe. "I am worried about my mother and father. Being here in Barbados is not good for either of them, but it is Father's duty, and Mother would never leave his side." I reached up to touch Sir Samuel's face, my longing begging to break free. "Perhaps it would be wrong of me to abandon them."

He grasped my hand and brought it to his lips, where he held it for a few precious seconds. "I understand your concerns and admire them. But there comes a time when each of us must live our own life. You know that, don't you?" He turned his gaze to the distant water beyond the docks of Bridgetown. "My dear Mary, you cannot imagine the treasures there are to see in this world. Mysterious, faraway places. People and cultures different from anything you have ever known. And not at all like Barbados." Again, he kissed my hand. "My beautiful bird in a golden cage—why must you only dream of flight when I am here to set you free? All you must do is say *yes*."

"I want to say yes, but …" His words were so incredibly sweet. How could there still be doubt in my mind? "You must give me a bit more time."

"My dear, one thing I have learned from war is that one must seize the opportunity when it presents itself. Act quickly or risk losing everything. Even life itself. It is a lesson one would do well to remember."

My heart sank. He would not wait. There were limits on his love. Perhaps what he felt for me was not love at all, but something else. Something he had expected to be more convenient.

"I'm sorry," I said, drawing my hand away, "but, as you saw tonight, my parents are not well. I fear their health is bound to deteriorate further the longer they stay in Barbados. If I could convince my father to resign his post and return home, I would. But I have no say in the matter, and he is a stubborn man."

His posture stiffened. "Then, you are refusing my proposal of marriage?"

I felt awful to disappoint him. But I, too, was disappointed. If he loved me, wouldn't he also care about my family? Wouldn't he at least try to offer a solution?

"I would prefer it if we said goodnight and talked about this in the morning," I said, knowing my words were the equivalent of a slap in the face. I had never felt more confused. About everything—my duty, my desire, my destiny.

"Very well, if you need more time, you shall have it. However, I must be on my way in the morning. My ship is scheduled to depart at ten. I will expect your answer by then."

I nodded, acutely aware of the rebuke in his tone. Perhaps he was right to be angry. Had I led him on, made him feel like a fool? A man like Samuel Hood was not accustomed to being treated so rudely. I had not meant to insult him. Certainly not to belittle him.

Was it really concern for my parents causing my sudden doubts? Could it be that I was afraid of becoming a wife? A mother?

But he had promised me freedom. Adventure ...

"I shall tell Cook to serve us breakfast together at nine. In the courtyard?"

"As you wish." He retreated a few steps back, the space between us now a chasm. "Allow me to see you to your room."

"Please, don't bother. It's lovely out here. You should stay a while longer."

His mouth settled into a firm line. I knew I had hurt him, and I was sorry. But further conversation was impossible. Right now, I had to be alone.

When I arrived at my bedchamber, I did not call for Sarah to help me undress. I was in no mood to speak with anyone. How had I managed to make such a terrible mess of what could have been the most wonderful night of my life?

He described me as a caged bird, longing for freedom. I had never thought of myself quite that way, but neither could I deny his assessment contained an element of truth. For years, I had chafed under the restrictions imposed by virtue of my sex. More recently, however, I had come to accept that being the eldest, whether male or female, inherently requires greater attention to duty than is demanded of younger siblings. Yet how had I gone about fulfilling that duty? What had I accomplished? I could do nothing to assist Father in his role as governor, nor could I control his gambling, resolve his indebtedness, or cure his gout. And Mother—were she dying of a fatal illness, still she would hide it from me and everyone else until the last possible moment, when it was too late. So, why was I trying to convince myself of my extraordinary importance to them?

Still, sometimes it seemed as though the fate of my family rested upon my shoulders, more than anyone else's. Was it the prophecy that had put such an idea into my head? The prophecy I claimed not to believe in. Not to fear.

But it was late, and I was too exhausted to think anymore. Perhaps when I awoke in the morning, the answers would be clearer.

I readied myself for bed and was about to climb under the covers when a knock sounded. My first thought was Sir Samuel. But surely, he would not be so presumptuous. I donned my dressing gown and padded with bare feet to the door, opening it just a crack.

"Father! What it is? Is something wrong?"

"I hope you weren't asleep."

I opened the door the rest of the way, and he stepped inside.

"Is Mother all right?"

He took my hand. "Come, my child."

We sat together on the bed, facing each other. "I need to tell you something," he began. "I should have told you before now. It would have made things easier for you. But I wanted to be certain myself before I spoke to anyone else about it—even your mother." He paused, staring down at his hands. "I've made a decision to leave Barbados. I plan to inform the Crown that, in the interest of my family's health, I must resign my post as governor, effective as soon as my replacement can be properly appointed."

I was stunned. Also puzzled. The timing of Father's announcement … it seemed suspicious that he would tell me this on the evening of Sir Samuel's marriage proposal. I wondered if he had gone to Father, after the two of us parted, and urged him to make this momentous decision. I had to know.

"Are you doing this for me, so I will accept Sir Samuel's proposal of marriage? Obviously he has told you of his intentions." I waited for his reply, but he offered none. "Father, I would be very pleased for our family to leave Barbados, but I would not want you to give up your post on my account."

"No, my dear. I have been thinking about this for some time. And yes, Sir Samuel has informed me that you did not accept his proposal. And he has indicated the reason why, or at least the reason you gave him. My question for you is, how do you really feel?"

"First, you must answer a question of mine—and answer it honestly. Is there anything about Mother's health that you are keeping from me?"

He seemed surprised. "The doctor says she is suffering from fatigue. Nothing more."

"I didn't know she had seen a doctor. Who is tending to her?"

"Dr. Williams. She is quite fond of him, you know."

I smiled, recalling when I had been rather taken with him myself, and perturbed by his indifference towards me. But none of that mattered now.

"So, are you going to answer me? Do you wish to be Lady Hood?" He patted my hand, chuckling. "Though you have not asked for my advice, I would deem it a wise decision were you to accept Sir Samuel's proposal. I have met no finer man than he, and I consider myself a fair judge of character."

It was as if the door to that golden cage of which Sir Samuel had spoken was suddenly flung open and the doubts I had entertained, less than an hour ago, were swept away in a rush of wings. "I believe I do love him, Father. And I know that you would enjoy having him as your son-in-law."

"I would. But that is quite beside the point. Do you wish to accept his proposal?"

My heart was racing. I took a deep breath. "Yes, I do."

"Then you must tell him straight away. Otherwise, he will be tossing and turning all night, wondering what you plan to say to him in the morning."

"I should let him suffer a bit in pursuit of love," I replied with a slightly wicked grin. "Won't he value its capture all the more?" It was odd how, suddenly, I felt so much older. Wiser.

Father kissed my cheek and stood. "You needn't worry about Sir Samuel's affections, my dear. But, despite them, you may find it impossible to keep him at home. The commodore is an adventurer by nature, and, for better or worse, war is his game. Can you live with that?"

"I shan't expect to change him," I said, not giving Father's warning a second thought.

CHAPTER THIRTEEN
JANUARY 1805

The silver moon was a perfect sphere, beneath which the entire lane leading up to Pilgrim House was ablaze with dozens of flaming torches. There were beeswax candles lit in every room of the house, the ballroom illuminated by hundreds of them installed in crystal chandeliers and wall sconces. Our guests were the elite of Barbados: British officials, wealthy plantation owners and their wives. The ladies in silk and satin gowns were bedecked with glittering jewels, painted fans, and India shawls. Most of the gentlemen wore full evening dress, except for the Royal Navy officers in their dark-blue uniforms with gold trim.

Mother was determined that my post-wedding celebration would be the most talked about affair in the history of Barbados and had arranged for a reporter from the *Mercury Gazette* to be in attendance, just to make certain. Samuel and I had been married for two months. The wedding itself had been a private affair, limited to family and the few people here that we considered friends. If only my dear Catherine could have shared my happiness. I thought of her fondly later that night, as I prepared to lay with Samuel for the first time. Recalling what she'd done with George, and how she'd described it, I was astonished that she could be so calm and self-assured. I was more nervous than I'd ever been in my entire life. Above all, I was afraid of disappointing my new husband. I'd never considered the possibility that he might disappoint me.

But he didn't. That first night, I learned how right I'd been to trust Samuel. He proved himself to be a kind and gentle lover, considerate of my needs, understanding of my uncertainties. I sensed that he enjoyed my innocence, for which I was grateful at the time. But I also was determined not to be thought of as a child. In the weeks that followed, I tried my best to impress him with both my ardor and imagination. I believed my efforts were successful.

Now, on this night of celebration, I wondered if the guests gathered at Pilgrim House could see the difference in me, as much as I was aware of it myself.

Not until one o'clock did the festivities move outside to several enormous tents, where everyone feasted on a lavish supper of roasted meats, fresh seafood, imported cheeses, and tropical fruits, alongside breads, puddings, tarts, and trifles. I made it my mission that every guest should feel welcome, including Father's political adversaries for whom I felt not the slightest affection. Dutifully, I stopped at each table to chat and encourage unrestrained indulgence in the abundant food and spirits. All the while keeping a watchful eye on Mother. Though she appeared lighthearted, I could see that she was under a great deal of strain. It showed in her face—the sallowness of her complexion and the absence of sparkle in her heavy-lidded eyes. I took heart in the knowledge that she and the rest of my family soon would be leaving Barbados. Samuel and I planned to sail for London in four months; I was hopeful that Father would be relieved of his governor's duties by then.

I was seated at a table surrounded by my family, and was about to take my first bite of food in over twelve hours, when Samuel came up behind me. He bent down, his warm lips brushing my ear. "Darling, could I speak with you for a moment?"

"Of course." I asked the others to excuse me as Samuel helped me from my chair. We stepped outside the tent.

Temperatures during the dry season in Barbados were generally pleasant, but tonight the air was chilly without my shawl, which I had left behind. Noticing the gooseflesh on my arms, Samuel removed his jacket and placed it around my shoulders.

"I'm sorry to drag you away from the celebration, but ... something has happened. Several of my men arrived in Barbados earlier this evening, bringing word that French troops from Martinique have just begun a new assault on the rock. We've already lost three men. With one of my lieutenants recently court-martialed, I'm short of officers who can handle an emergency."

"What are you saying, Samuel? That you have to leave?"

"I'm afraid so."

My heart stalled. "When?"

"Tonight. Immediately."

"You can't wait until morning?" He couldn't be serious about leaving me. Not in the middle of our wedding celebration.

"Mary, you know I would postpone it if I could. But there are lives at stake. And everything the Royal Navy has been trying to achieve over the last few months could be lost. I need to take charge of the situation before it's too late. Tonight the winds are favorable. We can make good time."

Father had warned me of this. But I didn't expect it so soon.

Samuel reached for my hand and drew me to him, kissing my mouth with a fierce passion that ignited my desire. But I was not to have him tonight. We were to be separated. Who knew for how long? I pulled away, an unspoken question hanging between us.

"It's impossible to say exactly when I shall return," he said, reading my thoughts. "But however long it is, promise you won't worry."

"How could I *not* worry?"

"My commission will be over soon, and we'll be on our way to London. You'll be surprised how quickly the time passes."

"It will not pass quickly at all. But, of course, I understand the necessity. You must go." It would not do for me to appear like a spoiled child.

I was a hero's wife.

•   •   •

Weeks went by with no word from Diamond Rock. No news of naval victories or defeats. Only uncertainty.

Mother and Father tried to cheer me, as did Frances and Caroline. Augusta avoided saying anything too insensitive. Charlotte and Helen were oblivious to my situation, or so I thought. But Charlotte surprised me one day by asking if I missed Sir Samuel, and when I acknowledged that I very much did, she planted a kiss on my cheek, saying, "That's from him."

Sarah was as great a comfort to me as anyone. She had always observed my moods closely and, should I appear melancholy, she would encourage me to speak of my feelings. "The best way to handle being stuck in a lonely place is to invite company," she'd often say. But it was difficult to talk about how I felt, my husband snatched away from me just as I was beginning to know him.

One morning in mid-April, I was summoned to the front door by Cunningham, who could not hide the twinkle in his eye. I imagined there must be good news of some sort, perhaps a messenger saying all was well on Diamond Rock. What I did not expect was Samuel himself. But there he was, standing on the threshold, dressed in civilian clothes and carrying a huge floral bouquet. I greeted him with a joyous shriek, flinging myself into his arms.

"My darling Mary."

So tight against him, I could not separate the beating of our hearts. "Please don't tell me that you are here only for a day or night."

"My commission is over. I am yours."

He kissed my lips—a long, deep kiss that left me weak. I paused to catch my breath before asking, "Did Father know you were on your way?"

"I'm afraid not. It's been difficult to communicate from the island, with no sailors to spare. The French have attempted several more landings, and they don't appear to be finished yet. But I've handed over the command to a very capable fellow and expect he will continue to hold them off."

"You're really done with it?" I still was afraid to believe he would not be leaving me again.

"Martinique is no longer my problem," he said, tucking a wisp of hair behind my ear. "All the arrangements have been made for us to sail for England in two weeks."

"Two weeks!" The fact of leaving Barbados for good had never seemed completely real until this moment. "My goodness, I have so much to do."

He kissed me again. "Such as?"

"Well—" Suddenly, I could think of nothing so very urgent. Except … "You must be tired from your journey. Perhaps you'd like to sleep for a while."

"A bed would be welcome." He gave me a gentle pinch. "But sleep is the farthest thing from my mind."

·   ·   ·

The day of our departure for England was bittersweet. Father still had no definite date for the family's return to Scotland, though he assured us a voyage was imminent. For now, the only member of the household accompanying Samuel and me to London was my faithful Sarah, deliriously happy at the prospect of returning to civilization.

Our voyage was expected to take between one and two months, depending on the winds and other weather. But what did I care for time, now that I was spending every second of it with Samuel? I would not have minded had we stayed in our cabin for entire days and nights, indulging in the pleasures of each other's bodies as often as we chose. Samuel had proved himself as bold in love as he was in war, and I was dizzy with desire for him. That he was twice my age only heightened the attraction. Why would I want a mere boy who knew nothing of the finer points of amorous adventure? At times, I was tempted to ask Samuel where he had learned all his delightful tricks, but, of course, it was not my business to know. What mattered was that now he employed them for my benefit.

The first two days at sea, we had clear skies and steady easterly winds. Soon we would be leaving Caribbean waters and heading across the Atlantic. There was a relaxed attitude among the passengers, many of whom spent the greater part of the day sitting in wooden chairs on the deck and admiring the view, an endless blue and tranquil sea. On the third morning, Samuel and I were enjoying a stroll on the deck of the *Sea Goddess* when one of the sailors called out that a mast had been spotted at twelve nautical miles. "Identity unknown," he shouted.

These waters were patrolled by both British and French naval vessels, but a passenger ship should not be under threat of attack from either. Pirates and privateers were another matter. There were far fewer these days, but occasionally one might run into them. Samuel had told me that the ship destroyed by a mysterious explosion at Diamond Rock, just a few months earlier, had been a captured privateer vessel unofficially sanctioned by the French.

"Will you excuse me for a minute, darling?" Samuel said, peering into the distance. "I'm going to the quarterdeck to speak with the captain."

"Why?"

"I'd like to borrow his telescope."

"Then I'll go with you."

"No, Mary. You stay here. I'll be back soon."

My lips settled into a pout, but I turned away without argument, allowing Samuel to leave me with his promise of a quick return. I would have liked to look through the telescope as well. But what annoyed me most was how easily Samuel could forget that he was not in command of this ship, only a passenger: No longer was he Commodore Hood; he was the distinguished Sir Samuel Hood, retired hero, accompanied by his wife, formerly The Honorable Mary Mackenzie, now The Honorable Lady Hood.

Lady Hood! Though I still was somewhat unaccustomed to that title, it sounded lovely.

Suddenly a horn blared from the ship's platform. "All crew to their battle stations! Passengers below deck!"

I looked around. Sailors were running about, shouting orders and herding the civilians on deck to safer territory below. It was fascinating to watch what takes place when a ship's crew believe they may soon be under attack. The excitement was contagious; I could easily imagine how commandeering a naval vessel in battle would be exhilarating to a man like Samuel. Perhaps he was feeling a bit of that familiar arousal right now.

"Madam, you need to go down below. Captain's orders." The young sailor who addressed me could not have been older than fifteen.

"I'm waiting for my husband, Sir Samuel Hood."

"You can't wait here, my lady."

"Have you determined the ship's flag?"

"Not for certain, my lady. Could be a privateer. Captain's not taking no chances. You need to go down below."

"Fine, I'll go. You run along and help the others."

He hesitated. Then, perhaps intimidated by my claim to be the famous Royal Navy commander's wife, he nodded and hurried on.

There was still no sign of Samuel's return. Making a peephole with my thumb and index finger, I closed one eye and tried looking through the aperture as I would a telescope. My vision seemed to sharpen a tiny bit, not enough to make a difference. The ship in question was still quite distant but moving towards us. Perhaps it was a privateer vessel, intent on boarding our ship and confiscating everything of value. Or staking claim to the ship itself. In that case, what would happen to the passengers?

A palpable thrill passed through me. I, for one, would not be forced down below to cower in the dark. Would I ever have another opportunity to witness such a battle? To have a small taste of what Samuel must have experienced in countless naval conflicts?

But I could not continue standing here, in the open.

My eyes darted about the deck, looking for a place to hide, until I noticed an area beneath the ship's rigging where some spare parts had been stowed. I went over to it and, making certain I was not observed, crouched down behind a pile of sailcloth.

By now, the sailors had cleared the deck of passengers, all of whom had been more than willing to scurry down below. Most were terrified. Perhaps being Samuel's wife was what endowed me with an extra dose of courage. Or maybe it was just my customary curiosity, which I might well regret were I to be discovered by pirates. How did I imagine I would talk my way out of such a predicament?

My ears picked up a conversation on deck, voices drawing close to where I hid.

"I'm quite confident, Captain." It was Samuel, now within several yards of me. "But it's always a good exercise to prepare for the worst."

"That it is, Sir Samuel. I'll go up and sound the all clear. Our passengers will be greatly relieved."

"No doubt they will. If you'll excuse me, I need to find my wife down below."

"Certainly, sir. I look forward to the two of you joining me tonight for dinner."

Peeking over the stack of sailcloth, I watched the captain set off for the quarterdeck. Samuel began searching for the closest passage to the area below deck, where he assumed I must be huddled with the rest.

I popped up from my hiding place. "Samuel!"

He turned with a look of surprise, which quickly turned to something less benign. "What are you doing up here, Mary? All passengers were ordered below."

"Yes, I know." I approached him with a defiant grin. "But I wanted to see what it was like to prepare for battle at sea. Besides, I heard your conversation with the captain. It was only a false alarm."

"This time, yes. But you had no way of knowing that, nor did I. You could have put yourself in the middle of a very dangerous situation. Hiding behind a pile of sailcloth gave you no protection whatsoever. I'm surprised you would be so foolish."

His tone was beginning to provoke me. I had done what I wanted to do and didn't need a lecture. "If you were so worried about me, why did you leave me on deck by myself?"

"Because I assumed you would have the good sense to follow orders."

"Is that what you expect of me? To follow orders?"

For a second, he seemed taken aback. Then he smiled. "My dear Mary, your father warned me that you've always had a bit of the daring in you. I told him it didn't scare me in the least. In fact, such a quality was precisely what I wanted in a wife."

"Are you changing your mind now?"

"Not at all. When I said that I would set you free, I meant it. Just don't get yourself killed in the process."

I slipped my arm through his. "All right—provided you can promise me the same."

A shadow flickered across his face, and I knew exactly what it meant. Though we were on our way to a new life together in London, Samuel's fighting days were not over.

CHAPTER FOURTEEN
LONDON, JUNE 1805

I had been aware that Samuel was a man of means, though he never spoke of it. All I knew was the address of his residence in the heart of London, 37 Lower Wimpole Street, in a fashionable part of Marylebone. The rest had been left to my imagination.

It was near the middle of June when I saw our home for the first time. We had been seven weeks at sea, and I was more than ready for a change of scenery. Still, I was nervous about becoming the new mistress of a household which heretofore, I assumed, had functioned quite well enough without me. Would I be welcomed, or might the staff resent my presence? And the residence itself: Would I be free to do with it as I pleased, or would Samuel's taste, firmly established, continue to prevail? Perhaps—and this I fervently hoped—there would be no conflict between our respective likes and dislikes.

As we pulled up in front of my new home I fixed a smile upon my face, determined to maintain it regardless. From the carriage window, the three-story brick townhouse appeared as stately as any I'd seen in London, its tall, multi-paned windows decorated with scrolled iron railings, and a portico supported by grand Corinthian columns.

A liveried footman opened the carriage door, offering me a white-gloved hand. Lining our path forward were members of the staff, positioned according to seniority as was the custom. I made a quick count of a dozen in attendance.

"Good to see you, Martin."

A black-coated butler, his hairless head smooth as a billiard-ball, stood at attention. "Welcome home, sir. And welcome to you, Lady Hood. I trust you will let us know how best to make you comfortable."

I acknowledged his greeting and each of those that followed with a nod and a smile. Ordinarily, I was good at remembering names and faces, but right now there were too many other things vying for my attention. I did notice, however, the surreptitious looks I received from some members of the staff. They could not be blamed for their curiosity about what sort of woman the master of the house had selected for his wife. While I would expect there to have been other women in Samuel's life before me, I wondered whether he had brought any of them here.

"I think it best if I take you on the grand tour later," Samuel said, escorting me into the spacious entrance hall. "Wouldn't you rather be shown to your apartment? Perhaps have a bath drawn?"

"Sounds delightful," I said, my eyes roaming the impressive entry, which exuded dignified elegance. Tiled in an intricate pattern of green and white marble, its mahogany-paneled walls were polished to a soft luster. An enormous crystal chandelier in the center of the high ceiling glittered like handfuls of diamonds. Though I was no stranger to opulence, the realization that I was mistress of everything I saw felt like a dream.

"Lady Hood's maid is outside with the trunks," Samuel said, addressing Martin. "Please welcome her and see that she has everything she needs to get settled."

"Yes, sir."

"Shall we, my dear?" Samuel steered me towards the winding marble staircase to the upper floors. I gripped the banister, intent on avoiding a careless stumble, knowing every eye below was upon me. Samuel and I did not speak until we were upstairs and had reached the end of a long hallway lined with oil portraits; I counted fifteen men and two women.

Finally, Samuel stopped in front of the open door to a spacious apartment.

"I hope you like it, Mary."

Stepping inside, my first impression was that the room needed a feminine touch. The draperies and furnishings were sumptuous but heavy and dark, and most of the room's decorative elements had a decidedly masculine flavor. Someone, however, had made an effort to brighten the place up. Scattered about the room were half a dozen porcelain vases crammed with giant red, pink, and yellow roses, their beauty and pervasive fragrance providing a delightfully sensual welcome.

"The dressing room is over here." Walking past the bed and fireplace, he led me through another open door. This adjoining chamber was also large, its tall windows draped in the same dark-blue velvet. Next to the fireplace were two rather stiff-looking armchairs upholstered in a blue and burgundy paisley pattern. Perhaps the same person responsible for the flowers had arranged several fancy perfume decanters on a mirrored dressing table. In the corner, a small writing desk and chair seemed an inviting spot to compose letters or make entries in my journal.

"I expect to spend a good deal of time in here, making myself presentable for London society," I said, giving Samuel's hand a light squeeze.

"You shall outshine all the ladies of London without even trying."

"Please, let us not deceive ourselves. I will need to work very hard at it." When last I lived in London, I was only sixteen. And not the wife of one of Britain's most notable naval officers, which naturally created high expectations.

"Where is your apartment?" I said, strolling back into the bedchamber.

"Upstairs, directly over yours."

"Ah, so you can put your ear to the floor and eavesdrop on all my private conversations?" I said, smiling.

"I hope we shall have no secrets from each other, my dear. But, having been a bachelor for so long, I admit that I'm not used to sharing. Not everything."

I took note of his comment, wondering if it might be meant as a warning, but quickly dismissed the thought. He was only being honest, and that could never be wrong. I knew, deep in my heart, that I could trust him.

"I realize these chambers are not exactly as you would want them," Samuel said with a hint of apology. "You are free to make whatever changes you wish."

My gaze rested a moment upon the huge canopy bed. "I suggest that we try out that bed straight away so I can decide whether it stays or goes."

He drew me into his arms. "After a bath?"

"Exactly what I was thinking."

•   •   •

We had been in London just over a week when Samuel sprung a surprise. It was the peak of the social season. Already we had attended two balls and three days of Royal Ascot, and dined out every other evening. But on this night he insisted we should stay home. I was perfectly happy to do so, having had barely enough time to catch my breath since our arrival.

For our first dinner alone, I wanted to look stunningly sophisticated. I chose my pale-blue velvet gown, a simple string of pearls, and asked Sarah to arrange my hair in a classical Grecian Knot.

Samuel and I were to meet in the drawing room before dinner. I was full of news about how I'd spent the afternoon shopping with my childhood friend, Kitty Pakenham, whose mother was my father's cousin. But upon entering the room, I saw that Samuel was in the company of a slender young man in the distinctive dress of the exclusive Harrow School—a long black coat, white shirt, knee breeches, black stockings, and buckle shoes. And there was a younger boy, also in a school uniform.

"Here she is now!" Samuel announced with a smile.

Both lads turned towards me, and I caught my breath.

"Oh, my goodness! William? Frank?" I rushed over to my younger brothers, embracing each of them in turn. "You've both grown so, I almost didn't recognize you!"

"It's been four years," William said in his new, deeper voice. At fourteen, he already was taller than I, still with that rather fragile look I remembered well. In contrast to his older brother, Frank had a strong, stocky build; physically, he seemed older than nine, but the eager innocence in his eyes gave him away.

"I take it this is all your doing?" I said, beaming at Samuel.

"You mentioned on several occasions in Barbados how you missed your brothers, though you were grateful for them being in London. Well, now you're in London, too, and you needn't miss them any longer."

"I was sorry you two couldn't attend our wedding," I said to the boys, "but two months there and back would have put you far behind at school."

"Mother wrote to us about it," Frank said. He looked up at Samuel with an expression of awe. "Someday, sir, I want to be in the Royal Navy."

"That would be a fine choice, Frank," Samuel replied. "But it's a little early for you to make up your mind about something so important."

"I don't care. That's what I want more than anything."

"Well then, when the time comes, I'm sure I can be of help. And you, William? What sort of future are you contemplating?"

William shifted on his feet. "After Cambridge, sir, I want to serve in Parliament," he said softly, as though admitting to such lofty goals embarrassed him. "Representing Ross-shire."

"Like our father." I patted him on the shoulder. "I think it's a fine ambition, William. And I'm sure you would make an excellent Member of Parliament. We need people who are not afraid to stand up for what they believe, even when it's unpopular."

"How do you know I would do that?"

His question was so unexpected that I was caught off guard. In truth, I didn't know. I'd been apart from my brothers for so long, we were practically strangers. But William, especially, had always been a sensible boy and well-spoken.

"I know simply because you have the Mackenzie spirit. You both do," I added, not wanting Frank to feel slighted.

"You must know that your sister is somewhat jealous of you," Samuel said, giving me a wink. "She wouldn't mind at all dressing up in one of your Harrow uniforms and masquerading as a boy, just to see what she could get away with. Isn't that so, Mary?"

I felt the color rushing to my cheeks. There was truth in his jest. Though I enjoyed my position in life, I couldn't help but begrudge men their limitless possibilities. "It might be fun."

"Mary doesn't yet realize the adventures that await her."

Frank's eyes grew wide. "What adventures?"

"Well, it wouldn't be right for me to tell you before I've told her."

Just as I was about to insist that Samuel explain himself, dinner was announced. I guided my brothers towards the dining room, aware of Samuel's admiring eyes on the sway of my hips beneath the simple drape of my gown.

Watching my husband that night—how he encouraged my young brothers to talk about their interests at school and probed their thoughts about the world—it was clear he would make a wonderful father. It was remarkable that Samuel had waited so long for the opportunity. I asked him once if he had ever loved another woman. He said not in the way he loved me, and I did not press him to explain.

"How many battles have you fought, Sir Samuel?" Frank asked, stuffing a forkful of roast duck with cherries into his mouth. "Were you ever wounded?"

Samuel chuckled. "I'm sorry to say I haven't kept count of the battles. It might be interesting to know. But as far as being wounded, I've been fortunate. Nothing serious. Still, every sailor knows what can happen in an instant when you least expect it. One must always be on guard and quick to respond to danger. Often a few seconds is all you have to make a decision that can mean the difference between life and death—yours and that of your men."

"Have you finished with fighting now?" William said. "I mean, is there something else you'd rather do?"

"No one enjoys combat, William. We engage in it because we must. As to whether my naval career is at an end …" He glanced at me, but I averted my eyes. I had expressed to Samuel that I hoped he would not seek another commission, but had received no assurances. "Trying to predict the state of the world is like trying to shoot a grouse while blindfolded. One is more than likely to fail. That is why I try to live day by day. And enjoy what happiness I can."

It was not exactly the answer I had wished to hear, but I hid my disappointment. "Frank, you said you wish to join the Royal Navy. But aren't you first going to follow your brother to Cambridge?"

Frank gave his brother a plaintive look, and William cleared his throat. "Well," William said, "not everyone goes to Cambridge."

"Of course not. But if one has the opportunity—"

"Mary, the boy is only nine," Samuel interjected. "He has plenty of time to decide what he wants to do."

For a second, I resented Samuel's interference. Frank was *my* brother, and I was entitled to look out for his welfare. But seeing how grateful Frank appeared to have avoided further questioning, I refrained from pursuing the subject. Perhaps Frank did not have a great interest in his studies, which would be unfortunate but not unusual. I had always thought young girls more suited than boys to serious learning. My opinion was not the popular one.

"So, tell us, William, what will be your first proposal as a Member of Parliament?" Samuel said, leaning back with a glass of port.

William sat up a bit straighter, seeming to grow an inch or two. "An end to slavery in Britain's colonies. Others have proposed it, but it never wins approval."

"God help us if it hasn't gone through before you get to Parliament!" I exclaimed, trying not to think of Father's dirty little secret. How would William feel if he knew about the plantation on Berbice?

"Too many competing interests," Samuel said. "Just like Lord Seaforth faces in Barbados. Even a man's best efforts cannot change the world overnight."

"Perhaps not," I said, "but William is very persuasive. If anyone can succeed in restoring morality to Parliament, it should be him. That's what true leadership is all about. Convincing others to do what they know in their hearts is right, regardless of the consequences."

"When you find a world such as that, you'll have to let me know," Samuel said with a sardonic smile. "I'd love to join you there, my dear."

"I didn't realize my husband was such a cynic." I was no longer naïve enough to doubt the truth of what he'd said. Still, I wished to nurture my brother's idealism. If he were to lose it at the tender age of fourteen, what confidence would he have in his future?

He must believe in that future.

CHAPTER FIFTEEN

I was eager to write to Caroline about the surprise visit from William and Frank, knowing it would please her to hear how well they appeared. I also asked that she keep me apprised of the family's plans to leave Barbados. It was imperative for Mother to insist that Father expedite his stepping down as governor. Aware of how he valued the prestige of his position, I worried he might have second thoughts about relinquishing it.

But most of the letter I composed to my dearest sister dealt with private matters. Caroline was the only one with whom I wished to share the details of my first months as Lady Hood—my thoughts about the complexities of marriage, my new life in London, and how I found myself unexpectedly eager for a child.

"Excuse me, my lady! Thank heaven you're here!" Sarah, her face flushed, burst through the door of my dressing room.

"My goodness, is someone chasing you?" I quipped.

"No, but you won't guess who is here looking for a position. Mr. Martin's speaking with him now."

"I didn't know that we were in need of additional staff."

"But don't you want to know who it is?" She was wildly impatient, which sparked my curiosity.

"Very well, who is it?"

"Ian Macleod! Remember him? Colin Macleod's lad? Farmed on the Seaforth property in Lochalsh?"

"Of course, I remember Ian. His family has been on that land for generations. I wonder why he decided to leave."

Sarah bit down on her lip. "Wasn't exactly his decision. The family was turned out of their home four years ago. Land taken over for sheep."

My throat went dry. "That's impossible. Father wouldn't give in to the sheep farmers. He'd sooner slit his own throat than throw his loyal tenants to the wolves."

"Aye, was surprising to hear it. But plenty has changed since we've been away. I guess the Highlands, like everyplace else, has to go with the times."

"No!" I slammed my fist on the desktop, and Sarah jumped. "I don't believe Father would consent to such a thing."

"Ian says it wasn't Lord Seaforth himself who went with sheep, but the one he sold his property to. Took him only six months to drive everybody out who'd been there forever. Now poor Ian is in London looking for work. A coincidence, it is. He didn't know you were the new mistress of the house till I happened to see him waiting in the kitchen for Mr. Martin."

I knew how my father felt about the Highland land clearances. For years he'd refused to remove tenants to make room for the more lucrative business of sheep farming. If he had changed his mind, it could only mean that his finances were in even more dire straits than I knew. It was unforgiveable enough that he had Africans working his plantation in Berbice, all the while claiming he loathed the practice of slavery. And now this—selling out his own clansmen. How could he?

"Don't be too hard on your father," Sarah said, seeing my distress. "So many of the landowners are selling just to survive. Times are hard for everybody."

I stood abruptly. "Was there anything else, Sarah?"

She hesitated. "Just that I wondered if you might want to talk with Mr. Martin. It's not my business, but if there was a place for Ian here—"

I interrupted her mid-sentence. "I'm on my way to the kitchen now, for just that purpose. We'll find something for Ian, I promise."

"Might I go along with you?"

It took me only a second to conclude the obvious. Sarah had more than a passing interest in the matter of a position for Ian Macleod. "I haven't seen him since we were children. What is Ian like now?"

Sarah looked away, a rosy flush returning to her cheeks. "A strapping lad, all right. Good-looking, I'd say."

"I see." I was trying not to laugh. And grateful for the distraction. There was nothing I hated more than questioning my father's principles, and the news Sarah had delivered troubled me deeply. "I take it you would welcome having him employed here?"

"Aye, to be honest, we could use a handsome lad. And a Scot on top of it. Nothin' wrong wi' addin' a touch o' home." she said, making her point with a touch of brogue.

"I couldn't agree more. Come along, let's see what we can do for him."

Sarah and I arrived at the kitchen just as Martin was seeing Ian to the service door. Apparently, the interview was over.

"Ian Macleod, what a surprise to see you here!" I said, approaching him with a lively step.

Ian dipped his head in deference, but I saw the conflicted look on his face. I remembered him as a bright-eyed, mischievous lad, slightly older than I, but a fine rough-and-tumble playmate. Not one to back down from a fight. "I hadn't any idea this was your home, Lady Hood, or I would never have bothered ye."

"Bothered me? Not at all. Have you just arrived in London?"

"Yes, my lady." He shifted his wool cap from one hand to the other. "After we lost the farm, we tried to make a go of it in the village of Dornie, but that wasn't the life for me."

I turned to Martin, who still seemed flummoxed by my familiarity with the young man he had been about to dismiss. "A dashing young footman such as Mr. Macleod would be a welcome addition to the staff. Please offer him a position, starting immediately." I hesitated, unsure how far to take my interference. But I was the mistress of the house, wasn't I? And I owed Ian as much, given that my father's actions, directly or indirectly, had led to his current predicament. "And please make certain Mr. Macleod's salary is commensurate with the other footmen, whatever his level of experience. I know him to be a quick learner and have no doubt he shall exceed your expectations."

Martin's face was bright red, and I could almost imagine smoke pouring out of his rather large ears. I surmised that Samuel had exercised little control over household matters, leaving Mr. Martin and Mrs. Bundy to make most of the decisions. While I had no desire to be overbearing, I was not averse to exerting my will as needed. Martin and the others would have to get used to it.

"Really, my lady, if ye're doin' this out of pity—" Ian undoubtedly felt caught in the middle.

"This has nothing to do with pity," I assured him, though it most certainly did. My heart was broken seeing him here, when he belonged in Scotland working the land to which he and his ancestors had devoted themselves for generations. I wished at least I could have offered him a gardener's position, but we had a fine gardener and there wasn't space for much of a garden anyway. "You've come at just the right time, Ian, and I'm grateful."

He looked at me with narrowed eyes. Was he thinking I had more than my share of conceit, offering to make him my servant after my father had destroyed the only life he'd ever known? Even if it wasn't Father himself who sold out to the sheep farmers, the clearances had finally touched our Mackenzie lands. Father had held out for years, but I was wrong to think he could do so forever. Partly because the world had changed, and partly because Father could not. He was as he'd always been—someone who lived beyond his means, ignoring that someday he and everyone else must pay the price.

CHAPTER SIXTEEN

In December, I was invited to a dinner party hosted by my friend Kitty Pakenham. On that night, Samuel was obliged to attend some honorary event of the Royal Navy, so I went alone. Dear Kitty, knowing my love of Scottish literature and history, arranged for Mr. Walter Scott to escort me to the table.

Mr. Scott had recently achieved a stunning success with the publication of his narrative poem *The Lay of the Last Minstrel*, a story of sixteenth-century Scotland. The setting was not the Highlands but south of it, at the border with England, yet the poem had stirred memories of my early life in Ross-shire. That warm feeling of belonging to a place, connected in almost a visceral way. I had been reminded how deeply I missed my home.

"Delightful to meet you, Lady Hood," he said, raising my hand to his lips. Walter Scott was a serious-looking fellow, probably in his mid-thirties, with sharp blue eyes and deep grooves across his forehead. Only his reddish, slightly tousled hair hinted at the rakishness one always expects in a poet.

"Looks as though our hostess thought we Scots had better stick together," I replied, settling into the proffered chair.

He chuckled as he took his seat, then repositioned himself for a better view of me. "Miss Pakenham mentioned that you were recently living in Barbados. That must have been interesting."

"Interesting at first. One might imagine it to be a tropical paradise, but life there is harsh in many ways. I was glad to leave, though I worry about the rest of my family. They must remain until my father, Lord Seaforth, vacates his post as governor. I've been told it shan't be too much longer."

"They're returning to Scotland?"

"I expect so. Mother is eager to resume renovations of Brahan Castle. Seems to be a never-ending project, and, of course, a castle tends towards decay when one is absent for so long. But it is our home, as well as a place incredibly important to Scottish history. A history about which you are said to be among the most knowledgeable of scholars," I added. A touch of flattery, perhaps, but nonetheless sincere. Mr. Scott's reputation as a historian was well established.

He leaned closer, appearing to welcome my invitation to talk about himself. "The chronicle of history has always fascinated me. But I must say, as a writer I am most intrigued by what propels history forward. By that I mean not only the human spirit, but supernatural forces as well, wielding their influence in our world to good effect or ill."

"Then you credit the supernatural with being more than just a poetic device?"

"Indeed." He regarded me with a curious smile. "But growing up in Brahan Castle, you must have encountered a ghost or two yourself."

"I have not." My response was overly emphatic, and he raised an eyebrow. "And you, Mr. Scott? Have you ever met a ghost?"

"Yes … and no." He paused, thoughtful. "I'll tell you a little story. One that I have found truly unforgettable. When I was nineteen, I had the opportunity to spend a night in the ancient baronial castle of Glamis. It's where Malcolm the Second, a Scottish king of old, was murdered. At the time of my visit, the castle's owner, the Earl of Strathmore, was spending very little time there, and the castle was only partially furnished. But there were a great many objects of antiquity hanging about—suits of armor and such—that lent a sober atmosphere to the place. My apartment for the night was in a distant corner of the castle which, as I said, was unoccupied but for an old caretaker and his wife. The room assigned to me was directly opposite what they called 'the king's room,' purportedly the site of Malcolm's murder. I will never forget that night and the strange sensations that came over me as I huddled in my bed. They were not what I would call pleasant. In fact, I cannot recall ever being more terrified, and yet of nothing I could actually see or hear. So, while I did not exactly *meet* a ghost, I believe that I experienced one."

"Have you considered that it might have been only the power of suggestion? Where a murder has occurred, one is easily induced to imagine a ghostly presence."

"True, though I am not so easily induced as most," he replied, sounding slightly piqued. "But do you mean to say, Lady Hood, that you never wonder about such things? The powers that exist beyond the mortal sphere?"

"I try not to."

"If I might ask, why?"

A quiet dread seeped into me like a subtle poison. But tonight, in the company of Walter Scott, I had the sudden urge to speak of the Seer, as I seldom did. Being a Scotsman well-versed in Highland history, he would know of the many prophecies attributed to Coinneach Odhar but surely confirm the Seer as only a fanciful legend.

"I will explain, Mr. Scott, but first tell me what you know of the man they call the Brahan Seer."

"Ah, so that is it," he said, rubbing his chin. "Forgive me, I should have recalled your family's connection to the Seer. As to what I know of him, I'm afraid no more than many others. That Coinneach Odhar is said to have been born Kenneth Mackenzie on the Isle of Lewis. That he may have worked as a laborer on the Brahan estate in the late 1600s, and that his execution was supposedly at the behest of the third Lady Seaforth. But you must know all this."

"Perhaps I do, but there may be something I have missed. Please go on."

"As you wish, though I can tell you nothing beyond the common knowledge." He withdrew a handkerchief from his pocket and dabbed at the tiny beads of sweat sprouting on his forehead. Had something in my insistence made him nervous? "According to legend, Odhar was not born with the Second Sight but obtained it rather by chance. The most popular account tells of a confrontation between his mother and the ghost of a Danish princess. The tribute demanded of the princess for the right of passage back to her grave was that Kenneth be given the Second Sight. As the tale is told, the next day he discovered a small stone with a hole in the middle. Through the stone's aperture, he was able to see the visions from which he made his many prophecies."

"A clever story," I said, though I had heard it before and always thought it foolish. "But why the stone?"

"A symbol's sway over the human mind is astounding. A sacred object can impart a certain *reality* to the abstract. Very useful to a would-be prophet. To a poet, also."

"But the prophecies themselves …" What I wanted from Mr. Scott was nothing less than his utter refutation of the Seer's curse upon my family. "Do you believe it's possible to see into the future?"

"Some say yes, pointing out, as proof of it, the prophecies of Coinneach Odhar that have come to pass. But if you are asking my personal opinion as to whether he is man or myth—"

"I am."

"My guess is that Odhar did exist and, as a result of the powers he claimed to possess, met an unfortunate fate. I'm afraid I cannot say with any certainty whether I believe in those powers—or not. Rather, to be more precise, I do believe in the gift of Second Sight, but it is very rare."

I must have looked disappointed, because Mr. Scott suddenly reached for my hand in a gesture of solace. "I'm terribly sorry if our conversation has disturbed you, Lady Hood. I should not have allowed your generous praise of my poetry to lead to a discourse so personally painful for you. It was extremely thoughtless."

"Please, don't chastise yourself. I am the one who raised the subject of the Seer. And I am not at all disturbed," I said, forcing a smile. "I was merely curious about your opinion of the legend. I have never believed it and never shall."

"Were I in your position, I would certainly adopt the same attitude." We were interrupted by dinner's first course, and our conversation during the rest of the meal was neither exclusively with each other nor of a serious nature. But before we parted that evening, Mr. Scott asked if he might write to me upon his return to Edinburgh.

I gave my permission and promised to reply.

CHAPTER SEVENTEEN
1806

Between renewing old friendships and making new ones, my social life in London accelerated rapidly. Despite having spent the greater part of my youth in Scotland, Father's service in Parliament had exposed me somewhat to English society. His subsequent elevation to the British Peerage as the First Baron Seaforth had added to my social capital, as did my marriage to Samuel, a hero of the British Royal Navy with considerable wealth of his own. But after my first year as Samuel's wife, I began to feel restless, as though something was missing. It did not require much soul-searching to determine what it was. I wanted a child.

Though Samuel did not speak of it, I was convinced he would welcome fatherhood. We had relations often enough—or it seemed enough to me—but month after month passed with no result. I became anxious. Was I doing something wrong? Or was I one of those sad, and frequently scorned, women incapable of conceiving?

One night after Samuel and I had shared my bed and he was dozing off, I could contain my worry no longer.

"Samuel," I said, touching him lightly on his bare shoulder. "May we talk?"

He awoke with a start. "What is it? Something wrong?"

"No, nothing is wrong. I just want us to talk."

With a sigh, he sank back into the pillows.

"It's about our—" I halted, suddenly wishing I had not begun. To admit openly that I had tried and failed to give him a child was excruciating. "I thought I would be expecting by now. Are you disappointed that I'm not?"

Several painfully long moments passed before he answered.

"You needn't be concerned, Mary. These things often take time."

"Mother gave birth to me within her first year of marriage."

Samuel propped himself up on one elbow. "Things happen, or not, for their own reasons. In our case—"

"Yes? In our case, what?"

"I was going to tell you in a few days, but it might as well be now. I've accepted command of a Royal Navy squadron that will be conducting a blockade of Rochefort, on the Atlantic coast of France. Our mission is to disrupt French naval activities and possibly mount an amphibious assault on the town, depending on conditions."

Had I really believed Samuel's naval career would end with our marriage? No, I knew this was coming. I had only hoped for more time.

"When are you leaving?"

"In two weeks."

"So soon …"

"I'm sorry, Mary, but we've a war to win. I hope it won't be for long, but look—" He swept a soft tumble of curls from my cheek. "You've made lots of friends here. You'll be fine without me."

I almost said *no, I won't be fine.* But I would be. I understood duty. My father had lived by it, as best he could. "Of course. I know how to take care of myself."

"So, you see …" He smiled. "It's better that you're not expecting now. I would worry too much about you. We'll work harder on it when I return, all right?"

"Every day and night?" I tried to laugh, but the tightness in my throat made it come out more like an embarrassing hiccup. "Are all British Navy wives so stupidly emotional when their husbands leave them?"

"I share those emotions, and they're not stupid. You don't think I want to leave you, I hope."

Though I shook my head, there was at least a kernel of doubt in my mind. As Father had said, Samuel was an adventurer, a man of war. The passion burning in his soul was not just for me.

•   •   •

The two weeks before Samuel left to assume his command were too brief to mentally prepare for his departure. Though the redecorating I had done over the past year had transformed our London townhouse into a comfortable home, the thought of living there alone was difficult. The strength of my feelings surprised me. I was not a person prone to loneliness, but something close to that had already set in by the day Samuel waved his final goodbye.

From the start, Sarah did her best to cheer me. But lately she was preoccupied with her own joy, the product of a blossoming romance with Ian Macleod. I could hardly expect her to share in my doldrums. Seeking solace, I turned to my good friend Kitty, who had married within the last few months. However, Kitty was in a worse state than I. She and her new husband, Arthur Wellesley, were not getting on well. Our time together was spent with her crying on my shoulder between tales of the latest insults Arthur had leveled at her. On top of that, she was already with child, about which I couldn't help feeling a twinge of envy.

Finally there came good news. I received a letter from Mother saying that Father's governorship had ended, and the family was now back at Brahan Castle. I instantly made the decision to go there. Samuel's absence was the perfect opportunity to see them and reconnect with my beloved Highland home. Sarah was not pleased, of course, preferring to stay in London with her new beau close at hand. I was sorry for the interruption of her love affair, but it was her duty to accompany me.

Our visit should be brief, I said, though I did not entirely promise.

The carriage journey took us over two weeks, stopping every night at an inn or tavern along the way to refresh ourselves and our horses. As we passed through the lands on the border of England and Scotland—the setting of Walter Scott's popular poem of the last minstrel—I wondered if he would ever write to me. I'd been surprised when he asked if he might and was confident that he had no improper motive, as I'd heard he was happily married. Perhaps it had been only my connection to the Brahan Seer that intrigued him, and he'd long since forgotten me. Still, I preferred to think he had enjoyed my company and found me intellectually bright. Though he would have no way to know, I was a fair writer myself. Not of poems or novels, but I was good at describing my observations of people and places.

As we made our way through Scotland, the temperatures turned cooler, evidence of early autumn visible in hues of gold, red, and orange dotting the landscape. The days were a mix of rain and sun, and the wind an ever-present companion, necessitating that we dress in layers that could be added or removed. It was a pleasant enough ride, but even had we encountered a snowstorm I would not have complained. I was going home.

There had been no time to forewarn my family of our visit. I could hardly wait to see their look of surprise when I alighted from my carriage in front of Brahan Castle. How I hoped I would find all of them well! I had received several letters from Mother and Caroline over the past year, assuring me that everything was fine. But my own eyes would better judge how each of them had fared since we were last together.

We arrived as the sun was sinking behind the summit plateau of Ben Wyvis. After passing through the iron gates, their stone pillars topped by an enormous pair of bronze stags, the carriage rolled to a halt in the cobblestone courtyard. Too excited to wait, I threw open the carriage door and stepped outside. A fine mist in the air softened the fiery sunset, making it a soothing mélange of lavender, pink, and tangerine. I breathed in the pungent scent of pines, harkened to the twilight calls of blackbirds, song thrushes, and wood pigeons. How long it had been since Mother Nature held me close like this! I could have cried from happiness and might have but for the interruption of Caroline's ecstatic squeal.

"Mary! Oh my, is it really you?" Lifting her skirts, she ran towards me, her fair hair streaming behind her. She flew into my arms, the two of us hugging each other so hard it literally took my breath away. "Why didn't you tell us you were coming?" she said, finally breaking free. "We would have planned for fireworks."

I laughed. "No, thank you! I much prefer the sunset. But darling, let me see you." I held her for a moment at arm's length. "You look well. And the others?"

"Recovering."

My smile vanished. "Recovering from what? Someone is ill? Mother?"

"The voyage from Barbados was difficult. It has taken all of us a while to readjust to home. But more of that later. Come in from the chill." She grabbed my hand. "You'll see for yourself, there's no reason to worry."

I turned towards the carriage. "Sarah, where are you?"

Sarah, carrying my brocade bag of toiletries, stepped down from the carriage. Caroline dropped my hand and hurried over to give her a warm squeeze. "It's wonderful to see you," she said.

"Thank you, Miss Caroline. Hard to believe we're here."

"I suppose I should tell you that Sarah is in love." I winked at Caroline. "With a Scotsman. You remember Ian Macleod?"

"Certainly I do."

"Well, he turned up in London, and Sarah secured a position for him in our household. Things have moved along quickly from there," I said with an impish grin.

Sarah blushed, and Caroline struggled not to laugh. "That's enough of embarrassing poor Sarah. I think it's wonderful about you and Mr. Macleod! You shall tell me more later. But for now, you both must be exhausted, and you still have the rest of the family to surprise." Hearing the crunch of dead leaves, all three of us turned to see the approach of a sturdy-looking young man in a rough wool shirt and trousers, his heavy boots caked with mud. "Good, Robertson is here. He can help your coachman and groom with the horses. We'll summon some others to tend to your trunks."

"I'll stay here to direct them," Sarah said.

I was glad to have Sarah taking charge. She'd been rather quiet throughout our trip, no doubt missing Ian and wondering how long they must be separated. I knew the feeling too well.

"I think you'll find your old room in order, Sarah," Caroline said. "The entire castle has undergone a good cleaning. As you can imagine, it fell into a bit of disrepair during our absence. Mother has been fretting over it ever since we arrived."

I turned to Sarah. "When you are finished, please come and say hello to everyone. They will be pleased to see you. And tomorrow, you shall be off for a visit to your parents."

As Caroline and I ascended the steep steps of the front entrance, I hastily smoothed my hair and gave both cheeks a hard pinch. I wanted Mother and Father's first impression to be that marriage agreed with me. No doubt they would be looking for evidence of a grandchild on the way. I had already planned to explain, should anyone ask, that Samuel and I had decided to wait until he returned from his current mission. They were likely unaware that he'd gone to war. It was a month since I'd last written, and, not yet knowing of their return to Scotland, my letter had been sent to Barbados.

"Mother and Frances are in the music room," Caroline said, pushing open the castle's heavy oak door.

"And Father?"

"Father is not here."

I paused in the doorway. "What? Why not?"

"When the rest of us left Barbados, he stayed on to finish up a few items of business. He boarded the ship for home over a month ago and will likely spend a brief while in London before coming here." She looped her arm through mine. "Come along, let's not stand here in the cold."

I sighed. "I could have seen him if I'd stayed in London! Well, perhaps he'll still be there when I return. But tell me, how is his health? Has he been awfully troubled by the gout?"

"It comes and goes."

So, that had not changed.

We passed through the entry hall, its stone walls decorated with mounted stag heads, Clan Mackenzie crests, and faded tapestries depicting well-known myths and fables. Climbing the circular stone staircase at the far end, we traversed the Great Hall, its gigantic fireplace ablaze with golden-orange flames. Next was the formal dining room with its gallery of ancestral portraits and a magnificently carved table nearly as long as the one at Pilgrim House.

As we came upon the music room, I recalled the lively evenings when Mother and Father's guests were entertained with recitals of piano, harpsichord, and chamber music. Sometimes I would be trotted out to perform, not brilliantly, but well enough to earn my allotted share of polite praise. Hearing the piano, I immediately recognized Frances's rapturous touch. Ah yes, it was good to be home at last! If it was wrong of me to prefer Brahan Castle to the London townhouse I shared with Samuel, I didn't care.

We entered, and Frances looked up from the keys. "Good Lord!" She sprang from the stool, rushing towards me with a smile of delight.

"Mary! Oh, it is so wonderful to see you!" She embraced me, kissing me once on each cheek. Over her shoulder, I saw Mother. She was sitting by the fire, staring open-mouthed at me. I left Frances and hurried over to her, bending down on one knee, and resting my head in her lap. "Mother darling. How I have missed you!"

She leaned forward to kiss my hair. "You naughty girl, not to tell us you were coming," she scolded. "But what a wonderful surprise it is."

I looked up, taking a moment to assess her appearance. Her face was thin, the lines deeper, her dark hair peppered with a bit more grey. But what concerned me most were the purplish half-moons beneath her eyes.

"How are you, Mother?" I asked, knowing what she would say.

"Just fine, dear. Glad to be back."

"Of course." In the nick of time, I thought to myself. I had seen that Mother was ailing those last months before I left Barbados, though the nature of her affliction was unclear. A few minutes ago, Caroline had said that everyone was "recovering"; I had understood her to mean Mother. I hoped that my sister's words had been truthful and not simply a well-meaning attempt to ease my homecoming.

"You must be starving, my child," Mother said. "We should be having dinner in an hour. Why don't you go to your room and freshen up. Someone has seen to your trunks?"

"Yes, and Sarah is with me."

"It will be good to see her. I hope you won't find it too dull here, Mary, now that you are accustomed to the London life." She glanced towards the door, appearing confused. "My goodness, where is your husband? Did he not accompany you?"

I did not wish for Mother to be burdened with my worries, but there was no way to make light of the fact that Samuel was again in harm's way.

"Samuel was commissioned to command a blockade squadron off the coast of France. He left London several weeks ago, just before I received your letter saying you had returned to Brahan Castle. The timing was perfect," I said, sounding as cheerful as I could. "He is on a very important mission, and he seemed confident of success. But then, when has Samuel not been confident? And rightfully so. It's quite something to be married to a legendary naval commander. I wish I could be there to witness him in action. How exciting that would be."

"You can't be serious," Frances said, plopping down on the fireside chair opposite Mother. "I can't imagine anything worse than being in the midst of battle. I know you crave adventure, Mary, but isn't that a bit much?"

I shrugged. "Maybe so, but the worst part of Samuel being gone is not knowing what is taking place from moment to moment. Not that I'm worried ..."

Mother shook her head. "What wife wouldn't worry, sending her husband off to war? But Samuel is an extraordinary commander, and he is fighting for Britain. I trust it is God's will that he succeeds in his mission."

God's will. That was how Mother had always accounted for everything that happens, good or bad.

I had never understood how life can be explained so simply.

CHAPTER EIGHTEEN

That night, tucked into my canopy bed with its linen gauze curtains, I struggled to fall asleep. Portions of Walter Scott's poem—which I had been reading again before I fell asleep—kept circling through my mind. Most vividly the scene in which the wizard Michael Scott's grave was opened. Though long dead, he appeared exactly the same as in life. In one hand he held his *Book of Might* and in the other a silver cross.

The Michael Scott in the poem was not only a wizard; he had the Second Sight and could foretell future events—just as Coinneach Odhar was said to have done. I reminded myself that the fabled Coinneach Odhar was no less an invention of the imagination than Walter Scott's fictional character. Still, it might have been wiser not to have immersed myself in Mr. Scott's strange poem. His tale had got under my skin, as had the telling of his ghostly encounter at the ancient castle of Glamis.

When I finally drifted into an uneasy sleep, it was only to suffer a most terrifying dream. I was wandering the windswept moors on a full-moon night, desperately in search of something—I didn't know what. Suddenly, without explanation, I found myself at Chanonry Point on the Black Isle. Waves crashed on the cliffs along the rugged coastline. The moon had disappeared, and the sky was black. I heard a chilling scream, then a wolf's howl. The earth began to rumble and shift beneath my feet, the ground where I was standing split open, and I was falling, certain that hitting the bottom would break me into pieces like fragile porcelain. But instead, miraculously, I landed on my feet.

Before me was the opening of a tunnel, illuminated by an eerie yellow light. With my first step towards it, a deep voice boomed, "Ye ken where it leads, dinny ye?"

The voice came from behind me, and I spun around, my eyes trying to pierce the darkness. "Who are you? Why have you brought me here?"

"I hevny brought ye anywhere. I've ainlie shown ye the way."

"The way to where?"

"To the end. Ye too, lassie, shall play yer part. Dinny doubt it—or do, if ye like. It makes nae difference." His laughter continued, louder and louder, until it filled the tunnel with a thousand echoes.

I woke up, my heart pounding. At first forgetting where I was, I imagined myself bedded in one of the inns along the route from London. But then I remembered: I was home. Brahan Castle, with its thick stone walls and its layers of history. The history of my family. My clan. Home.

I spread open the gauze curtain and swung my legs off the bed. Getting up, I lit a candle. The house was still, everyone asleep. With the light in my hand, I walked to the door, opening it without a sound. Then I tiptoed down the stone-tiled gallery to Caroline's room. I did not knock; she'd be asleep, and I hadn't yet decided if I should wake her. Letting myself in, I closed the door behind me, again making barely a sound. But it was enough that she stirred beneath her quilts and raised her head.

"Mary, what are you doing up?"

I went to the bed, setting the candle on her night table. "Do you mind if I climb in?"

"I would love it." She parted the curtain and threw back the quilts, moving over to make room for me. I slid next to her, quickly covering us both as the fire was low and the room quite chilly.

"Is everything all right?" she asked, wide awake now.

"Yes, I just needed to be near you." I felt rather childish to be so shaken by a dream but glad I had come to her. "Remember when we used to sneak into each other's rooms and whisper together all night long? Mother couldn't understand why she'd find us napping in the afternoons, like a couple of old hounds exhausted by the chase."

"I can't remember what we talked about," she said, smiling, "but I do remember the giggles. Poor Frances. I used to worry that she felt left out."

"Frances had weightier things on her mind, then as now. Sometimes she's too serious for her own good. But, Caroline—" I hesitated. Around my family, I had always avoided any talk of the Brahan Seer, as if speaking his name was an acknowledgment of his power. But tonight, he had wormed his way into my mind, and I seemed unable to cast him out. "I had an awful dream. About Coinneach Odhar."

Caroline was silent for a moment. "That doesn't sound like you, Mary."

"I know."

"What was the dream?"

I told her everything, and, afterwards, she was again quiet. "What do you think it means?" she asked finally.

"Nothing. It's just silliness." I was sorry I had said anything. Caroline knew the prophecy as well as I did, but her faith in God protected her from fear. I did not wish to tamper with that faith. Nor to admit that, once in a while, I perhaps would welcome a bit of it myself.

"Did I tell you that I saw our brothers in London?" I said, brightening my tone with the change of subject. "We talked of school and their ambitions for the future. William is still keen on Parliament, while Frank already seems set on the Royal Navy. They both looked well."

"Yes, you wrote to me of the meeting. We can take comfort in their good health," she said, astutely deciphering why I had brought it up, though I hadn't been aware myself. To her loving eyes, I was always transparent. "None of us can know what the future will bring, but whatever it is, we can be assured that it is God's will."

"You sound like Mother."

"If I do sound like her, I am proud of it." She propped herself up on an elbow. "You, above everyone else, have never let the Seer's curse shake your confidence in the future. What has changed?"

"My confidence is not shaken," I protested, the Seer's words still echoing in my head. *Ye too, lassie, shall play yer part.* "I'm sorry, Caroline. I don't know what has got into me tonight. If Samuel ever suspected I had the slightest inclination ... why, I'd sooner die than have him think me frightened of my own shadow."

"You've never spoken to him of the prophecy?" She seemed surprised. "I would guess he's heard of the Seer. Seems almost everyone has."

"The subject has never come up between us. It's not worth discussing." Talking about my nightmare had proved almost as disturbing as the dream itself. But at least now I felt more foolish than frightened. "Darling, I'm going back to bed, and you need your sleep as well."

I was about to throw off the covers when she took hold of my wrist. "Stay, won't you? It's been so long since we've been together. I've missed you."

I looked at her sweet face in the candlelight, those gentle, kind eyes that so perfectly reflected the tender soul within. Had Caroline ever entertained a cruel or selfish thought in her entire life? I doubted she had.

I laid my head back upon the pillow and snuggled closer to her. My weariness had disappeared, as had my apprehensions. I was back in control. "Remember Kitty Pakenham? Well, she just married the most awful fellow, and he is already making her life completely miserable."

"Oh my, the poor thing. You must tell me all about it."

CHAPTER NINETEEN

The castle had held together fairly well in the family's absence. A few structural repairs were sorely needed in the older sections, but the more recent areas were intact. A major extension had been built ten years earlier, which included a new kitchen wing, nursery, and children's bedrooms. At that time the front of the castle to the east was redesigned, and the gardens were laid out to reflect modern English tastes. Father had added many elegant touches: an exquisitely carved chimney, ornate stone pilasters in the library, and a variety of fine furnishings and paintings purchased from London's best galleries. I had rarely questioned the luxury in which we had always lived.

But now, most of the servants employed here before the family left for Barbados were gone. Only eight remained. When I asked Mother if she planned to hire more, her response was vague. I surmised it was a matter of money. I didn't ask if Father's investment in the Berbice plantations proved successful. Neither did I question her about the land sale that had evicted Ian Macleod's family, and many others, from their farms. When Father arrived home, I would find the proper time for us to talk. It was not my intention to humiliate him. On the contrary, I wanted to respect him. His hypocrisy in becoming a slave owner, albeit a kinder version of one, did not do his character justice. If he had not already divested himself of the Berbice plantations, and freed the Africans he had brought there, I would try to convince him to do so.

And the land clearances—I hoped he had allowed no more than I already knew about. There must be another way to resolve the estate's debts.

By the end of my fourth week at Brahan Castle, with Father still absent, the opportunity to speak with him of these serious matters seemed about to slip away. Soon I must return to London. I was worried about not being there to receive any letters Samuel might have sent me. And the weather was changing. Unless I wished to remain in Scotland for the entire winter, I had to be on my way before the roads became impassable. I knew the family would beg me to wait for Father, and I planned to stay a bit longer. But Father's schedule, like so many of his whims, was impossible to predict. Since he had planned to spend time in London before heading home, I might yet have the chance to see him there.

I was enjoying tea in the drawing room with Mother, Frances, Caroline, and Augusta, and was about to bring up the subject of my departure, when our butler Hinkley appeared in the doorway.

"Pardon me, my lady, but this was just delivered," he said, addressing Mother but eyeing me. He seemed nervous as he approached. "It's addressed to Lady Hood. The dispatch rider who brought it is in the hall, should you wish to send a reply. He said to take your time."

"Dispatch rider?" I glanced at the front of the folded and sealed letter. It was clearly something official. Staring at it dumbly, I felt the beginnings of panic.

"What is it, Mary?" Mother said, setting down her teacup.

Caroline reached over to lay a hand upon my arm. "We are here, darling," she said. Her words of comfort only increased my sense of foreboding. Caroline's intuition was seldom wrong.

Frances and Augusta remained silent, though Frances's face showed the same signs of worry as Mother's.

"You may tell the rider to wait." My voice, thin and tremulous, betrayed my worst fears.

"Very well, my lady. I will tell him." Hinkley turned on his heel, hurrying off to carry out his orders.

I waited until he was gone before breaking the seal. Unfolding the letter, I scanned its contents. The message was brief.

"What is it, Mary?" Mother asked. "What does it say?"

I shut my eyes for a moment, then opened them, furiously blinking back tears. "It's from Admiral Brighton of the Royal Navy. About Samuel. He's been injured but—" I stopped to swallow the lump that had sprung to my throat. "It happened on the twenty-fifth of September. He was hit in the wrist by a musket ball. They say he is out of danger now and recovering. Except—" I stifled a sob. "He's lost an arm."

An unnatural stillness settled over us as everyone struggled to absorb the news, each in her own way. Mother was first to speak. "Thank God it's no worse. He will be coming home to you. That's all that matters."

I sat motionless, paralyzed with shock. Mother was right, of course. But it wasn't me I was thinking of. It was Samuel. What effect would the loss of an arm have on him—and on the career that he loved, perhaps even more than he loved me? Would he be forced to give up his command? Samuel was strong, but he was also a practical man. A realist. Or was he? Mother said to be grateful he was coming home, but I wasn't at all certain what he planned to do. Especially in light of the letter's last paragraph.

"Samuel has been promoted to Rear Admiral," I announced.

Caroline took her hand from my arm, leaning back in her chair with a pensive look. "He won't be assuming his command for a while. In the meantime, he will need you all the more."

"Will you still want to be married to him—with only one arm?" Augusta blurted, to my horror and everyone else's. She had a habit of bluntness, but this was inexcusable.

"As Caroline said, he will need me. And, to answer your question, Augusta—yes, I love him and will try doubly hard to be worthy of him. I am certain he will not let this mishap change him in the least or stop him from pursuing our enemies with the same vigor he has always shown. I am terribly proud of him, and I cannot wait to tell him so."

"We all are proud of him," Frances chimed in. "And of you, Mary. I know he will find great comfort in your presence during his convalescence. You must go to him as soon as possible—even though it rips our hearts to lose you. We were hoping you might stay longer, at least until Father returns."

"Even before this, I had a feeling that I was needed in London. Now I know why. But the letter doesn't say where Samuel is—or was. It's addressed to me at the townhouse, with no mention of him being in London or on his way there. By now, of course, he could have been sent home."

"He won't be discharged until it is safe for him to travel," Caroline said. "But London is where you belong—waiting for him."

"Of course you must go," said Mother. "Your father will understand why you couldn't stay longer."

"There is a chance Father may still be in London," I reminded her.

"Yes, though his last letter said he would come to us as quickly as he could, after taking care of business—whatever that means. You know your father. He is easily distracted."

I feared Mother was referring to Father's gambling, for which London offered many opportunities. "If I find that he is still there when I get back, we shall have a chat and then I will send him on his way. If necessary, with a scolding." My attempt at humor was lame, and the next second, my eyes were again filled with tears. What must my husband be going through? His promotion to Rear Admiral was indeed an honor but could hardly compensate for what he had lost. Still, I doubted if Samuel would spend a single moment feeling sorry for himself. He was dedicated to the Royal Navy. To Britain. He was a hero, and he thought in the way a hero thinks. No sacrifice was too great.

"If you'll excuse me," I said, standing, "I must write a brief message to send with the dispatch rider for Admiral Brighton, saying that I am on my way back to London."

"Let us help you, however we can." Mother rose from the sofa, not easily.

"Thank you, Mother, but Sarah is all the help I need. Except perhaps someone could tell the groom to prepare the horses for travel, and my driver should be informed that we will leave first thing in the morning."

"I can do that," Augusta offered, wearing a mildly sheepish expression. I was glad if she had realized how insensitive her earlier question had been. But I had already forgiven her; she was young and had much to learn.

Thinking of what lay ahead, I realized that I did as well.

CHAPTER TWENTY

I had to wait several weeks after my return to London for Samuel to come home. I had hoped to receive a letter from him with details of his plans, but instead was informed of his expected arrival by another official correspondence. It worried me that Samuel had not picked up a pen to write to me himself. But then it occurred to me that perhaps he couldn't. He was right-handed, and no one had yet told me which arm he had lost.

I prepared for his homecoming to be a joyous affair, but a private one. There was no telling what his state of mind might be, or how well he was adapting to the difficulties losing an arm presents to even the simplest aspects of daily life. But, knowing Samuel as I did, he was more likely to be worried about me than himself. My most important task, besides providing whatever support he needed, was to show him through my every word and deed that nothing between us had changed.

The exact time of his arrival was unknown, and I was on tenterhooks all day and into the evening. By seven, when he still was not home, I began to wonder if his transport had been delayed. But finally, at half past, the door to the drawing room opened. I was sitting by the fireplace, trying to distract myself with a good novel, when suddenly there he was. Standing tall as ever, dressed in his new Rear Admiral's uniform—and smiling. The left sleeve of his jacket hung loose from the elbow down. Thank goodness it was the left arm and he still had the upper part, which could be useful. Overall, he looked remarkably well, better than I'd expected, though he'd lost a great deal of weight.

Rushing over to him, I threw my arms around his neck. With his one arm, he held me close, and I struggled to blink back my tears. It would not do to cry like a baby. I must be as strong as my husband. Or, if need be, stronger.

"I'm sorry I didn't write. I meant to but …" His voice trailed off.

"It doesn't matter now. I'm just grateful that you are here. How far did you travel today?"

"Oh … about two miles."

I pulled back to look at him, puzzled. "Only two miles?"

"I didn't want to arrive looking weary and bedraggled. Better to make a proper first impression."

"There is no way you could have made any impression other than a proper one. But if it made you feel better …" I stood up on my toes to kiss his cheek, unsure what to say next. Should I ask how he was feeling and acknowledge his injury, or wait until he brought it up himself? I decided the latter was a safer choice. "Are you hungry? I had Cook hold dinner, hoping you would be here in time."

"Maybe later."

"Very well. Then perhaps—"

"Aren't you going to tell me how much you love having a one-armed man for a husband?"

His sardonic tone put me on guard. I must choose my words carefully.

"I love having *you* for a husband, so clearly the answer to your question is yes. I am very much in love with a one-armed man, and very grateful for that one arm—and the rest of him, of course."

Samuel chuckled, and I breathed a sigh of relief. We would get through this.

"Are you having any pain?"

"Some, but nothing like in the beginning. My surgeons were top-notch. I have no complaints. They took excellent care of me. The rest is just a matter of time." His eyes drank me in, and I felt a faint stirring inside. "But Mary, I hope you'll understand. My strength isn't quite up to what it was. Not yet."

How joyful it was to hear him say *not yet.* "Don't worry. I'm a bit out of practice myself. We'll work up to it together."

"But for now, please don't deny me the exquisite pleasure of feeling your skin next to mine. It's what I have dreamed about for months, what kept me alive."

"Are you suggesting that we go upstairs now?" I said, fingering the top button of his jacket.

"Are you willing to help me undress? Those buttons are still a bit tricky with one hand."

"I think we can manage."

"Good." He tucked a wispy curl behind my ear, just as he always used to do. "Who knows, I may rebound faster than either of us imagine. After all, if you are to be expecting by the time I go back to my command, we'd best get busy."

Back to his command ... I could not begin to contemplate such a thing. Not now. Samuel's injury would not be the end of the world, neither his nor mine. He was just as brave about it as I'd believed he would be, standing up to his fate with courage and optimism. But with the worry of these last few months finally past, I was eager to start an entirely new chapter in our lives. One without the specter of war.

The question was, would I be able to convince my husband?

•   •   •

Samuel remained in London for almost a year, and I began to imagine that we might never again be parted. But in December of 1807, he left for the coast of Portugal to oversee operations against Madeira, a strategic location for French naval operations. I still had not conceived.

Samuel made light of my failure. It was taking longer than we had hoped, but I was young, he was strong, and we had plenty of time. I appreciated his optimism but felt a growing sense of hopelessness—and shame. I had disappointed my husband, who had postponed marriage until his forties, only to end up shackled to a woman unable to give him children. Perhaps he was starting to wish he had made a different choice.

The night before Samuel's departure to assume his new command, as he was about to leave my bed, he pulled me close. I often told him that his one arm was as powerful as two of any ordinary man, and that seemed to please him. I loved seeing him happy. Which is why I had not tried to dissuade him from returning to battle, even though I feared the loss of his arm might make him vulnerable.

"Do you remember, before we married, what I promised you?" he asked.

"There were many things, as I recall."

"But the one that mattered to you most was your freedom."

My heart stopped. Was he going to tell me that he no longer wished for me to be his wife? And could I blame him? "Yes, you compared me to a caged bird, longing for flight. Honestly, I had never thought of myself that way."

"That is how I saw you, with your innocent beauty and your exuberance for life. But I fear that I've not upheld my part of the bargain. Going off to war and then my injury and recovery—you have had scant opportunity to spread your wings. Though I had intended otherwise, there has been a decided lack of adventure in your life."

"I have been perfectly contented," I said, though it was not completely true. I was too often worried about one thing or another. My husband's safety, my family's stability. And sometimes bigger things. Whether the Highland way of life was dying a slow death. Whether my father and those like him were the ones killing it.

"My darling, I want your assurance that while I am away you will enjoy yourself. Get out more often. Spend time with people who stimulate you."

"But I do already. I have many friends in London."

He hesitated a moment. "I hope you know that, in your socializing, there is no need to deny yourself the companionship of men. I believe your nature is more inclined towards their sort of conversation. Do you not love a good debate about politics? More, I think, than gossiping over needlepoint." He smiled. "If you tend to enjoy yourself in the company of men, there is no crime in it. I do not fear the loss of your loyalty, my dear."

Samuel's words were no doubt inspired by my behavior at a dinner party just a few nights earlier. I felt compelled to correct a prominent member of Parliament who claimed the recent passage of the Abolition of the Slave Trade Act had ended slavery in the colonies when, in fact, it had only banned the further importation of slaves. He did not take kindly to my criticism that the Act had fallen far short of a moral solution.

"You flatter me, Samuel. But about this adventure—what exactly did you mean, and when should I expect it?"

He hesitated only a second. "For that, you must wait a bit longer. But don't worry, my darling. I will not disappoint you."

PART II

CHAPTER TWENTY-ONE
SEPTEMBER 1811
PORTSMOUTH, ENGLAND

The loss of his arm did not prove a hinderance to my husband's naval career. After his command of the operations against Madeira, he was assigned to the *Centaur*, a seventy-four-gun frigate supporting Sweden in the Russo-Swedish war. For his role in the conflict, Sweden's king awarded him the Grand Cross of the Order of the Sword. His most important mission, however, was protecting British interests in the Baltic. For that, George the Third granted Samuel a baronetcy. Every year had brought a new conflict, a new assignment, new honors. Father had warned me that being a naval commander's wife would not be easy. But during those London years, I cultivated many friends among the aristocratic, political, and literary elite, and these friendships served to greatly enliven the long stretches when Samuel was at war.

I knew of the gossip that attended my cordial relations with powerful men, but such idle talk did not concern me. If one would define *infidelity* as sharing a love of poetry or the theater, or spending a lively evening wrangling over the record of Parliament or British colonial policies, then I would plead guilty as charged. But I remained true to Samuel, holding no secrets from him; and he had never swayed from his belief that I must seek stimulating companionship wherever I might find it. How I loved him for that!

I was perhaps most proud of my friendship with Walter Scott, whom I considered a true literary genius. We corresponded with some regularity and occasionally had the opportunity to meet in London. He insisted that the Highland heroine of his poem "Lady of the Lake" was inspired by me. Whether or not that was true, the poem proved an enormous literary success. The popular consensus was that Scott had done more for the good image of Scotland than any writer in recent history.

The Napoleonic Wars continued to rage, but my husband had a new assignment. On a blustery day in late September, Samuel and I boarded a ship bound for Madras, India, where he would take command of HMS *Illustrious* in his position as Commander in Chief of the East Indies Station. Sarah accompanied us, as did her husband Ian Macleod, who now served as Samuel's personal valet.

Amidst the excitement of my first voyage to India—the first of the adventures that Samuel had promised me—I felt a touch of sadness to think how long it would be before I saw my family again. Next year, William would be twenty-one, and he planned on putting himself forward as a candidate to represent Ross-shire in Parliament. My brother Frank was set on enlisting in the Royal Navy as soon as he finished his studies at Harrow School. I found it remarkable that all my sisters remained unmarried, and that no one seemed bothered by it. Likewise, to their credit, neither Father nor Mother had ever asked me why, after seven years of marriage, I remained childless. I was grateful, because I had no answer for them. Mother would have said it must be God's will.

On our first few days aboard HMS *Owen Glendower* we encountered bad weather and were forced to dock at Lymington. It was a full month before we set out again, and when we did, our progress was similarly hampered by blustery gales and choppy seas. Most of the passengers and crew found the voyage quite miserable. I suffered my share of seasickness but hated being ordered to stay below, often sneaking out to the deck, even in the worst weather, to absorb the sounds and smells of the open sea. During periods of respite from the storms, I sat outside in a wooden chair, soaking up the sun, reading, or writing letters that would not be sent until the completion of our several-months' journey around the southern tip of Africa.

Our cabin, near the stern, was the ship's most spacious accommodation. Still, it was cramped, and the bed much narrower than I was accustomed to. That did not stop Samuel and me from putting it to good use; we took advantage of many an uninterrupted afternoon to reexplore the familiar territory of each other's bodies. Intimacy with Samuel had always been wonderful and still was. But it was different now. We no longer thought of it as having a purpose beyond ourselves; we had accepted childlessness as a permanent condition. And, like the Seer's prophecy, it was a shadow over my happiness that I mostly managed to ignore.

We docked in Madras on the thirteenth of February. I was impressed by my first glimpse of the city from the ship's deck. All the buildings sprawling out from the administrative center of Fort St. George were single-story and white, which gave the urban landscape a clean, classical look. Samuel said the English had recently begun moving farther from the confines of the fort, and the governor was building a new mansion on Mount Road, wherever that might be. For the moment, I was most interested to see where we would be living. I did not have long to wait.

Soon after our arrival, we were transported by carriage to our official residence, the Admiralty House. Overlooking the Bengal Bay, it was an integral part of East India Company's administrative and military center. Since the Company first established itself here in 1639, it had become a corporation not only with diverse trade interests in the region but commanding a massive military that had conquered vast areas of the country. With tacit approval from Britain, the Company had license to do whatever it wanted, which included deposing local political and religious leaders, and installing its own ruling administrators and diplomats. Several men of my acquaintance in London held important posts in the East India Company. They were all exceptionally intelligent, and entirely unapologetic about the

Company's India agenda. I had not yet formed my own views on the subject but should now be in a position to do so with some measure of authority.

Admiralty House was a flat-roofed ochre-colored house of notable elegance, with tall shuttered windows and wide steps leading to a white-pillared portico. As our carriage halted in front, my gaze roamed the broad expanse of well-tended lawn, lingering for a moment on the green and white palanquin tipped on its side beneath a shady tree.

"Well, what do you think?" Samuel asked me.

"It's lovely. I see we even have our own sentries guarding the door. I shall sleep well tonight."

Samuel turned his attention to the gentleman standing at the bottom of the stairs, the household staff flanking him on either side. "Lord Minto, Governor-General of the Presidency of Fort William," he said. "Born in Edinburgh, studied under the Scottish philosopher David Hume. You two should get along well."

"My philosophy credentials are not so illustrious, but I shall have a go at captivating him with my Highland charm."

A liveried footman hurried over to help us from the carriage, while two others went about retrieving the trunks we had brought with us. The rest of our belongings were still being unloaded at the dock, under Sarah and Ian's watchful eyes. I expected it would be a while yet before they arrived with them.

Samuel straightened his jacket, offered me his arm, and together we approached Lord Minto.

"Your Excellency." Samuel made a slight bow, which was returned with a nod from Lord Minto. "May I introduce my wife, the Honorable Lady Hood Mackenzie, daughter of Lord Seaforth."

"A pleasure, Lady Hood," replied Lord Minto, again bowing, though his steely gaze quickly passed from me to Samuel. "I'm afraid I cannot stay long; I have a most important meeting. But when I heard your ship had docked, I wanted to personally welcome you. I am certain you and Lady Hood shall be quite comfortable here at Admiralty House."

"Very kind of you, Your Excellency," Samuel said.

Lord Minto gestured towards the servants on either side of him. "The staff is eager to serve you. Do not hesitate to ask for whatever you need." Then, resting a hand on Samuel's shoulder, he said, "Before I go, may I have a private word with you, Admiral?"

"Certainly, Your Excellency."

Lord Minto turned towards a greying gentleman wearing a butler's black suit and snapped his fingers. The man scurried over to us. "Lady Hood, Jansen here will take you inside and, when you are ready, show you to your quarters."

Lord Minto guided Samuel towards the carriage, from which all our items had been removed, and the two of them immediately fell into deep conversation.

After acknowledging each of the servants in turn, Jansen ushered me into Admiralty House. I anticipated an interior as classically elegant as the exterior. But one never knows about the personal tastes of others, and I assumed quite a few others had occupied this house before us.

"How lovely," I murmured, my eyes sweeping over the spacious granite-tiled hall, its pale green walls decorated with large, gilt-framed paintings of scenic Indian landscapes.

"Here we have the reception room," he said, indicating an open doorway on the right, "and beyond it, the drawing room. On the left, the formal dining room. If you would like, we can stroll through the public rooms now, or—"

"I'd prefer to be taken to my apartment first, if you don't mind. And if you could see to the delivery of my trunks as quickly as possible?"

"Certainly, Lady Hood. Please, follow me."

He led me down a corridor past a library and meeting room on the right, a billiard room on the left. Then through a wide arch with another corridor running perpendicular to the first. "Your private living areas are in this section of the house. Your apartment, Lady Hood, is at the very end of the corridor on our right."

I was relieved when Jansen had finished pointing out the features of my apartment, which overlooked a lovely garden, and I was finally left to myself. Exhausted, I sank into a deep armchair in front of the fireplace and closed my eyes. There was no question that Samuel and I would be comfortable at Admiralty House. But this stately mansion, decorated in the European style, was not the India I most wished to know. Thinking of the palanquin tipped on its side in the front yard, I smiled to myself. I would have many official duties as the Vice Admiral and chief commander's wife, primarily of a social nature. But Samuel had made me the promise of adventure, and I would hold him to it. Exactly where to take me first was up to him, but take me he must.

CHAPTER TWENTY-TWO

O n the evening of the third of July, almost five months after our arrival in Madras, I left Admiralty House to begin my tour to the Kingdom of Mysore. I was, at first, disappointed that official business prevented Samuel from accompanying me. However, always concerned for my amusement, he had arranged what promised to be a remarkable journey in pleasant and stimulating company. I was not unaccustomed to being on my own and, though I would miss my husband, in some ways it made the journey seem even more of an adventure. I should have many stories to tell him upon my return.

Our new friend from the British administrative office, Mr. Belfour, drove me the first seven miles along Arcot Road in a canopied curricle. The ride, though swift, offered no escape from the hot winds of the Carnatic plateau, which sent temperatures soaring. Overheated and windblown, I climbed into a waiting palanquin, which would take me twenty-seven miles to my first destination, Stuperma, where I would meet up with the rest of my traveling party: Miss Elizabeth Casamajor, whose father was one of the Council at Fort St. George, and Mr. Miles Cunliffe, who had arranged our various accommodations along the way.

Twelve men were assigned as my palanquin bearers, four carriers at a time, in succession. I was assured that the men were not forced laborers, were well paid, and actually considered their work an honor.

Having no other option, I chose to believe it was true. Their strange grunting and moaning, which made it seem as if they were in constant agony, took some time to grow accustomed to but apparently was considered a sign of respect for the one being carried. In addition to the bearers who transported me, my entourage included half a dozen horses loaded up with my personal items. All other supplies were to be provided, at least initially, by Mr. Cunliffe.

We arrived in Stuperma around midnight, which I thought remarkable considering the distance. The first leg of the journey had not been without excitement. At one point along the road, we encountered a tiger feasting on a fresh buffalo carcass. Peering through the curtains of my palanquin, I met the golden gleam of his eyes, but at the shouts of our torch carriers, the hungry beast fled. I was sorry to have interrupted his dinner, for which he undoubtedly had risked his life.

Joining with the rest of my arranged party, the next day we traveled by palanquin another fourteen miles before stopping at the Rajah Choultry, one of many such places across India designed for the respite of travelers. Such stops along common routes usually were built by the local rajah or another person of substantial wealth. Fatigued from the forty-one miles traveled thus far, we welcomed spending the day resting and sheltering from the heat in tents. This was the first choultry I had ever seen, but Mr. Cunliffe explained that virtually all of them were arranged in the same manner, enclosed on three sides and open to the south. Here, one could dine in the choultry, and, outside, water was provided by a large stone-lined tank; a group of women stood on its steps, washing and drawing water. Our tents were pitched on one side of the tank, another cluster opposite, with two camels and an elephant tied nearby.

We were not to stay long in this picturesque spot. By six that evening, we set off in a hot wind for Vellore and the residence of Major Marriott, who was in command of the fort there. I was unprepared for the "Englishness" of his dwelling and décor, which was as comfortable as a gentleman's country home. At dinner that night, I asked the major about the history of his outpost.

"Have you had an opportunity to admire the view from your room, Lady Hood?" he replied.

"Do you mean the pagoda?"

"That and the barracks. Both were scenes of a bloody massacre of fourteen British officers and one hundred and fifteen Englishmen of the 69th Regiment." He seemed to announce this shocking bit of news almost gleefully.

Miss Casamajor set down her fork in genuine dismay. "How could such an awful thing happen? Who was responsible?"

"Was a mutiny of Indian soldiers, supposedly under British orders, who got it in their heads to restore the power of the Sultanate. And it all started with a hat."

"A hat?" I echoed.

The major chuckled. "Well, it's a bit more complicated. You see, the sepoys had the notion that we British were going to force them to convert to Christianity. Most of them are Hindu. We'd already insisted that they get rid of their beards and trim their Rajput moustaches. And no more earrings or caste marks on the forehead. The traditional turbans, too, had to go. That's when we introduced a new model of turban for them, which to their eyes was nothing other than a British hat. Set them off like a firecracker."

"So they decided that they preferred a Muslim ruler to the British."

"The Hindus and Muslims in India, despite periods of conflict and conquest, have a long history of coexistence."

"You mentioned the barracks," said Miss Casamajor. "I assume they are empty now."

"As a matter of fact, no. The women who once belonged to harems of the defeated Muslim rulers have been confined there for the last thirteen years."

"But why?" I demanded. "What did they do to deserve imprisonment? Did they fight alongside their husbands?"

Major Marriott laughed. "No, no. That's not what these women do."

I took his comment to be salacious, and unfairly so. If they were allowed no greater purpose in life than to satisfy the sexual whims of the Sultan, it was no fault of theirs. "If they did not participate in warring with the British, why after all this time are they still being held as prisoners?"

"It is unfortunate, of course, but to free the women might stir up support for the late Sultan's sons, who are being held at Fort William. Think of it this way: *Out of sight, out of mind.*"

"What you describe is not the usual course of British justice," I argued, knowing full well that justice in the colonies was as malleable as needed to protect British interests. Hadn't I seen its workings firsthand in Barbados, where the murder of Africans was treated like a petty offense, if that?

"I can assure you the women are well cared for, and their life is not so different from what it was before. As the Sultan's harem, they were prisoners of a different sort. It is a way of life to which they are well accustomed."

No doubt he was correct about their prior life, but I hardly thought it a justification for their incarceration by the English. I glanced at Elizabeth Casamajor, with whom I had begun to establish a comfortable friendship, but she seemed intent on attacking her roasted chicken leg. Perhaps she was smarter than I, deciding to hold her tongue. But my London acquaintances who were employees of the Company had led me to believe that British administrative authorities in India were committed to improving the lives of women, not subjecting them to further abuse. It had been one point upon which we could agree.

"I have heard Company men say there is much to be admired in the women of India," I said.

"I, and many others, would agree. In years past, you had high-ranking Company men taking Hindu and Muslim wives, adopting their style of food and their way of living, even their religion. But since Arthur Wellesley took over, that sort of behavior is frowned upon;

you'd lose your post over it. Wellesley says the British should remain British. Why would we want to emulate those we have conquered?"

The mere mention of Arthur Wellesley raised my shackles. I was aware of the esteem in which his military and diplomatic career was held, but to me he would always be the man who broke my dear friend Kitty's heart.

"Perhaps not *emulate*, but one can show respect for another culture in those aspects that are not injurious to its people."

"Respect certainly has its place here, as you shall see," the major replied. "When you visit Mysore and the domain of the Rajah, I believe you will be greatly impressed."

"To change the subject," said Mr. Cunliffe, perhaps thinking it best to do so, "the ladies have expressed an interest in taking a closer look at the pagoda and the choultry within it. I understand the carvings are quite exceptional examples of native sculpture."

"Very likely they were, but their condition has deteriorated badly. No one bothers with them much anymore. The pagoda is no longer used as a place of worship. The locals consider it contaminated by our presence. And the choultry has been appropriated by the Company for weapons storage." He thought for a moment. "I recall there was an artist who had executed some fine drawings of both the inside and out. I'm not sure where he is at present—the General banished him for having composed a detailed sketch of the fort, which was immediately confiscated—but if the ladies are interested, I can try to locate him."

"Thank you, but I doubt there will be time for that," said Mr. Cunliffe. "If we are to stay on schedule for our arrival in Mysore, we must be on our way tomorrow at sunset."

"Ah, a pity. Before you leave, I would be delighted to be your guide for a walk around the fort. It's quite interesting, with many picturesque ramparts and bastions ... but you'll need to watch your step. There is a broad ditch that circles all the way around. And, by the way—" He paused dramatically. "It is filled with crocodiles."

Major Marriott's words had the desired effect. The horrified look on our faces set him to laughing, and we readily agreed not to chance a turn around the fort without him.

As all of us were weary, following dinner Elizabeth and I returned to our tent to prepare ourselves for bed. Concerned by how quiet she had been all evening, I asked if anything was wrong, suggesting that perhaps she was troubled to learn of the women imprisoned in the fort.

"It seems very cruel," she replied, sitting on her cot. "But what the major said brought to my mind another story. One connected to my sister Jane."

Elizabeth had told me that Jane died a few years ago, at the age of twenty-one and only two months after her marriage to Henry Russell, a young Englishman who held a position in the higher echelons of the East India Company. Though I did not mention it, I had met Mr. Russell once—at a party in London, well before his brief marriage to Jane Casamajor. He had made a memorable impression on me and surely every other woman present, being an extremely attractive bachelor about town.

"Do you wish to tell me?" I asked, seating myself beside her.

She stared at her hands, tightly clasped in her lap. "My sister's husband, Henry Russell, once had an affair with a Muslim woman of a very high rank," she said. "They were lovers before he met Jane. But my sister told me on several occasions that she wasn't certain Henry had completely abandoned the affair. That was one reason she initially refused his offer of marriage."

I was intrigued. "How did Mr. Russell come to meet such a woman?"

"She was married to James Kirkpatrick, the Company Resident under whom Henry worked in Hyderabad. The affair with Henry wasn't until Mr. Kirkpatrick had passed away," Elizabeth added hastily. "Apparently, the woman loved her husband greatly. Choosing an Englishman and someone born to a different faith nearly cost her life. But she married him, and they were happy. After his death, though, her children were taken away from her by Mr. Kirkpatrick's family and sent to England. Later, when her love affair with Henry became public knowledge, her powerful uncle banished her from Hyderabad. Henry tried to help her settle elsewhere, but there were difficulties. Eventually, they lost contact. And then he met Jane."

"You say your sister knew all this when she and Mr. Russell married?"

"Bits and pieces, mostly from the gossip around Madras. I listened to more of it than Jane did. She would rather not have known. But people like to talk. Henry was wealthy and very good-looking. I'm sure there were those who observed he had a high opinion of himself, which made them eager to criticize. Though when he took up with Jane, everyone seemed to look favorably upon the relationship. Henry and Jane were the perfect couple."

"And his former lover? What became of her?" I hoped Elizabeth didn't mind my questions, but Mr. Russell's love affair with a Muslim woman struck me as rather exotic.

"I've never heard anything more about her. But . . ." She appeared conflicted. "Henry is now the Company Resident in Hyderabad—where she used to live. I've heard that when her uncle died, she was allowed to return there."

"Ah ..." Now I understood. Elizabeth was distressed by the thought her brother-in-law might have reunited with the woman he loved before Jane. But from what Major Marriott had said earlier, the Company's current policies strongly discouraged relationships between its representatives and local women. Serious relationships, that is. "I am sure Mr. Russell holds dear the memory of Jane and would do nothing to disgrace it."

"I believe you are right. His grief over Jane's death was immense and apparent to everyone. He swore he would never love again."

"Hyderabad is several hundred miles from anywhere our travel will take us. You need not worry about encountering your brother-in-law—or the woman you have spoken of."

"I'm not so sure. At least about Henry. He knows of our journey and wrote to me, promising an official visit to Mysore to coincide with our arrival."

"And you think he has arranged for it?"

"Possibly, though chances are he was only saying so to be polite. There were several times he was in Madras and could have seen me, but he didn't. It was almost as though he were hiding something."

"I doubt that, Elizabeth. Perhaps seeing you would be too painful a reminder of Jane."

"If that's true, then he shan't be in Mysore."

"No, he shan't."

From what Jane had told me, I doubted we would see Mr. Russell. But if we did, I hoped for her sake that he would be as chaste as she wished to find him.

CHAPTER TWENTY-THREE

Continuing our expedition through southern India, the scenery became grand and wild, in parts surprisingly reminiscent of Scotland. The hot winds that had trailed us all along were gradually replaced by cooler breezes. One day, in a lush green valley where the air was filled with the aroma of sweet-smelling shrubs, we came upon a resting flock of small, white-breasted vultures, which the natives regard as sacred. I smiled, imagining them as winged messengers sent by the Rajah to remind us that we would soon be leaving Company territory and entering his dominion.

At this point in our travels, we were met by an associate of Mr. Cole, Resident at the Court of the Rajah. He provided us with comfortably furnished tents as well as carriages, horses, an elephant, and servants to satisfy our every need along the final leg of our journey to the Kingdom of Mysore. We typically began each day's travel at about five in the morning. To accompany us, the Rajah had sent an impressive escort. When Elizabeth and I were riding the elephant, ahead of us on foot were forty spearmen and two others whose sole duty was to blow an enormous trumpet, called a collery horn, upon our approach to any habitation. If we were riding in the bandy, however, the elephant and spearmen followed behind, along with a contingent of twenty-five riders on beautiful Marwari horses. In front of us were another twenty-five, and at the very head of the entire procession was a man on a camel.

Arriving at the first village, a large group came rushing out to greet us with tom-toms, gongs, and horns, and the chief magistrate draped garlands of fragrant white flowers around our necks. I did not yet know that this ritual was to be repeated at every village until our arrival at the Court of the Rajah on the twenty-seventh of July, twenty-four days after departing the Admiralty House in Madras.

•   •   •

We had been told it was the Rajah's birthday. Whether or not that was true, the plan was for us to witness an impressive tribute to the ruler of Mysore. Or, I should say, the nominal ruler. As we were duly informed, an act of diplomacy between the Rajah and the English had been the simplest way for all parties to avoid further bloodshed, leaving the young Rajah free to enjoy the pleasures of his privileged life while Englishmen went about the business of advancing British interests—though perhaps less overtly than in territories openly ruled by the Company.

Knowing this did not substantially lessen my enthusiasm for a glimpse of the Rajah's court and its rituals. Mr. Cole placed himself completely at our disposal, and it was with him that Elizabeth and I arrived that first evening at the Durbar Court, an open gallery with stairs leading down to a square where the birthday ceremony would take place. Colored-glass lanterns cast a many-hued glow, and hundreds of the Rajah's subjects who were gathered to honor him, all wearing traditional native dress, made the scene appear much like a magnificent theater production.

In the center of the square, the Rajah sat upon a silver throne. He wore a long, belted jacket of gold brocade studded with jewels, and a silk turban decorated with pearls, from which a lovely crest of carved ivory fanned out like the feathers of a peacock. Our party, met by two court attendees, was taken to him straight away. Mr. Cole, though exaggerating somewhat, had told the Rajah I was a British woman of the highest rank, so I was prepared for the young prince to welcome me accordingly.

"Your Highness." I inclined towards the Rajah, palms flat against each other in an attitude of supplication, as I had been instructed. An uncommonly striking young man of twenty-two, the prince had the most piercing black eyes I had ever seen.

He nodded in acknowledgment, and then addressed me through his interpreter. "His Highness is almost as gratified as he would be if your husband had come."

I glanced at Mr. Cole uncertainly. Was this the Rajah's idea of humor, or did he mean to knock me down a peg or two? I supposed it was well that a court attendant then appeared to escort me to my seat, giving me no opportunity to respond. Otherwise, Mr. Cole might have had cause to question the wisdom of inviting me here, especially on such a momentous occasion.

Every person holding a government position, or of high rank by birth, must present the Rajah with a tribute. Only following all the presentations by native subjects did we British have our turn. Mr. Cole made a grand show of gifting the Rajah a great number of magnificent gems, after which the Rajah presented him with a gigantic breast jewel hung from a string of pearls. The irony was that all such gifts to the Rajah were only ceremonial; afterwards, they would be diverted to the Company's treasury in payment of the prince's ongoing debt for British protection. Mr. Cole's stunning breast jewel would meet the same fate, since servants of the Company were not permitted to accept gifts of value from a native prince.

Given that my husband was not employed by the Company, Mr. Cole had informed me that I would be allowed to keep any gifts I might receive. On this occasion, the Rajah presented me with an ornament of pearls and flat diamonds, which he deftly tied around my neck without need of touching me. Despite this symbolic act of cordiality, I could not help feeling as though my presence was not entirely welcomed by the Rajah. His initial greeting, though possibly altered in translation, I had found insulting. But beyond that, while he displayed no animosity towards Elizabeth, he could not look at me without a slight scowl.

I was relieved when we were dismissed at the close of the official birthday ceremonies without an additional audience with the prince. Riding in the carriage with Mr. Cole, I wasted no time in expressing my concerns about the evening.

"Judging from his manner towards me, I must have greatly displeased the Rajah."

"You noticed." Mr. Cole appeared amused.

"He seemed perturbed whenever he looked at me. Is there something wrong in the way I am dressed?"

"You are exquisite, Lady Hood. Please, put your mind at ease."

"But then, what is it? Why do I feel so uncomfortable about his reaction towards me?"

"Let me explain." The light from the coach lantern cast shadows on Mr. Cole's thin, careworn face. I knew very little about him, except that he was a dedicated servant of the Company, but I trusted him to tell me the truth. "Here in India, the concept of traveling for curiosity or pleasure is not commonly understood, particularly if the traveler is a lady. When I told the Rajah you would be visiting Mysore without Admiral Hood, he was immediately suspicious of a different motive for your journey, convinced that you were being sent by the British at Fort St. George to spy on him."

"Spy on him! For what purpose?"

"The Rajah has a Favorite, a very clever woman. She has managed to usurp the role of the young Ranee, who has, through certain channels, complained of her husband's woeful neglect. The prince believes you have been sent to deliver a lecture to him on behalf of the government, and he is not pleased."

"But surely you informed him that is not the case. I know nothing of the Ranee's situation—though, from what you have told me, the Rajah could use a good talking-to."

"I am glad you feel that way, Lady Hood. In all honesty, I have allowed him to believe his intuition about your visit was correct. The

Ranee is a charming young woman, but she is only fourteen and very naïve. Also, I hear, very much in love with the prince. Her life must be difficult enough without suffering this sort of humiliation. Though I suppose it's none of my business, I hoped the threat of a spy from the fort might have some positive effect on the prince's behavior."

"And has it?" I was beginning to enjoy this unusual sense of power, the threat of which was enough that even a Rajah was intimidated by me.

"Indirectly it has. When the Favorite heard of your impending visit, she decided it might be prudent to seek the Ranee's forgiveness. She begged her not to say anything on the subject to you. Apparently, she is just as worried as the Rajah that you will disapprove and deliver an unfavorable report to the government."

"Well then, I mustn't disappoint them. I shall be ever watchful, and if the Rajah steps out of line even once ..." I smiled. "A sharp rap on the knuckles?"

"I will leave the punishment up to you."

Though the situation was laughable, I was intrigued by the possibility of exerting my influence on the royal couple. But how? According to Mr. Cole's description of the Ranee, she was little more than a child. Perhaps what she needed was a lesson in feminine wiles. But such forms of persuasion do not free one from the yoke of slavery; they only make it somewhat more bearable. If the young Ranee could learn to assert herself, perhaps her husband would find her more interesting. Yet it would take more than a brief meeting to effect such a transformation. Considering his suspicions about me, the Rajah was unlikely to permit any meeting at all.

·   ·   ·

Our entire party was staying at the British Residency, a large English-style house that was well suited not only for its full-time occupants but for the comfort of official guests. We returned that night to find a new arrival lounging in the drawing room, sipping from a small tumbler of arrack.

"Hello, my friends!" Rising from the sofa, Henry Russell set his glass on a side table before coming over to greet us. "Mr. Cole. Lady Hood," he said, bowing to each of us in succession, after which he turned to Elizabeth. "My dear Elizabeth," he said, lifting his former sister-in-law's hand to his lips. She seemed stunned to see him, having believed he had no intention of coming despite his promise to try.

"Mr. Russell," she murmured.

His attention quickly returned to me. "You probably don't remember, Lady Hood, but we met once in London."

"I do remember. It was during a party at Kitty Wellesley's townhouse."

"Very good. That's exactly where it was. I understand you and Admiral Hood are living in Madras now."

"We are. And you have returned to Hyderabad?"

"I've assumed the Residency there. A great honor to follow in the footsteps of my beloved mentor, James Kirkpatrick."

"We've just returned from the Rajah's birthday celebration," said Mr. Cole. "A rather long and dull evening, I'm afraid. But tomorrow night promises to be a good deal more exciting. The Rajah and I have arranged a tiger fight for the amusement of these lovely ladies. You'll join us, Henry?"

What seemed an irresolute look passed over Mr. Russell's face, but he replied, "Of course, I'd be delighted."

CHAPTER TWENTY-FOUR

O ur group for the event at the Rajah's court consisted of Mr. Cole, Mr. Russell, Elizabeth, myself, and two other ladies— wives of British officers—who had luncheoned with us at the Residency and were invited to come along. The six of us sat on a wide balcony overlooking an area of a hundred paces square, enclosed by strongly woven rope netting. The Rajah's interpreter was positioned between us and the prince, who was seated on a carved-ivory throne.

Mr. Cole was on my right and Mr. Russell on my left, with Elizabeth seated next to him on the other side. She seemed to have warmed towards him since last night, when the surprise of his sudden appearance had clearly flustered her. Over luncheon, he told us of his heartbreak at having commissioned the famed sculptor John Bacon to create a magnificent monument to his late wife, Jane, only for it to be lost at sea before reaching St. Mary's Church in Madras. Undaunted, he had recommissioned it, with some minor alterations to the lengthy epitaph he had personally composed in her honor; it was to be installed at the church sometime next year. Elizabeth was visibly moved by his account, taking it as evidence of his continuing devotion to her sister's memory, and her fears concerning a rekindling of Mr. Russell's former love affair in Hyderabad appeared thoroughly assuaged.

I found Mr. Russell's company more agreeable than expected. I had remembered him as charming, but with a widely acknowledged propensity for conceit. Perhaps the tragic loss of his beloved wife had produced a change in him for the better.

The event began with little fanfare. I was both curious and apprehensive about the fight we were about to witness, imagining a ferocious and bloody battle between two tigers. However, the first animal admitted to the ring was a cheetah, whose exceptional grace of movement we were permitted to admire for a time. He was rather small, probably not much more than nine stone, with black spots on his golden-yellow coat.

"He won't be pitted against a tiger, will he?" I whispered to Mr. Cole, thinking such a match unfair to the smaller beast.

"Just watch," he replied.

Instead of another wild creature, several men wearing loose, knee-length tunics and rope sandals entered the ring. They began baiting the cheetah with fireworks and discharges of small shot. And then the spearmen took over. The cheetah struggled long and hard against the men's brutal assaults, showing a tenacity of spirit that should have put his tormentors to shame. I was appalled. Growing up in the Highlands, I regarded hunting as a noble pursuit, a competition for survival between man and beast from which either might emerge victorious. But this horrid exhibition of slaughter could claim no justification. The animal was a trapped target, with no chance of escaping the handlers' weapons. When they finally dragged him from the ring, I could not raise my eyes to look at the bloody pulp, all that remained of the poor creature.

Suddenly, the door of the tiger cage at the end of the arena was raised, and a beast at least three times the size of the cheetah came forth in all his grandeur. The handlers began their baiting, this time with a wooden figure of a man, which the tiger readily pounced upon. Having discovered it to be a mere decoy, he showed no interest in a second figure that was pulled about with ropes to attract his attention. Fireworks followed, before a bowman at one side of the arena started shooting arrows. Though at least ten of them pierced the tiger, he remained on his feet, walking about. After nearly half an hour of torment, he was attacked with small shot. Unlike the cheetah, who screamed out with every hit, the tiger made not a sound—not a single cry or groan. It was only with a shot to his head that he succumbed, falling to the ground in a lifeless heap.

Throughout this dreadful display, the Rajah was quite obviously annoyed by my visible distress. It was clear that he was the orchestrator of the barbarity we had just witnessed, having given the signal for every new attack by a subtle inclination of his head. However much I wanted to berate him for his disgusting behavior, I was not at liberty to do so. Instead, I swallowed my words of reproach, maintaining a sullen silence.

As we waited for the battered carcass to be dragged from the arena, Mr. Russell leaned towards me and whispered, "This was not the way I would have arranged for you to spend your afternoon."

"It appears the Rajah's need to feel powerful requires sacrificing the most majestic creatures in his domain in the cruelest and most cowardly way possible."

"I do not enjoy such displays any more than you do. There is much to admire about India and its traditions, but some practices are antithetical to the Western mind."

"And hypocritical as well. The Rajah obviously has no affection for me, even resents my presence, yet every morning he sends trays of sugar candy, almonds, and fruit, and a messenger on horseback to bring him an account of my health."

"The Indian etiquette is quite elaborate."

"And the rules for women? I believe I should rather be dead than to be one of the Rajah's harem."

"Even as a man, I find it insufferable that any woman should be forced to live in such a way. Though there are many among the Rajah's subjects who would trade places with them in an instant."

"I suppose they must live in great luxury."

"You would be surprised. Perhaps Mr. Cole can arrange for you to visit the zenana. Would you be interested?"

"I would, but it is doubtful the Rajah would wish for me to have contact with his women." I smiled. "He may fear an uprising."

"The Rajah likely has good reason to fear you," he said amiably. "I have heard you are a woman of strong opinions."

I wondered what strong opinions he was referring to, as I had kept most of them to myself since arriving in Mysore.

"So far, I have no plan worthy of his consternation. But I am still thinking."

I had not taken Mr. Russell's suggestion of a visit to the zenana too seriously, but on the way back to our lodgings, Mr. Cole made an unexpected announcement. "Lady Hood, I am pleased to tell you that tomorrow night, around eight, you will meet with the Ranee in her apartments."

I was both stunned and delighted. "The Rajah has agreed to it?"

"Apparently, he's decided that his interests may best be served by cooperating with your official investigation," Mr. Cole replied with a chuckle.

"I see."

"I should mention that the Rajah wanted his Favorite to also appear at the audience, but I told him you would consider it an affront to your dignity and that of the Ranee. He readily dropped the idea."

I smiled. "Well, it's a start."

•   •   •

On my third trip to the Rajah's court, I was accompanied only by Mr. Cole and Elizabeth. It was to be our last visit before starting back to Madras. The first order of business was my interview with the Ranee.

Since last night, I had given a great deal of thought to my purpose in having an audience with the Rajah's young wife. I recalled that night in Barbados when Samuel told us of the African slave who warned the British on Diamond Rock of a surprise attack by the French. Samuel rewarded him with his freedom; he became a sailor in the Royal Navy. At the time, I had thought to myself how wonderful it must be having the power to change a life. To give a man his freedom! If only I had such a power …

Perhaps now I did.

Elizabeth had been given permission to accompany me for my interview with the Ranee, and I was counting on her rudimentary knowledge of Hindustani. Mr. Cole was permitted to escort us only as far as the door to a long passage leading to the women's apartments. The moment Elizabeth and I passed through, and the door closed on Mr. Cole, the Rajah appeared before us. His demeanor was entirely different from before, cheerful and friendly.

He led us down the passage to another door, behind which his wife and five "mothers"—the widows of his father—were waiting. After a brief but gracious introduction, he departed, leaving us alone with the six highest ranking women in his entire kingdom and two interpreters. There were chairs already arranged for us. Elizabeth and I were positioned opposite the six of them. Such were their manners that not even the Ranee would take a seat until we had done so.

Mr. Cole had described the widows as "old, fat, and poorly dressed, lacking even a single ornament." I had thought his assessment harsh, but now was forced to concede its accuracy. I supposed there was little cause for concern about appearances, considering their lack of contact with the outside world. But I found it disturbing that the reason for their isolation and forced austerity was the mere fact of being widows of a powerful man.

The Ranee did not suffer the same material deprivation. She wore a costume nearly as grand as the Rajah's, and she had decorated herself with jewels and pearls. She was a pretty but slight young woman, her delicate countenance bearing a look of perpetual melancholy. I recalled what Mr. Cole had said about her: She was in love with the Rajah, but he had little time for her, preferring another from his harem. Such a situation would drive any woman to despair, especially one who hadn't the experience or guile to outsmart her competitor.

My plan had been to take the Ranee aside and, with Elizabeth's assistance, offer my advice. To tell her how the British view marriage and the rights of women. Though our system was far from ideal, at least women of means typically weren't held as prisoners by their husbands. Not literally, anyway. I hoped to stir her spirit, give her confidence and courage. I envisioned her confronting the Rajah with a list of demands, invoking my name as needed to ensure his compliance. Contemplating all this the night before, I had felt nearly giddy with power.

But now I felt nothing but a fool.

Elizabeth's familiarity with Hindustani seemed of no use; a direct conversation with the Ranee was impossible because, we were told, etiquette forbade her from opening her lips. The mothers were allowed to speak, but only Canarese. Every exchange must be conducted through the interpreters provided by the Rajah.

I was defeated. Useless. I could do nothing to bolster the Ranee's sagging spirits, other than by my presence in the women's midst and the assumption that someone with influence was behind it.

Disillusioned, I tried to make the most of our meeting by learning as much as I could about their daily lives. To satisfy my curiosity, the widows spoke of such things as their favorite pastimes and the celebrations they were permitted to attend. All this was related with an attitude of acceptance, even pride. Numerous times, they referred to the Rajah as "the poor boy," which I found ironic. But then, what did I know of his life? His country had been torn apart; his rule was a sham. Whatever privilege he still enjoyed must feel precarious.

Still, he was in a better spot than the Ranee, who must answer to him. Throughout the entire session, her exotic almond eyes were trained on me. I felt she longed to reach out but was afraid. She was so young, so alone. And constantly watched.

But as we were about to say our goodbyes, I had an idea. Hastily removing my gold and sapphire pendant necklace, I pressed it into Elizabeth's hand, whispering in her ear, "Give this as a gift to the Ranee and as you are fastening it around her neck, speak to her softly in Hindustani. Tell her that, in light of the Rajah's improper behavior in showing preference to a woman other than his wife, the British are seriously considering whether to strip him of his power. If she wishes to spare him such humiliation, she need only give me a nod. But tell her she must be sure the Rajah understands what she has done for him—and that, just as easily, it can be *un*done."

Elizabeth appeared anxious. "My Hindustani is not very good, you know. What if it comes out completely wrong?"

"Just do the best you can," I said, rising from my chair along with everyone else.

"May Miss Casamajor present the Ranee with a gift from me?" I asked one of the interpreters. Suspecting nothing, he gave his assent.

Approaching the Ranee, Elizabeth smiled and held up the necklace for the young woman's closer inspection. The Ranee seemed pleased by the ornament, though her own jewelry was far more valuable. Then, just as the Rajah had done when presenting me with pearls, Elizabeth carefully placed the necklace around the Ranee's neck, fumbling long enough with the gold clasp to deliver my message, or at least try.

Finally, she stepped away. I held my breath, waiting to see what the Ranee would do. Several moments passed. I began to fear that either Elizabeth's grasp of Hindustani was insufficient to convey my message, or the Ranee had chosen to ignore it.

Suddenly, the young woman raised her head and looked at me. Perhaps I saw only what I wished to see, but there seemed the hint of a sparkle in those dark, almond eyes. Was it amusement? Hope? The fragile beginnings of self-confidence?

Then, discreetly yet quite definitely, she nodded.

CHAPTER TWENTY-FIVE

That night's dinner at the Residency was a long, drawn-out affair. It was our final evening with Mr. Cole, and Mr. Russell would also be leaving early the next morning. As a surprise, we were treated to a dessert of ice produced with water, cream, saltpeter, and sal ammoniac; it was excellent, if slightly too hard. At half past midnight, Mr. Cole retired to his bedchamber. Lacking a gentleman willing to stay up with him, Mr. Russell invited Elizabeth and me to join him in the sitting room for a glass of arrack and a puff or two on the hookah pipe, a popular habit cultivated by many of the British in India. I had indulged only a couple of times but thought it pleasant and a fitting way to end our stay in Mysore. Elizabeth declined, saying she was exhausted from the day's events.

In the sitting room, I took a seat on the sofa next to Mr. Russell. At his request, a servant had prepared our drinks and left them on the low table in front of us. He reached for the first tumbler, handing it to me before taking the other for himself.

"To you, Lady Hood," he said, raising his glass. "Everything I have heard about you is true—all of it sterling."

His tribute embarrassed me, as I could not say exactly that about him. What I had heard of Henry Russell was not always glowing. Now that I had spent time with him, I considered much of the criticism leveled against him undeserved. Yes, he was rakishly handsome and carried himself as though he knew it. But there was a sensitive side to him. I had seen no evidence of disloyalty to his late wife, though years had passed since her death. Besides, after a respectful period of time, one should not be faulted for wishing to again find love.

"I hope this shan't be the last we see of each other." I took a sip of my drink. One tiny taste was all I could tolerate. "The Admiral has talked of a voyage up the coast in November. Perhaps we could arrange an inland journey to Hyderabad. I would love to see the area."

"Then it's settled. You and Admiral Hood shall be my honored guests." He swept a hand through his dark hair, a gesture that seemed not entirely unselfconscious. I could see how others might assume him to be vain. He had a right to be. "Your husband—how is he doing? I was sorry to hear of his injury some years back, but he seems to have overcome it famously."

"The loss of an arm would be difficult for anyone, but he never once complained."

"I am certain your affection was a great comfort to him after such an ordeal."

"His indomitable spirit has only made me love him more."

"And a lucky man he is, Mary." He smiled. "I hope you don't mind if I call you by your given name? At least while we are alone."

"Then I shall call you Henry." There was an awkward silence as we digested our new familiarity.

"I had the hookah prepared for us. Let us put it to good use before the charcoal cools, shall we?" On the table was a beautiful specimen of a shisha, its ceramic base and bowl painted with traditional designs, and the hose covered in a rich gold fabric. "I brought some special tobacco, infused with rose and mint."

"I should like that very much."

He used tongs to transfer the red-hot charcoal pieces to a screen just above the bowl. "If you don't mind, I'll test it to make sure everything is right." Henry drew on the metal mouthpiece, causing the water in the base to make a soft gurgling sound. He sat back, savoring the tobacco before exhaling. "Perfect." He handed me the hose. Having only smoked a few times, I was cautious not to inhale too deeply.

We passed the mouthpiece back and forth, enjoying the sweet aroma of the tobacco. It surprised me how comfortable I felt with Henry, a man whose reputation, in the beginning, had both intrigued me and given me pause.

"So, now that you have experienced India for yourself, what do you think?" he said. "Have you fallen in love with it, as I have?"

"I might more easily fall in love with India as it used to be. Doesn't it sadden you to see so many of the great mansions and palaces, masterpieces of architecture and art, falling to ruin out of sheer neglect and indifference? And the sacred places so esteemed by the natives, contaminated through the disrespect of European conquerors?"

"I share your sentiments. In my own small way, at the Residency in Hyderabad, I am attempting to restore some of the native observances and customs that my mentor, James Kirkpatrick, chose to honor when he was alive. Unfortunately, his immediate successor did not see the worthiness in such an attitude. He did not take the time or trouble to understand the people and culture of India."

"I have heard it said that General Arthur Wellesley is behind the lack of tolerance."

"It's true that Wellesley has little use for anything or anyone beyond the British."

I thought back to my visit with the Rajah's wife and mothers, suddenly questioning whether I should have interfered in the relationship between the Ranee and her husband. What right did I have to judge another people's traditions and beliefs? Perhaps I was no better than Arthur Wellesley, who wished to erase the old India in order to remake it in the image of Britain.

Henry poured himself another arrack. "You may be new to India, but you've seen British colonial life firsthand. As I recall, you were in Barbados for several years before you and the Admiral married."

"Yes, I'm afraid our countrymen have made Barbados a land with no heart and no respect for justice. Commerce is all that matters."

"And that surprises you? What you describe has been the way of the world since recorded history began."

"Members of Parliament pat themselves on the back for having passed an act to end the transatlantic slave trade in the Empire. But everyone knows that slavery still exists in the colonies. Those who were in bondage before the legislation are still in bondage. For them, nothing has changed."

"Slavery is an atrocity, but it has made Britain the world's leading industrial power. I am not defending it, mind you. I am merely stating a fact. Whether it's greed, love of country, belief in the inevitability of what we like to call *progress*—there are many reasons for what we do. Many excuses for the harm done to others. And aren't we—you and I— as guilty as anyone? The life we enjoy, with all its comforts, is due in large part to the labor of those we have subjugated. Here in India as well as Barbados. The circumstances may be different, but, in some ways, the end result is the same."

He scrutinized me with an air of amused curiosity. "Tell me, Mary—and please be honest. Would you be willing to give up your luxurious style of living, and the privileges you enjoy as the wife of a British Royal Navy admiral, in the name of justice and equality?"

I did not like being confronted with my own hypocrisy. But there was no escape from it. There had never been. "It is easy to tell oneself that the world's problems are someone else's. I would like to think myself better than that. But I am not."

"I do not mean to criticize you," he said, perhaps sorry for having confronted me in such a way. "If either of us is deserving of moral condemnation, it certainly would not be you. I, on the other hand, have often behaved in a manner I regret. Worse yet, I have a tendency to repeat my mistakes—even when I know better."

"And what mistakes are those?"

His mouth twisted in a tiny grimace. "A great many involve women. My deep appreciation for beauty has been known to cause me trouble. I suppose that's why Elizabeth is still skeptical about me."

"I don't believe that she is. Not anymore."

"Her sister was the great love of my life, and I have made no secret of it. But there have been other loves."

I waited for him to say more, thinking he might tell me of the Muslim woman in Hyderabad.

"Another round with the hookah?" he asked, smiling.

The weightiness of our conversation had tired me, especially the questions I had been forced to ask of myself. It wasn't that I had never thought of them before. But I had always managed to put the blame on others, more than on myself. "It's getting late, don't you think?"

"But it's such a special night. Our last night together. In fact," he said, finishing off his second arrack in a single swallow, "you can protest all you like but I refuse to accept *no* for an answer."

He proceeded to fire up the hookah again, and, silently, we shared another smoke.

"You know my biggest regret about this journey?" I said finally.

"That I did not join your group sooner?"

There it was, that touch of conceit. Tonight, I could forgive him for it; most likely it was the arrack talking. "We have enjoyed your company, certainly. But I was referring to my ignorance of the native language. There were so many questions I might have asked of the people we've met. I could have learned a great deal."

"What about India fascinates you most?"

"I am greatly moved by the sacred places I have seen, even the abandoned ones, though I know so little of India's spiritual side."

"Hinduism? Islam? Buddhism? I have studied them all. Ask me anything. I may have the answer—or if I don't, I will admit to it."

A question had quietly burned within me as I journeyed through the ruins of India's past.

"Very well. The Hindu law of karma is that a person's present actions have consequences in future lives. But what about one's ancestors? Could their actions, good or evil, affect the karma of generations to come?"

He thought for a moment. "Without a doubt. In fact, we see it all the time, don't we? The mistakes of one generation affecting those that come after? The Bible calls it 'the sins of the father.' In that sense, the concept of karma is not unique to the Hindus."

I took another sip of arrack, its harshness burning my throat.

Suddenly, Henry's face loomed in front of me. "Forgive me, but a lash has fallen upon your cheek, and I am obsessed with it. May I?" He proceeded to gently sweep it away—if indeed there was a lash—and then he smiled. "I have wondered what it would be like to be this close to you, Mary."

I should have looked away, but it seemed I couldn't. Never had I been drawn by such powerful attraction to any man, except Samuel. Yet how different the two of them were. Samuel's eyes, blue as the open sea; Henry's, dark with secrets.

"Mary, I forgot to—"

Halting in the doorway, Elizabeth wore an expression of shock and confusion. Henry hastily withdrew his hand from my cheek, where it had lingered.

"You decided to join us?" he said with a smile that could only be described as sheepish. "Come in, come in."

"I didn't mean to interrupt." Elizabeth's tone was terse.

"You're not interrupting." I rose from the sofa. "I was about to go upstairs. Shall we retire together?"

"Don't leave on my account," Elizabeth replied. "You seem to be enjoying yourself." She might as well have added *with my sister's husband*. That was what she must be thinking, and I could not fault her for it. I was ashamed of the desire Henry's touch upon my cheek had created in me. I was not entitled to such feelings, nor did I wish to have them. I loved my husband. There was no room in my heart for any other.

Elizabeth had not waited for me and was already halfway down the hall. I knew what she would do once she was in her room. Fling herself across the bed, sobbing for the lost honor of her sister Jane.

"Oh dear …" I gave Henry a plaintive look. "I feel awful. Elizabeth is so sensitive about Jane—and you. Your visit has been wonderful for her. I wouldn't for the world upset her."

"There's nothing for her to be upset about. Is there?" He broke into one of those easy smiles for which he seemed never at a loss. But I could not get over feeling that we had been caught doing something wrong. "Listen—if you are going up to bed, I had better ask you now. May I write to you in Madras? We will need to make plans for your visit in the autumn. Yours and the Admiral's, that is."

"Of course." How quickly he could move on. I supposed it was a useful talent.

"You and Marie will like each other," he added blithely.

"Marie?"

"Yes, my wife. Marie Clotilde—daughter of Benoit Mottet de la Fontaine."

"Oh—" This was the first I had heard of Henry having a wife. So casually spoken, one would have thought it a matter of little importance—as his behavior tonight might also suggest. "How long have you been married?"

"Soon it will be two years."

"Does Elizabeth know?"

"I told her yesterday. Odd that she'd not heard already, but she took it quite well."

"I'm glad." But what must she have felt to discover Henry and me on the sofa, gazing into each other's eyes in a cloud of smoke? "Well, I'd best be heading upstairs. Perhaps I'll check on Elizabeth."

I could not forget that look of hurt surprise on her face. I had become exceedingly fond of her and found it unbearable that she should think poorly of me. But as I wearily climbed the stairs, I felt too exhausted to confront her. And not in the proper frame of mind.

The following day, I explained to Elizabeth that Henry had been slightly drunk but completely respectful. Just to be certain she felt no ill will towards him, I embellished the truth by saying that he'd shed a few more tears over Jane and appeared utterly inconsolable. I reminded her as well of the memorial due to arrive in Madras next year. Throughout the long journey home, we were on the best of terms.

The trip back from Mysore, though by the same route as our original journey, seemed much longer. Samuel was waiting in a carriage to take us the last seven miles to Madras. After more than six weeks away, I was excited to see him. Though we were accustomed to separation, it had always been his adventures stealing him away from me. This time, I had my own tales to tell.

None of them included Henry Russell.

CHAPTER TWENTY-SIX

In late November, Samuel made good on his promise of a voyage up the west coast of India. I should have realized that an inland journey to Hyderabad, far to the east, made no sense. In truth, I was relieved.

It was January when we docked in Bombay, and I had the unexpected pleasure of a visit from my brother Frank, who arrived into port on a frigate from China. He had fulfilled his dream of joining the Royal Navy and was now serving as a midshipman. His surprise visit was Samuel's doing, and it meant the world to me. Frank looked sharp in his Navy uniform, grown up and proud to be serving his country. We spent the next several days on inland excursions. My favorite was the one to Malabar Point with its curious passage among the rocks through which one can barely squeeze, if not too large a person. We were told the Hindus consider it a sacred place; they believe that passing through the rocky corridor cleanses the soul of all former sins.

Near this place of absolution were the ruins of a pagoda, partially destroyed by the Portuguese, and a bit farther on was a small temple with a well-preserved bas-relief of Vishnu reclining on a lotus. We walked to the Brahman village. It was the day of a partial eclipse of the sun, and everyone was engaged in some sort of worshipful activity— bathing in a cistern of fresh water and afterwards the sea, or devotions at one of the village's several pagodas, or washing their sacred utensils in the common water tank. Inside a pagoda sheltered by banana trees, we observed how the Hindus note the passage of time by the dripping of water from one vessel to another; when the vessel is emptied three times, an hour has passed.

How lovely to measure one's life by the slow drip of water!

Upon our return in February, Samuel received his new flagship, *Minden*; I was again on my own at Admiralty House. I relied on a busy social schedule to help keep me occupied. As the center of the British military and administrative command in India, Madras was teeming with officials, many of whom were accompanied by their wives. The Governor-General had recently completed a new residence that boasted an enormous ballroom, which he was eager to put to good use. But when I was not mingling with people of importance, I spent time studying the many books on Indian history, religion, and culture that were tucked away in the Admiralty House library.

One afternoon, I discovered among the leather-bound volumes an English translation of *The Bhagavad Gita*, the seven-hundred-verse Hindu scripture that explains the law of karma, to which it claims we in the mortal sphere are bound. The Hindus believe certain aspects of one's karma, or fate, are predetermined by the past, but not everything. One's present choices can influence the future. Which started me thinking: Were there choices I could make, in the present, that might *cleanse* my family's karma of the sins of our ancestors? Render powerless the last prophecy of Coinneach Odhar?

Horrified, I snapped the book shut. Why had my thoughts turned to Coinneach Odhar? What would it take to purge him from my mind, once and for all? The legend of the Brahan Seer was pure fantasy. My family was perfectly fine, and so was I. Yet the fear remained, mostly in the background but always somewhere.

Sarah popped her head around the corner. "My lady, shouldn't you be getting ready for the unveiling?"

I glanced up at the longcase clock. "Oh dear, I forgot all about it."

"I've readied your toilette."

"Very well, I shall be there shortly."

Sarah ducked out and I replaced *The Bhagavad Gita* upon the shelf where I had found it. How could I have overlooked that today Henry Russell would dedicate the memorial to his late wife Jane Casamajor?

· · ·

St. Mary's was the oldest Anglican church in India. Consecrated in 1680, its four-feet-thick walls and rounded roof were built to withstand cannon fire. There would be none of that today, only sighs and tears. In the lush garden outside the nave, a group of a hundred or more milled about in anticipation of the dedication of Henry Russell's monument to Jane Casamajor.

Spotting Elizabeth, I hurried over to greet her. She looked worried.

"Sorry to be late. Is everything all right?"

"Henry isn't here. He was supposed to arrive last night. We can't unveil the memorial without him."

I was well aware of all he'd done to recommission and transport the new sculpture after the first one was lost at sea. It was inconceivable that he would be absent from the unveiling. Unless something had happened to him . . .

"What should I do, Mary? Tell everyone the dedication is postponed?"

I thought for a moment. The eulogy inscribed on the monument was written by Henry as his eternal tribute to Jane. It would be incredibly moving to hear him recite it. But wasn't it more important for those in attendance this afternoon to be given the opportunity to honor Jane's memory, with or without Henry? "Do you feel able to speak on Henry's behalf?" I asked Elizabeth. "Could you read the inscription aloud?"

"Me?" Her eyes grew large. Much like my sister Frances, Elizabeth was shy by nature and not fond of attention. "I have read it silently, to myself, many times. I almost know it by heart. But to speak on Henry's behalf? I would find it difficult to speak of his devotion to my sister when, only two years after her death, he married someone else."

"You will do an excellent job of filling in for Henry," I said, brushing off her objection. Though not entirely surprised by Elizabeth's attitude, I could not support her in it. Fair or not, society typically held different expectations of widowers than widows; it was not unusual for a man to remarry within months of his wife's death, while a woman would be criticized for doing the same. After two years, however, it was not unreasonable for either a man or woman to again seek conjugal happiness. Appearing apprehensive, Elizabeth glanced towards the arched entrance to the church. The memorial, covered with an enormous gold cloth, was to its immediate right. "Very well. I'll do my best. Can you help me to herd the group inside?"

I was about to get started, more concerned about Henry than I wished to admit, when he suddenly appeared in the doorway. Behind him were several male companions, none of whom I recognized. Nor did I pay them any mind, as it was Henry's severely battered state that sent a wave of shock through me and the others gathered in the garden. His arm was in a sling, his face badly bruised, and as he approached Elizabeth and me, I saw that he walked with a limp. Nevertheless, he was smiling and still had all his teeth.

"At least give me credit for knowing how to make an entrance," he said, first kissing Elizabeth's hand and then mine. "Ran into a little trouble on the way from Hyderabad. Bandits. I'm afraid they took the gifts I had brought for you—both of you," he said, giving me a wink. "In fact, they made off with a good deal more than that. Thankfully, no one was killed. Just knocked around a bit."

"You hadn't any guards with you?" I asked, surprised he would be caught defenseless.

"Apparently not enough. But let's not talk about it now. These good people have been waiting long enough for the dedication. And so have I."

Everyone who witnessed Henry's arrival was full of questions. But with gentle prodding, Elizabeth and I managed to shepherd them into the nave. All chatter ceased as we stood before the monument. Henry faced us, his expression somber.

"I had prepared a speech for this moment," he began, "but now I find myself without words. For I have inscribed in stone everything that was—and shall always be—in my heart. My darling Jane, I know you are watching, listening. You will never be far from me."

He nodded for his three associates to remove the gold cloth. The marble sculpture, glistening in the light from a high window above, was a deathbed scene. A young woman reclined on a chaise; a man, hovering over her, cradled her head against his chest. Two other women stood by, their slumped shoulders bespeaking grief, while a servant, on her knees, covered her face with her hands.

Commencing his recitation, Henry's deep voice rang out strong and clear. "Could I, dear saint, to this cold stone impart each deep impression on thy husband's heart. Could I in language to my sorrow just record this last sad tribute to thy dust. Even strangers, then, who read the faithful line, should pause, in solemn silence at thy shrine. Should mourn with me my late espoused bride, untimely severed from her Russell's side."

He paused, and I thought he might shed tears, but he cleared his throat and went on. "In joy's first dawn, in early beauty's bloom, torn from the nuptial altar to the tomb, then should they see thee: lovely in thy youth, serene in virtue, dignified in truth, firm without rashness, gentle without fear, sedate though cheerful, polished yet sincere. So wise, so soft; so gay and yet resigned. So fair in person and so pure in mind. Should here they contemplate with admiring eye, a model how to live; alas, and how to die."

Looking about, I saw not a single dry eye. For my part, I had rarely been so moved, not only by the eulogy's fine words but the obvious sincerity of the speaker. I glanced at Elizabeth, who pressed a lace handkerchief to her lips, tears streaming down her cheeks. Though five years had passed since Jane's death, it was as though we were witnessing her final moments yet again. If my friend had any doubts of Henry's enduring love for her sister, surely this moment had quelled them forever.

One by one, the guests passed in front of the memorial, each stopping briefly to bow their head and perhaps say a silent prayer for Jane's eternal peace. I was overtaken by a realization of how fleeting is our earthly life, and yet how lasting the impression left by each departed soul. But throughout it all, I could not take my eyes from Henry's face. Scraped and bruised, and in the throes of wrenching emotion, he had never seemed quite so human. So vulnerable.

Witnessing Henry's pain might have been easier for me if Samuel were by my side. As it was, I could barely restrain myself from rushing to his side to offer what comfort I could. But that was for others to do, not the wife of Sir Samuel Hood.

Henry was soon busy accepting condolences and congratulations, as Elizabeth made the rounds, thanking everyone for coming out to honor her sister's memory. No one noticed me quietly slip away.

On the ride home, I was filled with a vague foreboding. Death comes quickly, and often without warning. And here I was, a world away from my family. Any one of them could pass on, and it would be months before I'd ever hear of it.

These morbid thoughts settled upon me like a cloak of sorrow I could not shake off.

CHAPTER TWENTY-SEVEN

I did not know how long Henry planned to stay in Madras, nor did I expect to see him again before he left. But later that evening, to my surprise, he called at Admiralty House.

We sat together in the library, sharing a bottle of Madeira and inhaling the musty smell of old books. Speaking fondly of our time in Mysore, the conversation soon turned to Henry's future—and mine. When I told him of my desire to return to Scotland, he was skeptical.

"So, you believe the Admiral will agree to becoming a country gentleman?"

I shrugged. "I might convince him."

"Well, if anyone could lure him away from the high seas, it would be you. I'd wager there isn't a man alive who would dare deny you anything you asked of him."

"I know that Samuel wishes to please me. He always has tried his best. But you may be right. Some men are born sailors and will remain so until the day they die. They can't be happy any other way."

"Sometimes we don't know what might make us happy until we try it. Take me, for instance. I used to think I would always remain a bachelor. What could be better than flirting with every young lady who strikes your fancy and never committing to any of them?" He laughed. "But then I met Jane."

"She was your one true love. No one who heard you speak this afternoon could doubt it."

"I suppose you are right." Looking thoughtful, he swirled the wine in his glass. "Has Elizabeth forgiven me for not telling her sooner of my marriage to Marie?"

"Forgiven you?" I wasn't sure how to answer him, though I had a good idea of how she felt. "That is a conversation you must have with Elizabeth, not me."

"I imagine she thinks of me as something of a cad. I saw the look on her face that night in Mysore, when she walked in on us at … I suppose one could call it an *awkward* moment."

"I explained it to her the next day, and she was fine. Elizabeth does not think poorly of you, Henry. But she is extremely protective of her sister. Probably more now than when Jane was alive."

"Maybe so. At any rate, I am grateful to you, Mary."

"Grateful? Whatever for?"

"For treating me as a friend. For not sitting in judgment of me, as so many have."

"We all are judged at one time or another, and usually by those who could not themselves withstand similar scrutiny."

He eased himself out of the chair and came over to stand behind me. With one hand, as the other was hampered by his arm being in a sling, he began to massage the back of my neck. My heart was pounding. Was this the behavior of a friend … or something else?

"Relax, Mary. You feel very tense. Are you not comfortable with me?"

"Henry—" I turned my head to look up at him. Even with his face scraped and bruised, Henry Russell was possibly the most attractive man I had ever met. More than once I had imagined what it would be like to kiss him. To feel his hands in places he had no right to touch. Alone with him now, in the home I shared with Samuel, such emotions were not only out of place, but frighteningly reckless.

"What are you thinking, Mary? Is it the same as what's on my mind?

"I wouldn't know what's on your mind. How could I?"

"Then I should tell you. Or, better yet, show you." He bent down, lightly kissing the top of my head. "You must know that I am very fond of you."

I tried to slow my breath, to calm myself. "One can be fond of many things that, in the end, cause regret of the most painful sort."

He kissed me again. "I wonder, do you speak from experience or simply fear of the unknown?"

I could stand it no longer. "Henry, stop!" I slithered from my chair, moving away from him, out of reach. "I cannot allow this. And you shouldn't either."

He stood, silent, looking at me almost brazenly. For a moment, though I knew it was crazy, I imagined he might try to take me by force. Finally, he dropped his gaze. "I've offended you. I'm sorry."

"It's not that you've offended me. I—I know it's been a trying time for you. An emotional afternoon."

"The emotions I feel tonight, here with you . . ." He shook his head. "How can I explain? Instead of pain, you give me joy. It's a welcome change. A pleasure I've not experienced often enough in my relationships with women. Not since losing Jane."

How did he do it? How did he succeed in making me feel as though I was cruel to refuse his advances?

"Surely your wife Marie—"

"Marie can be difficult." He smiled. "Don't misunderstand. She's a wonderful woman, beautiful, intelligent. But she is a bit on the abrasive side. One might say, extremely demanding."

"Perhaps she has reason to be," I said, thinking of how I might behave if my husband were as free with his affections as Henry appeared to be.

Henry gave an amused sniff. "I shall not try to defend myself. In fact, I plead guilty as charged. But remember—you promised not to judge me." He picked up his hat from the side table. "You were most kind to receive me without invitation, but I should be going. It's late, and I've barely slept in three days."

Now that he had said he was leaving, I didn't want him to. But, of course, he must not stay.

"You still are planning a visit to Hyderabad, are you not? Marie and I would welcome it. Oh—and I have a few gifts to send you. Replacements for those that were lost." He turned towards the door.

How smooth he was. How effortlessly he let it all go.

"I will let you know about the visit," I said, not mentioning that Samuel and I had already made our voyage.

CHAPTER TWENTY-EIGHT

T he letter I received from Caroline in September brought both encouraging and troubling news.

"For a while, Father's strength was failing him badly," she wrote, "but more recently he has taken a turn for the better. He enjoys riding about the properties of Brahan Castle in a specially designed low carriage that allows him to view the scenery from a reclining position. His spirits have risen considerably, and he spends most evenings in our company, appearing in exceptionally good humor."

Her report concerning our brother Frank assumed a different tone. She related that Frank had taken a sudden strong aversion to the Navy, abandoning his post only a short time after seeing Samuel and me in Bombay. Since then, he'd been feeling poorly. His last letter to the family said he was on his way home to Brahan Castle.

Though I told myself it must be nothing serious, the chill in my veins was insistent. Frank, by nature the more robust of my two brothers, was ailing. Just as Father appeared to be gaining strength.

It was then I had a terrible thought, for which I was instantly ashamed. But I could not deny it. If my father's end were near, then the Seer's prophecy could never come to pass. But if something were to happen first to Frank . . .

"Excuse me, my lady, but could I please have a word?" Sarah stood at the door to my dressing room.

"Of course, come in." I was glad for the interruption. "But you must tell me something to make me smile. I could use a bit of cheering."

"I hope you will be happy, but ..." She fiddled with her sleeve.

"Out with it! You know I can't stand to be kept in suspense."

"Well ... Ian and I—we're expecting."

I was speechless, though there was little reason to be surprised. Ian and Sarah had been married a good many years now; I'd lost track of how long. It was surprising a baby had not come sooner. I used to think that Sarah might be waiting out of respect for me, not wishing to precede my joyous news with hers. But, of course, mine had never come.

"Sarah, darling!" I jumped up to embrace her. "How long have you known?" I asked, stepping back for a good look at her. Nothing was showing yet.

"Not long. Wanted to be sure before I spoke to you. I reckon I'm about three months now."

"And Ian—is he pleased?"

"Pleased is hardly the word for it. He's already making a list of names for the bairn—all of them boys' names."

"Naturally." I pressed my palms together, thinking. "Well, we'd better start preparing for change."

Sarah's face fell. "I hope you won't think of replacing me. The bairn won't interfere with my duties, you can be sure."

I took Sarah's hands in mine and held them. "Do you know how dear you are to me? What I meant was that you and Ian will need a more private living arrangement. A family home. And I'll find a nurse to look after the baby."

"A nurse? That's for rich folk, not the likes of me."

"Don't be silly. Your baby must have the best of everything."

"You'd do that for me?" Sarah's eyes glistened with tears.

"Under one condition. You and Ian must allow Sir Samuel and me to be the baby's godparents."

Her jaw dropped. "Oh, my lady! Such an honor!"

I let go of her. "Now, promise to take proper care of yourself. Watch your diet and get plenty of rest. I am ordering a chaise for you; they say it's the best thing to lie upon when you're expecting. And I will tell Ian to speak of nothing unpleasant for the next few months so that you remain calm and relaxed."

"You warm my heart, but you know I'm sturdier than all that. My mother claims she had me whilst in the kitchen, stirring a kettle of soup, and she never once dropped the spoon. I think I've got it in me to have an easy time of it."

"Tell me, I know about Ian, but what do you wish for—a boy or a girl?"

"I'd be happy with either, truly. But there's something about a little girl . . . I should like to dress her up, put ribbons in her hair. Silly nonsense like that."

"It's not silly at all. A baby girl would be lovely to have around here."

"I'm grateful you feel that way, my lady."

"How could I not?" I said, sending Sarah off with a kiss on each smooth cheek. Then I sat down at my writing desk, and I cried.

CHAPTER TWENTY-NINE
FEBRUARY 1814

My dearest Mary,

It is with a mother's heavy heart that I write to tell you of your beloved brother Frank, who passed from us into the Kingdom of the Lord on the sixth of November. In God's mercy, He saw fit that your father should be at Brahan Castle for his dear son's passing, attending his bedside for two days and nights with no thought of nourishment or sleep. I regret that I had remained in Edinburgh. We have recently rented a residence there at 21 George Street, and I wished to prepare it for your father's arrival. If I had known we were to lose our sturdy, spirited boy, there is no power on earth that could have kept me away. But perhaps the Lord, in His greater wisdom, meant to spare me the pain of that moment when our most darling Frank slipped away forever. I was told he did not suffer greatly; the fever that took him was sudden and quick. But suffering takes many forms; since his arrival from India, his usual vigor had appeared greatly diminished, for reasons unknown.

I fear your father is in a state of anguish that cannot but weaken his own precarious condition. I shall insist that he join me in Edinburgh next month. Until then, Caroline is devoting herself to his every need, as are your other sisters excepting Frances, who is engaged in an affair of which I highly disapprove and would prefer not to discuss at such a time as this.

Reading Mother's letter, my eyesight clouded by tears, I felt myself sinking into despair. My little brother was dead! His life had only just begun, and now it was over. What might he have become if given the chance? How might he have distinguished himself in the world? We would never know.

But I couldn't shake the feeling there was more to his untimely death than met the eye. What had happened to Frank made no sense. Joining the Navy had been his lifelong dream. He seemed enthusiastic about it as recently as last February in Bombay. Had the rigor of service proved too much for him? Had he come to realize he was not suited for war? Could it be that his exposure to the gentle and devout inhabitants of India during the days we spent together had somehow altered his perspective, caused him to think differently about Britain's role in the world?

I would guess such thoughts too lofty for a young man of seventeen, especially one who had set his sights on the Royal Navy since childhood, but what did I really know of my brother? We had spent far more time apart than together. I had no right to assume anything about his innermost thoughts and feelings.

And what did it matter now? Frank was gone, his promising young life over. His passing left only questions, doubts ... and a terrible unease.

Our family had arrived at a crossroads, and I could not be the only one to see it. Surely the rest of my family were thinking the same as I was. Now it was up to William to thwart the next phase of the Seer's prophecy—his prediction that all Lord Seaforth's sons would die before him. William, whose constitution had always been on the fragile side. Who, as a child, was prone to illnesses of one sort or another.

But he had always recovered; that was the important thing and what we must remember, now more than ever. William was strong when he needed to be.

Strong—as I used to believe I was.

Now I wasn't sure. I was fast losing my long-fought battle with the Seer. At times, I had the sensation he was controlling my mind. Turning my thoughts in directions I had always turned away from. Making me see the dark hand of fate in everything that happened.

Or might happen.

CHAPTER THIRTY

Samuel turned over the command of his flagship, *Minden*, to Captain George Henderson in April 1814 and by late August was back at Admiralty House. For me, the months since learning of Frank's death had been emotionally draining.

Caroline and Frances were at Brahan Castle; my other sisters were living in Edinburgh with my parents. My brother William was back and forth between Ross-shire and London, his duties in Parliament requiring him to split his time accordingly. I wished to see all of them, of course; but, at the moment, William was the focus of my concern. I still found it difficult to admit that the root of my growing fears was the Seer's prophecy that William would be the next to die. Better simply to tell myself, and Samuel, that I was worried about my father's failing health. All I knew for certain was that I must go home, without delay. And, if Samuel were agreeable, it would be to stay.

My husband had been back only a few days when, after a late dinner, I broached the subject of his retirement.

"I know you feel a responsibility towards your work, darling. But when will you decide that you have done enough for the Royal Navy?"

"I suppose, if it were up to you, I would decide right now."

"I can't deny that my father's precarious state of health weighs heavily on me. I would be heartbroken if he were to pass before I can see him again. Of course, I could go to Scotland alone."

"If I didn't know you better, I might take that as a threat," he said playfully.

"I'm speaking from my heart. My brother Frank's death has devastated all of us, especially my father. Samuel, my family needs me. I must go to them as soon as possible. Will you go with me?"

Samuel set down his fork, fixing his quiet stare upon me from across the table. "Forgive me for making light of your needs, and those of your family. I don't mean to. In fact, considering what you have told me, Mary, I must give you some important news. Right away."

I braced myself for the worst. Had he accepted a new commission? Would he be leaving on another mission?

"I've decided to retire."

His words floated across the space between us, sounding so light and inconsequential that it took me a moment to realize what he had said.

"Oh, Samuel! Do you mean it?" I wanted to leap out of my chair and throw my arms around his neck. But there was still one important question. "When?"

"By the end of the year. I've already posted my resignation, effective on the first of December."

Now there was nothing that could stop me. Abandoning my seat, I flew the length of the table. He had already pushed back his chair so I could slide onto his lap. We kissed long and hard, with no regard for what the servants might think should any of them walk in.

Finally I came up for air. "We shall go to Edinburgh first. I will arrange for William to meet us there. And then—"

"Hold on, hold on." Samuel chuckled. "These are not decisions we need to make this very moment, are they?"

"No, but very soon. I must write to everyone and let them know we're coming."

Samuel pressed my hand to his lips. "I understand, my love. Yes, we will visit Lord and Lady Seaforth in Edinburgh. That is our first duty."

"Thank you, darling. It will mean so much to them. Especially now."

But in the midst of my unexpected joy, doubts quickly emerged. December was four long months away. What might happen between now and then? And once I was home, what could I possibly do to keep William safe? I had no magic wand to wave, no incantation I could chant to override the Seer's evil curse upon my family. If, indeed, there was such a curse.

"Should we plan for a ball before we leave?" Samuel said, oblivious to the detour my thoughts had taken. "You'll want to say goodbye to all your friends."

Why was Henry Russell the first who came to my mind? But it was doubtful that Henry and I would see each other again—and probably for the best.

"An excellent idea. I'll start planning for it right away. And I can't wait to tell Sarah of your decision. She and Ian will be pleased beyond words. Lately, she has been bemoaning that her parents back home might not see their little granddaughter until she was half grown."

"Then I suppose everyone is eager to leave India."

I looked into his eyes, those gently inquisitive eyes that had captured my heart the first time I dared let them try. "Including you, Samuel? You are not doing this only for me, are you?"

He paused, and I had a moment of doubt. Was he truly ready to retire, or had I pressured him into it? Was I taking him away from what he most loved?

"Aristotle once said 'It is not enough to win a war; it is more important to organize the peace.'" He kissed my cheek. "No, Mary. I am not retiring only for your sake. It is time. Perhaps there will be some better use for this old, battle-scarred sailor."

I snuggled closer to him. "I can think of one right now."

"I was hoping you might."

I slid off his lap and offered my hand. "Your chariot awaits, my lord."

• • •

The servants had orders to pack up our personal household items following our departure for London on the thirtieth of December. The plan was for Sarah and Ian to remain behind and then accompany our boxes on the next ship out of Madras. They were to take everything to the townhouse in London and await our further instructions from Edinburgh.

My anticipation grew with each passing day. In many ways, I had enjoyed my time here, and I had learned a great deal about India's people and customs. But what some called *progress*, I often saw as destruction of the beautiful and sacred; what others labelled *order* easily lapsed into tyranny. I had once applauded the administration's stated goal of elevating the status of India's women, a proposition that had planted fear in the heart of the Rajah of Mysore. But I doubted such sweeping change would occur anytime soon, nor that it was a priority of the highest order for the British.

Samuel and I had not settled on any specific plans after our visit to Edinburgh. He had asked that we take things one step at a time. The idea of retirement was an adjustment for him; I must do my part to make it easier. I hoped, initially, we might live part of the year in Ross-shire and the other part in London, on a schedule more or less coinciding with William's. For reasons I would have been hard pressed to articulate, it seemed important that I stay close to my brother, the last male heir of the Seaforth line.

With only a month until we were to set sail, Samuel surprised me by asking whether I would object if he took a farewell voyage on the *Minden* with his friend Captain Henderson, to Trincomalee on the island of Ceylon. Trincomalee was a highly strategic harbor and one of the Royal Navy's most important bases in the Indian Ocean. Samuel explained that he had been asked to advise on proposed reforms to the base's organization. Though on the eve of his retirement, and under no direct order to go, he wished to accept the invitation.

I was not enthusiastic about the idea. Sailing the Indian Ocean was never predictable. Changing wind patterns and weather conditions could either expedite or delay travel. Under the best conditions, the voyage to Ceylon would require a week in each direction.

"Don't make me sail without you, Samuel. You know how important it is that I reach Edinburgh as soon as possible."

"Don't worry, darling," he assured me. "I'll be back in plenty of time."

CHAPTER THIRTY-ONE

Samuel left for Trincomalee on the second of December. On the third, I received a letter from Caroline that drove me to my bed. Pulling the covers over my head, I sobbed for the better part of an hour, stifling the urge to scream, to vent my anguish on a God who surely was not listening. What had happened was inconceivable, and yet hadn't I imagined it a hundred times? Maybe a thousand? Since Frank's death, it had almost seemed inevitable. Such is the folly of the superstitious mind. By imagining, believing, it grants evil the power to succeed.

I lay in bed the rest of the afternoon, too sapped of strength to do anything else. Finally, dry-eyed and numb, I went to sit at my writing desk. Picking up my quill pen, I dipped it into the ink, then held it aloft, staring at the blank page before me.

What was there to say? I could insist that, beyond the darkness of our shared grief, there was still light. But I would only be pretending.

My brother William was dead.

"William was a sensitive soul," Caroline had written in her delicate hand. "He took Frank's death very hard, and he was so conscientious about his duties in Parliament. I fear he wore himself down with it all. Then, too, he was concerned, as are all of us, about Father's health. I should mention that Mother and Father no longer are renting on George Street, but have purchased a quite fashionable house on

Charlotte Square and also are leasing a summer residence, Warriston House, just a mile outside Edinburgh, which is where poor William drew his last breath on the twenty-fifth of August. Father has not spoken a word since, either by voice or sign. He is completely mute. It is as though he is with us in body but his spirit is elsewhere. William was buried at Fortrose Cathedral, carried to his gravesite with great honor by virtually all the able-bodied men of Ross-shire, but of course Father could not be present."

I threw down my pen, sweeping aside the blank paper upon which I had foolishly imagined I might compose a letter of comfort and hope, words of wisdom to bolster the sagging spirits of my sisters, my mother—perhaps even my father. But Caroline had said Father was unreachable. Perhaps he would remain that way forever.

I heard Sarah at my door and was about to call out that she should return later. But why? If I had ever needed someone who might understand, it was now.

"Come in."

She entered the dressing room. Seeing my red, swollen eyes and blotchy cheeks, she rushed to my side.

"What is it, my lady? What's wrong?" Sarah bent down, her eyes searching my face. "Is it the letter you received from your sister?"

I nodded, my lips trembling though I had no tears left.

"News of Lord Seaforth?"

"Father is not well. But William. He's—" I couldn't bring myself to say the word *dead*. "Our dear William has fallen ill . . . and perished."

Sarah's hand flew to her heart. "Oh no! William? I can't believe it. Oh, my lady . . . I am so terribly sorry."

I stared at the floor, seeing nothing, hearing nothing. Forgetting Sarah was there, until she laid her hand on my knee.

"Poor darling. Both your brothers gone, and your father ill. It will be a comfort to your family once you're back in Scotland. And a comfort to you."

"Comfort?" I raised my eyes. "You must realize what William's death means? The last of Father's sons." And then I began reciting the hated words of Coinneach Odhar, words that I once had vowed would never pass from my lips: "*I see a chief, the last of his house, both deaf and dumb. He will be the father of four fair sons, all of whom he will follow to the tomb. He will live careworn and die mourning, knowing that the honors of his line are to be extinguished forever.*"

There was more, much more. But I went no further.

"There's not a speck of truth in that old legend," Sarah said firmly. "You've insisted on it yourself, many times."

"Please, don't coddle me. The heirs to my father's title are dead. Father is still alive, deaf as ever and now either refusing or unable to speak." My tone was harsh, though I had not intended it to be. "I'm sorry, Sarah, if I sound angry. You're the only one here who can truly understand." Exhausted, I let my head drop. "It's so confusing, everything that's happened. I can't make sense of it. Poor William … and Frank."

"It's awful. Both of them so young."

"But Sarah—" I looked up at her. "Whatever happens in the future, promise you won't desert me."

"I would never, my lady."

"I know." I sighed. "I can't think anymore. I can't . . ."

"Let me draw you a bath. A good soak would be the best thing for you."

I gave her a weak smile. "Thank you. And please—not a word of this to anyone. I don't need sympathy or gossip, either one. If you must tell Ian, then do," I added, knowing she would find it difficult to keep any secret from her husband. "But only him. He remembers William and will be grieved to learn of his passing."

Sarah retrieved the blank page that had dropped to the floor and handed it to me. "Were you planning to write to Miss Caroline?"

"I thought I'd try to offer some words of consolation. But there were none to be found."

"Words for others can wait. You need first to take care of yourself."

•　　•　　•

That night, I awoke from a dream much like the one during my last visit to Brahan Castle, soon after I'd met Walter Scott. I was wandering the moors under a full moon, an aimless wandering but with a sense of anxiety. And then, somehow, the scene switched to Chanonry Point on the Black Isle. The moon had disappeared. The roar of waves crashing against the rocks grew louder and louder. As before, the ground beneath my feet rumbled and a giant chasm opened like the jaws of an enormous beast, sending me hurtling into the bowels of the earth. Again, I heard a voice that came from nowhere, filling the darkness around me. A taunting voice that called to me by name.

"Mary—or should I say *Lady Hood*? If ye're seeking yer brothers, they've gone. Ye'll no' lay eyes on them again. But yer sisters …"

"Do not speak of them, I beg you."

"Ye sound frightened, Lady Hood."

"You will not touch my sisters. They have done nothing wrong."

"Right and wrong no longer have aught to do wi' it. What's writ is writ. My words canny be scrubbed out. They'll bide for all eternity."

"What if I atone for the past? Anything—I will do anything to save my sisters."

"Only one, Lady Hood. Only one maun die."

"Not by my hand, she won't. Please …"

"I near pity you, Mary. Near."

I heard a scream, a wail of such sorrow—or was it agony? I sat up in bed, awake and shivering, as if I still crouched in that cold, dark pit.

I threw back the covers, eager to leave my bed. Afraid of sleep. But either way, asleep or awake, I had lost control. A shadow was chasing me, a shadow without substance but powerful enough to drown me in its void. What I had called *lies* now appeared as truth. I had tried reason, telling myself that fathers frequently outlive their sons; it was not unusual, especially in times of war. But the rest—the prophecy of a deaf and dumb chief: How "usual" was that? And there were other details that I had always glossed over. Descriptions of four neighboring Highland chiefs, supporters of my father, whose distinguishing features—one buck-toothed, another hare-lipped, a third half-witted, the fourth a stammerer—were signs that the Seaforth line was soon to fall. I had argued that observing such traits in others may be more subjective than actual. An occasional hesitancy in speech does not make one a stammerer. And a person can be less than brilliant without deserving the pejorative of *half-wit*.

Such were my earlier attempts to embrace logic over emotion. Attempts that now seemed altogether futile.

Pacing back and forth across my room, I became angry with Samuel for leaving me alone. He did not have to go to Ceylon; he wanted to. He liked being needed, feeling as though the entire Royal Navy would fall apart without his guidance. He must be thinking *how can they ever do without me?*

"It is your wife, Samuel, who needs you," I cried. "What about your duty to *her*?"

Hearing my words, I was ashamed to have spoken them or even permitted myself to think them. Samuel was not to blame. As a husband, he could be faulted for nothing.

I paused in front of my dressing table, studying my reflection in the mirror. Worry did not become me. Neither did fear.

But they owned me now.

CHAPTER THIRTY-TWO

I had hoped for Samuel's return before Christmas. On the twenty-first of December, around two o'clock in the afternoon, I received word that his ship had docked in Madras. Trying my best to shake off the deep melancholy that had enveloped me since learning of William's death, I scurried about Admiralty House, checking to make certain everything looked perfect, with freshly cut flowers in the drawing room, dining room, and both our apartments. Cook was instructed to begin preparation of Samuel's favorite dinner. I changed into the forest-green dress that I knew was his favorite. This would be his last homecoming to Admiralty House; despite everything else, I wanted it to be a memorable one.

But when Samuel had not arrived by five, I began to question whether the news of his landing had been a mistake. By six, having received no further messages, I became concerned. About to send Ian out to investigate, I was suddenly informed of a sailor from the *Minden* waiting to speak with me.

"Where is Admiral Hood?" I asked, entering the foyer.

"Good evening, my lady." The young man, avoiding my eyes, appeared nervous.

"Is the Admiral on his way?"

"No, my lady. I'm sorry to say that Admiral Hood has taken ill. It was decided to transfer him directly to hospital. Just a precaution, my lady."

"What sort of illness?" I demanded.

Sarah came up behind me and placed her hand at my elbow.

"All I know, my lady, is that he's got a fever."

Abruptly, I turned to Sarah. "We must go directly to hospital. Please grab whatever we might need and arrange for the carriage."

Sarah hurried off while I remained in the hall, my mind racing. A *precaution* could mean anything. And a fever—that told me nothing either.

"You have no further information about my husband's condition?"

"I'm sorry, my lady. I wish I knew more."

Frustrated, I dismissed him. But, as he was turning to leave, I thought of something else.

"Wait!"

He swung around. "Yes, my lady?"

"Find out which doctor is treating Admiral Hood, and let him know I am on my way."

The Madras General Hospital was not far; within twenty minutes our carriage had passed through the iron gates and I was being helped down the step. A young nurse, a white bonnet covering her hair, met me at the entrance.

"Lady Hood?" She peered at me through the evening fog. "I can take you to the doctor."

She led me up a short flight of steps into the one-story building. I was familiar with the place, having been here as a volunteer visiting injured servicemen. I followed the nurse down a long corridor and through an enormous open ward with beds lining every wall.

"Come this way, please," she said, directing me to a short passageway. "Down here are the private rooms. We generally save them for high-ranking officers, or cases requiring isolation."

Isolation? "I will be able to see my husband, won't I?"

"The doctor will explain everything."

A grey-whiskered man in a long coat appeared at the end of the corridor, approaching us with a grim look that sent chills through me.

"Lady Hood, welcome," he said. "My name is Dr. Mitchell, and I am in charge of your husband's case. He is resting quietly at the moment."

"I was told he has a fever, but that was all. I want to know everything about his condition."

Dr. Mitchell's nostrils flared, his lips pursing in a manner that portended the gravity of whatever he was about to say. "Admiral Hood's fever is quite high, and he is suffering severe abdominal symptoms. Unfortunately, his illness began at sea and, by now, his condition is critical. Presently, he is not eating, but we are giving him clear fluids and, for the pain, opium."

His condition is critical. No, not Samuel. With all he had survived in his brave, gallant life, he would not be defeated by some silly fever. "There surely is more that can be done. There has to be. Are you the only doctor attending my husband?"

Dr. Mitchell raised his whiskered chin, looking down at me with an air of impunity. "I assure you, Lady Hood, I am doing everything possible to save your husband."

"And what do you think are the odds of your success?"

"I have never been a gambling man, and certainly not when it comes to my patients. I simply do my best and leave the rest to God and nature."

His evasiveness was maddening. "I have no doubt you are doing your best. Forgive me if I seemed to imply otherwise. Perhaps if I could see the Admiral now—"

"I would not advise that, Lady Hood. Admiral Hood has been placed in isolation. The nature of his illness is unknown."

"But I am his wife. I have a right to see him."

"I understand and certainly sympathize, but I'm afraid that right is subject to hospital policy. Perhaps tomorrow, if—"

"According to you, my husband could be dead by tomorrow! I want him taken out of here at once and moved to Admiralty House. He will fare much better, I believe, in his own bed—and under the care of his private physician, whom I will summon now to accompany him."

"Lady Hood, please. Moving your husband in his weak condition is not a good idea. I beg you to reconsider." He hesitated before heaving an annoyed sigh, "If you insist, I will allow you to see him. Perhaps then you will understand why he is better off where he is."

I had won the battle over visitation. But now, suddenly, I wasn't certain I could bear to see Samuel in such a dire state. What if I broke down in front of him? What he needed was strength and optimism, not an anguished wife in doubt of his recovery. The weight of all I had suffered of late—the deaths of my brothers, the dread of more ill fortune to come—rained down upon me in a torrent of emotion. I pressed a handkerchief to my face.

"Are you all right, my lady?" The nurse laid a gentle hand on my shoulder. "Would you like to sit down?"

Shaking my head, I lowered the handkerchief. "May I see my husband, please?"

I hadn't realized we were standing in front of the room to which Samuel had been assigned until Dr. Mitchell opened the door and stepped aside for me to enter. "Best if you keep your distance," he said.

The shade was drawn over the room's single window, the only light coming from an oil lamp next to the bed. As the doctor had said, Samuel was sleeping. The sight of him, lying in this barren room, alone, only convinced me more that he belonged at home.

"Thank you, Dr. Mitchell," I said, pivoting towards the door. "I've seen what I needed to see."

I returned to the corridor. Dr. Mitchell followed, shutting the door to Samuel's room. "If you like, I can send word in the morning of his progress," he said, obviously trying to smooth over the bumps in our earlier discourse. I did not wish to insult him or make him feel inadequate; none of this was his fault. As soon as I was out of here, however, I planned to contact Samuel's personal physician Dr. Lowry and order him to arrange my husband's immediate transfer to Admiralty House.

CHAPTER THIRTY-THREE

S amuel did not arrive until ten o'clock the next morning. I had not slept all night, worrying whether I had done the right thing in removing him from hospital.

I stayed out of the way while he was being moved into his apartment, understanding that Dr. Lowry and his nurse required time to organize what they would need for his continuing care. Finally, I could stand it no longer. Announcing myself from the hallway, I opened the door to the bedchamber. A single step inside, and I froze.

"Lady Hood!" There was a note of panic in Dr. Lowry's voice. The nurse standing next to Samuel's bed glanced up, her eyes red and watery. A white sheet covered my husband's face.

"No …" I staggered forward. Dr. Lowry rushed over and grabbed me by the arm.

"Please, sit down, my lady."

"I don't want to sit," I snapped. "Why did no one tell me? How long has he been—"

"He expired shortly after we arrived. Within minutes. I was just now getting ready to find you."

I allowed my anger to rise, unchecked. It was the only way I had to keep from completely falling apart. "Did he know where he was? That I had brought him home? Did you bother telling him?"

"There was no opportunity. He was unconscious the entire time. Probably the opium." Dr. Lowry shook his head. "I'm sorry you didn't have a chance to speak to him. I know you were hoping for that."

Suddenly, my anger dissipated, leaving me to feel as though I'd been punched in the stomach, the air knocked out of me. But even in the midst of the most excruciating grief I'd ever known, there was a question I had to ask. And I was terrified of the answer.

"Is it my fault?"

Dr. Lowry was still holding me by the arm, but more gently now. "No, my lady. How could it be?"

"I'm the one who had him moved from hospital. Should I have left him there?"

He paused, longer than I would have wished. "I'm certain he would have found comfort in being at home, but … well, it was not to be."

"But might he have recovered?" My tone was insistent. "If I had left him in hospital, as Dr. Mitchell urged, might he have lived?"

"No, Lady Hood. Even in hospital, he was very near the end. Exactly how near, it was impossible to say. I thought perhaps he might have a little time left. But recovery?" Again, he shook his head. "It would have been nothing short of a miracle."

I took a tremulous breath, still unconvinced. Dr. Lowry knew, of course, what I needed to hear. He would not offer me less. But nothing that anyone could offer would help me now. My husband was dead, snatched away without even the chance to say goodbye.

"Would you like for me to arrange for the undertaker?" the doctor asked delicately.

I was tempted to say that I wanted to keep him here, at least for tonight. To lie beside him one last time. But the truth was, I hadn't even the courage to walk over to the bed and pull back the sheet. To look at my beloved husband's face. Touch his cold cheek. Stand beside death, close enough to smell it.

If I were to do any of those things, I feared I might go insane.

"Yes, Doctor, please make the arrangements."

· · ·

In Madras, the color of mourning is white. White, symbolizing purity and simplicity. Withdrawal from worldly pleasures.

I wore a white sari to Samuel's burial at St. Mary's Church; it seemed only right. My heart must now—and always—remain in India.

The Governor-General attended the ceremony and afterwards told me that a plaque honoring Samuel's distinguished service and outstanding character would be installed in the church. "I hope you will return one day to see it," he said.

I considered delaying my departure from Madras, scheduled for a few days after Samuel's burial. But staying longer at Admiralty House would only preserve my grief at its rawest. Every room held some memory of us together. The library, where we would sometimes read late into the night, side by side, in front of the fireplace. The dining room, talking and laughing over long dinners alone. And, worst of all, my bedchamber. Since Samuel's passing, I could not bear to sleep in the bed we had shared. Of course, it didn't really matter where I was: Samuel was with me day and night, awake or asleep. With me, yet not with me.

I dreaded the voyage back to England nearly as much. It was not the danger of the seas, but the prospect of being alone, with only my morose thoughts to occupy me. And when I finally reached Scotland, what would be awaiting me? Father was ill. And Mother? I had received no letters from her recently. Not even to tell me of William's passing. For all I knew, something untoward had befallen her as well.

Two days before I was to board the vessel for England, Sarah was helping me to lay out my clothes on the bed before packing them when suddenly she stopped.

"Sorry, my lady, but I can't do this."

"What do you mean? Are you unwell?" I started towards her, poised to check her forehead for fever.

"No, I'm fine. But you're not."

I turned my face away. These days I was so emotional, almost anything could make me cry.

"I refuse to send you off to England by yourself," she said. "Either you must delay and travel with us and your cargo, or I'm going with you now. Ian can manage looking after your things. He doesn't need any of my help."

"But the baby—"

"Ellen has to make the trip sometime; might as well be now. But we'd best see straight away if there's an extra cabin this late. If not, we'll have to cancel your fare and rebook for the next ship out, with us."

I was not accustomed to being ordered about by my lady's maid, though I was grateful for it now. Sarah was a friend, indeed. Still, I had to get to Edinburgh while my father was still alive. I would never forgive myself if I missed the opportunity to offer what little solace he might still find.

"Do check on the cabin, Sarah. And thank you. But, regardless, I will be on the ship leaving the day after tomorrow."

•　　•　　•

On the thirtieth of December, Sarah, baby Ellen, and I boarded the vessel for England. I wore my mourning dress and a hooded cape, both white as the ship's sails, and took with me as many books as I reasonably could. Among my chosen volumes was *The Bhagavad Gita*, which I'd "borrowed" from the Admiralty House library. It was the least I was owed by India, after what it had stolen from me.

I found it a welcome relief to be on the open sea, surrounded by nothing but water and sky, a brisk wind whipping the sails overhead. From the ship's deck, I sometimes imagined I was viewing the horizon through Samuel's eyes, as he must have done thousands of times. Perhaps searching for an enemy frigate, an impending storm, or the first outlines of a destination harbor. And I occasionally mused it might have been better had he died at sea. It seemed a more fitting end for a naval hero—and the man I loved.

The peaceful start to our journey was not to last. Three weeks into the voyage, we ran into our first gale, worse than any storm I had encountered on previous crossings. We were ordered to our staterooms and told, for safety's sake, to stay in our berths. The noise was awful, vicious gusts of wind roaring through the rigging; boxes and trunks tossed about the cabin, crashing into the walls and everything else in their path. The waves battering our ship were high enough to breach the sides. I could hear the fast, heavy footsteps of sailors overhead, their shouts and cries, and the captain barking his commands.

I was worried about Ellen. How must a baby experience such a terrifying ordeal as this? Her mother holding her close was the only thing that quieted her, and not for long. Her fits of crying and Sarah's attempts to soothe her brought back memories. Being the eldest child in my family, I had often been the one from whom my brothers and sisters sought reassurance if they were frightened or confused. Perhaps it would be like that again, once I was back in Scotland. But would I be strong enough to keep my grieving family afloat, with their faith in God's goodness in tatters?

Or was it only me who doubted? Me, who for so long had staunchly denied my vulnerability, believing if I chose to ignore evil, it would simply disappear. How foolish I was to imagine myself, and my family, immune to tragedy. How self-indulgent to witness the misery of others—the indentured, the enslaved, the conquered—and consider it not my own. Now I understood: The misery of one belongs to all. And all shall know it, sooner or later.

Halfway to our destination, we enjoyed a stretch of good weather. On one delightful morning, Sarah and I, with Ellen contentedly bouncing on her mother's lap, sat on the deck, lulled by the tranquility of a quiet sea. I glanced up at the billowing sails; how white they were against the bright blue sky. What is it about *white* that calms the spirit so?

I pulled my hooded cape a bit tighter around me to blunt the chilly breeze. Perhaps my family would find it strange to see me dressed in white, being accustomed to black as the color of mourning. I would have to explain about the custom in India and that I thought Samuel would approve of my observing it.

Suddenly, I gripped the arms of my deck chair. It was as if I'd been slapped in the face by an icy wave. An awakening of sorts—a cruel and bitter one. How could I have failed to put it all together, what had happened to Samuel and the prophecy. The line that came after the death of my brothers, after my father's sinking into the grave.

... and the remnant of his possessions shall be inherited by a white-hooded lassie from the East. Turning to Sarah, who was resting with Ellen held tight against her chest, I said quietly, "The Seer knew."

Her eyes flew open. "I'm sorry, my lady, what did you say?"

"The Seer knew—about Samuel. He knew my husband would die before my return to Scotland. And that he would die in India. Remember the white-hooded lassie? Look at me, Sarah. Look at what I'm wearing."

She frowned. "Aye, I see what you mean. You coming home, all dressed in white. And being the eldest daughter, the lands should go to you someday. That's the Scottish law."

Strangely, what I felt at that moment was not fear but anger. I knew very well the rest of Coinneach Odhar's last prophecy and the part I was meant to play. But I was tired of cowering. Instead of the Seer's taunts echoing in my head, for once I heard my own voice, strong and clear:

God or devil, prophet or whatever you may be—you have tried to destroy me and what's left of my family's legacy.

But the rest shall not be yours.

CHAPTER THIRTY-FOUR
LONDON

I did not plan to remain in London long. Barring any unforeseen complications, I would leave for Edinburgh in two days. The voyage from Madras has afforded me plenty of time to think about what I would say to my father when I saw him. And what he might say to me—if he spoke at all. The last I had heard from Caroline, Father was completely mute, neither speaking nor signing. Her letter gave the impression that his condition was not as much physical as mental. I imagined, like me, he had spent his entire life silently doing battle with the Seer—refusing to believe in him, yet unable to ignore him. And now, with the predicted death of his sons an established fact, he no longer saw any reason to live.

But I would give him a reason. The Seer's curse had devastated our family, but not destroyed it. Father still had an heir. His titles could never be mine, but whatever was left of his estates would someday pass to me. I would find a way to correct the mistakes that had been made in their management.

And when Father was gone, I would be ready to take his place as chief of the Mackenzies.

On my arrival at the townhouse on Lower Wimpole Street, I found several letters awaiting me. One from Mother, another from Caroline, and a third from Mr. Scott, who for some time now had signed his letters as *Walter*. I broke the seal on the letter from Caroline, but could not yet bring myself to read it. What if I was too late and Father already was gone, having died a broken man without hope?

I set her letter aside, reaching for the one from Walter Scott. His correspondences were generally cheerful, always thought provoking. I looked forward to the opportunity to see him while in Edinburgh.

I unfolded the letter and began to read, skipping past the opening condolences for my brothers' deaths, hoping for something to enliven my spirit. But when I reached the third paragraph, I realized the futility of any such hope.

"And now, you face perhaps your greatest challenge," he wrote. "It was with enormous sadness that I watched your father's funeral procession from my Castle Street house. Most likely the snow storm kept away many who would otherwise have been there to pay their respects. The sight of his body passing by, with so little of the fanfare he deserved, left me quite melancholy."

The page fell from my hand. I could read no more. Inured to death, weary of weeping, I simply sat, stone-faced. My father had his failings—a few of which had disappointed me greatly—but he was a good man with much to be proud of: accomplishments that were the envy of men born into somewhat easier circumstances, with none of the physical challenges he faced throughout his life. A devoted father, he had a family he loved and who loved him. If only I could have been there to remind him of all this. But, like the others I had lost—Frank, William, Samuel—he had passed without a word, or a touch, from me.

Leaving me to carry on.

As early as Barbados, I had been aware of Father's overspending and his gambling. Later on, Samuel told me of the substantial loan my father had requested from him. But it was years since I thought seriously of having a talk with him about financial matters. Knowing he would consider it none of my affair, I had let it go and convinced myself that one day William would take over and set things right. In the meantime, my parents had seemed to manage well enough. Their recent purchase of the Edinburgh townhouse in Charlotte Square, one of the city's most desirable locations, suggested that, by whatever means, they were still able to afford a luxurious style of living.

But now, with no grasp of the estate's annual income and expenditures, or the demands of its creditors, I would need to educate myself quickly.

As much as I longed to see Mother and my three sisters, I decided to postpone a visit to Edinburgh in favor of going straight to Brahan Castle in Dingwall, a base from which I could best assess the condition of the Seaforth estates. Caroline had stayed to manage things as best she could, and the thought of seeing her brightened my mood.

Samuel's nephew and heir, Alexander Hood, was eager to take possession of the London townhouse but accommodating of my needs. It was decided that I would leave for Brahan Castle as soon as possible, while Sarah would stay in London waiting for the ship bearing our cargo. She and Ian would arrange to store my possessions—those coming from Madras and my personal items from the London townhouse—until I decided where I wanted them permanently. When all was settled, they would join me at Brahan Castle.

It was June by the time I arrived in Dingwall, feeling as though I had swum oceans and climbed mountains to get there. The castle did not look well, with ill-kept grounds and a general sense of lassitude about the place. A lifelessness that reflected not only the absence of its lord and master, but also its pared-down staff. There was much work to be done.

Standing by the carriage that had brought me all the way from London, I rejoiced at the sight of Caroline scurrying down the steps and across the courtyard. She hurtled into my arms.

"I wrote to you as soon as I learned about Sir Samuel, but I doubt my letter arrived before you left London," she said. "How are you holding up?"

"It's been difficult, of course. Everything."

She was silent for a moment before looping her arm through mine. "Well, you are home now. It's just you and me—and the servants.

But …" She bent down to peek inside the carriage. "Sarah isn't with you?"

"She will come later, with the baby and Ian. I needed her to settle a few things for me in London."

"Then I shall wait on you myself—hand and foot. After all, you *are* the new mistress of Brahan Castle."

"At the moment, a dubious honor," I said wearily. "I expect there is a great deal we don't know about Father's business."

"But, Mary—" She looked questioningly at my white hooded cloak. I had thought about discarding it in favor of black, but there was no reason now.

"In Madras, women in mourning wear white."

"Ah—lovely," she said.

•   •   •

"The estate is badly in debt and has been for as long as anyone can remember." Mr. Ross, the estate factor, eyed me over his wire spectacles. "Lord Seaforth was repeatedly urged to sell off property and trim the family's living expenses, but he was a difficult man to reason with. No disrespect, of course," he added hastily. "He took his role as clan chief to heart and wanted to protect his tenants. I can appreciate that. But now, the burden falls upon you, Lady Hood, and it won't be an easy one—especially for a …"

He left his sentence unfinished, but I knew what was in his mind: It was a pity there were no sons to inherit Lord Seaforth's estate—and to take over as the Mackenzie chief.

"Especially for a *woman*? Is that what you meant to say? Perhaps you are one of those who believe a woman is not suited to manage an estate or, even less, to be a clan chief?"

Mr. Ross's face reddened. "Again, Lady Hood, I mean no disrespect. But you've been away for a good many years now. Things have changed. Agriculture has suffered. Kelp, which was doing well seven or eight years ago, is worth just a quarter of what it brought then. The annual interest payments on loans are barely covered by the estate's rental income. And then, too, you have annuities to pay." He loosened his collar. A drop of sweat rolled past his temple. "As for being chief, no one can say you are not entitled, Lady Hood."

His sincerity was questionable, as I was certain he must be aware that some were questioning my right to assume the title of chief. Sweeping economic and social change had greatly weakened the clan system, but the chief's symbolic role was still important to Highland cultural life. I would not relinquish that role to another simply because I was a woman.

I stared at the dozens of papers spread out on the table, all of them filled with figures for profits and losses, income and expenditures—an overwhelming amount of information requiring decisions I was unprepared to make.

"Can you tell me, please, what is the total amount of the estate's debt?" Though I tried to sound calm, inside I was quaking. How bad would it be?

He searched through the papers, then shoved one of them towards me. "There it is. One hundred and forty-five thousand pounds."

I swallowed hard. The figures on the page in front of me were a blur. "I see. Well, it will take some time to sort through all this and decide what to do."

"Are there any other questions I might answer for you?" Mr. Ross's skeptical frown suggested he doubted my ability either to ask the right questions or reach the correct conclusions.

Suddenly I remembered what I'd vowed would be my first action as the Seaforth heiress. "Berbice. I believe my father bought a plantation there?"

"Two plantations, actually. Turned out to be a poor investment. The first couple of seasons, the weather was bad and spoiled the cotton. After that, it wasn't much better. Still isn't."

"I want to sell them."

"If there's anybody interested," he said, with a shrug. "Of course, there are over two hundred African slaves, which ought to make the proposition a good bit more attractive. Lord Seaforth took good care of those slaves. Didn't lose too many of them to disease, which is a good thing seeing that Parliament has made it impossible to replace them."

"The Africans shall not be part of any sale."

Mr. Ross gave me an impatient sniff. "You don't understand, Lady Hood. They're the best thing you've got."

"Perhaps so, but you are going to arrange for their freedom."

"Lady Hood, I must advise you that—"

"There is no argument about this, Mr. Ross. I want it taken care of immediately. Do *you* understand?"

He rose, lifting his hat from the table. "Very well. I urge you, however, to act more wisely in your other transactions—and to act soon. Your creditors may be less forgiving now that Lord Seaforth is gone."

I saw him out myself, as our butler had left upon learning of Father's passing. Caroline was just coming in from her morning ride.

"How did your meeting go?" she asked.

"Quite well." There was no reason to tell her about the slave plantations in Berbice. I preferred that she remember our father at his best. As for the rest, I did not wish to worry her. "The finances will take some work, but I'll straighten them out."

"That's good to hear," she said, smiling. "If there is anything I can do to help, you must let me know."

How glad I was to have her here, even if I must keep certain things from her. "Promise that you'll stay with me, Caroline. I would be terribly lonely without you."

"Of course I'll stay. Why wouldn't I?"

I put my arm around her shoulders. "Tell me honestly, is there no gentleman in your life?"

"A gentleman?" She seemed genuinely surprised.

"Just look at you—so lovely. I can't imagine that you've had no offers of marriage."

"None I would care to consider. Besides, I have no desire to end up like Frances, ridiculed and broken-hearted. She's in love with a Danish sculptor who is much in demand, and I'm afraid success has gone to his head. After promising to marry Frances, he dragged her along with him to Italy, where he proceeded to fall in love with someone else. This was after he had taken quite ill, and Frances had singlehandedly nursed him back to health—only to be told that he no longer needed her."

I had heard none of this before. My heart ached for Frances. Artistic as she was, I supposed it was inevitable she would fall for a sculptor or painter, or even, heaven forbid, a musician.

"I met him when I visited Frances in Italy," Caroline said. "He speaks no English, or so he claims. I think he simply wishes to avoid conversation. He dislikes even his own countrymen, having declared Denmark as fit only for nettles and wild beasts. In my opinion, the latter description suits him rather well. He might be a decent looking fellow if he didn't wear his hair hanging down in a manner everyone agrees looks bizarre."

"Frances is better off with a broken engagement than what sounds like a disastrous match. But whatever her predicament, it should not discourage you from finding a husband, Caroline. I can tell you, from my own experience, marriage is wonderful when one has the proper mate."

Her expression softened. "I know you loved Sir Samuel very much. I'm so sorry for what happened. And now to come home, only to find that Father is gone, and all his responsibilities are yours ..." She hesitated. "Will you have to sell Brahan Castle?"

She had seen through me, but I would not admit to it. "No. I shan't ever sell it. Father may have made mistakes, but if there was one rule he lived by, it was to honor our heritage. That means not only Brahan Castle, but all the land for which the Mackenzies of Kintail have fought and died. As much as he could, he protected our people and their homes."

Even about this, I could not be entirely truthful. Father had indeed cleared some of his lands for sheep; Ian's family was among those displaced. But he could have carried it further than he did. "I'm not saying that Father always adhered to his highest principles; he did not.

But, Caroline, our father had a good heart, and, in ways that may be hard for others to understand, he had a difficult and often lonely life. When he inherited the estate from his brother, it was seriously in debt. Perhaps he could have done well with it if he had started with a clean slate. I don't know ... but now, it doesn't matter what Father did or didn't do. As you say, the responsibility is mine."

And mine alone, I thought to myself.

PART III

CHAPTER THIRTY-FIVE
MAY 1817
EDINBURGH, SCOTLAND

W̲e had met, not really by chance, at a time when I often felt myself drowning with no hope of rescue. The challenges of managing the Seaforth estates, without resources to meet the needs of my tenants, had become overwhelming. I had just received from the solicitor of the Treasury a letter demanding loan payments in arrears. And, that very day, a visit from several chieftains of Clan Mackenzie, whose role was to serve beneath the chief. Beneath *me*.

Their mission on that day, however, was quite the opposite.

"Out of respect for your time of mourning, we have waited to approach you with our concerns." The one who spoke was George Falconer Mackenzie, fourth of Allangrange.

"To what concerns are you referring?" I asked, curious to see how he would phrase his condemnation of womanhood.

"Forgive me, Lady Hood, but surely you understand that, in order for a chief to be effective, he requires the confidence and acceptance of his clan members."

"Or hers," I corrected him.

"The tradition of the chiefdom passing through the male line is a long-honored one. It is regrettable that your brother William could not take over when Lord Seaforth passed. You have our sincere condolences in that regard, as well as for your other losses—needless to say." He glanced at his somber companions, who nodded in unison. "You undoubtedly have your hands full managing the Seaforth estates. Relinquishing the chiefdom should ease your burden considerably."

"I thank you for your sympathies—all of you—and your concerns," I said, not wishing to stir animosity, any more than was necessary. "But I have no intention of relinquishing the chiefdom."

Beneath the portrait of my father, George Mackenzie shifted uneasily in his chair. "As I said, Lady Hood, the support of one's clan is essential. Without it, a chief cannot fulfill his role as a uniter, and the clan, as a whole, suffers. As for our relations with the other clans, the Mackenzies will not abide any loss of prestige."

"As a female chief would automatically produce?" I queried with a raised brow.

"I'm sorry, Lady Hood, but such is the way of the world."

I smiled. "The world is bound to change, Allangrange."

"Perhaps, but not yet."

I struggled to hold my temper. "I have many supporters. The people of Ross-shire stand with me, and I with them. There is no precedent for removing me from my rightly inherited role as chief. Nothing precludes me from succeeding my father. My arms have been recorded, and shall be passed to my male heirs. All has been done with the legal authority of the Lord Lyon." I stopped to take a breath. "Now—may I respectfully suggest that, if our aim is to unite Clan Mackenzie, all of us shall do our part to avoid any appearance of conflict within our ranks. Do I have your agreement on that point?"

"It is a worthy aim," Allangrange conceded.

The silence was tense as I personally escorted the gentlemen to the door. Our meeting had ended abruptly, but I had stated my position and presumably forestalled any further rumblings of discontent—though only time would tell.

That afternoon, I took the carriage to Fortrose Cathedral, wishing to visit the graves of my father and brothers. It was winter and bitterly cold, but I didn't care. It was only the dead in whom I could confide my frustration. Knowing they could not hear me—decaying flesh and bones was all they were now—still I found the ritual of kneeling at their gravestones somehow consoling.

I was on my knees before the monument to my father when a man's voice came from behind me.

"Are you all right, Lady Hood?"

Startled, I turned my head to see who had spoken. The man standing a few feet away was wrapped in a heavy wool cloak, his cheeks ruddy from the cold. A handsome man, I couldn't help but notice, with liquid brown eyes and a mop of curly dark hair. His was a sensitive face, made more so by a look of genuine concern.

"We haven't met before, but our mothers are well acquainted, as both live in Edinburgh. My name is James Alexander Stewart. I hope I've not intruded, though of course I have. But I wish to offer my condolences, belated as they are, for the loss of your brothers and father. I had the honor of attending Lord Seaforth's funeral procession and was greatly moved by it."

I shivered from a sharp blast of icy wind. "Thank you. You are very kind."

"I, too, have family buried here. Whenever I am in the vicinity, I like to stop by and pay my respects. I—I saw you arrive and recognized you from your portrait. The one in your mother's drawing room . . ."

His voice trailed off, and I did not try to fill the silence.

"As I said, I hope you'll pardon the intrusion."

I stood and, brushing dead grass and leaves from my cloak, turned to him. "I'm afraid you have caught me at a bad moment, Mr. Stewart."

"There is no such thing as a bad moment. I believe every moment is precious, even sorrowful ones. Sometimes the only way to understand the depth of love is to experience loss."

I smiled wistfully. "There should be an easier way."

"Your burdens are great, Lady Hood. And, I am certain, difficult to support … alone."

"I cannot deny it. There are times when I wonder if I truly can. But there is no other way when so much depends upon you. Not only the lives of people, but the land we all love so dearly. Even Brahan Castle cries out for help," I said, shaking my head. "But forgive me, I shouldn't be talking this way. I am fortunate to be entrusted with so much."

"I hope you will not think me forward, but I have always wanted to see Brahan Castle from inside. Might I stop by sometime?"

It was indeed very forward to invite himself to my home. And with no introduction other than his own. But since our mothers were friends, I supposed it would be rude of me not to make him feel welcome. "Of course, you must come by. I have thought about arranging for a party of some sort. Perhaps in the spring."

"I shall look forward to it. But, in the meantime, I would very much like to offer my assistance."

"In what regard, Mr. Stewart?" His boldness was slightly unsettling. I was not long out of mourning and had grown accustomed to my solitude. Encouraging the attentions of a gentleman was far from my mind.

"In whatever regard you might allow me, Lady Hood."

The very next day, he arrived on my doorstep with gifts of chocolate and lace. And a Bible. The latter seemed peculiar, until I remembered his acquaintance with my mother. I wondered if she might have encouraged his interest in me—and my lapsed faith? James Stewart was just the kind of man I could imagine her choosing for me. A fine, God-fearing Scotsman. Only later did I learn of his pedigree—grandson of the sixth Earl of Galloway, nephew of the seventh Earl, and his late father, Vice-Admiral Keith Stewart, was a revered officer of the Royal Navy.

Having James in my life was the miracle I had wished for, without knowing it. The second son in line, he had no capital to speak of, but he made up for it with his talents. He had a knack for architectural drawings and a practiced knowledge of construction, having overseen the renovation of his family's ancestral home in southwest Scotland. In the first several months of our acquaintance, he surveyed the Seaforth estates in their entirety. Though I had not yet shared all the details of my indebtedness, he became aware of the dilapidated condition into which some of my properties had fallen, especially Seaforth Lodge on the Isle of Lewis. But James seemed to relish a challenge, and his innate energy and enthusiasm had made me believe that, together, we could achieve something. Mend what was broken, restore what had been lost, make a better future for the people of Ross-shire.

And now, it was all about to begin.

"What a joyous day this is!" Mother said, beaming. We had found a quiet corner, apart from the hundred or so guests invited to the wedding reception at her spacious Edinburgh home, the one she and Father had bought not long before his death. How they had financed such a purchase, I was still trying to unravel. "My dear Mary, I have prayed that you would find happiness again, and now you have. And with such a devout Calvinist! Dare I hope you have finally returned to your faith?"

"You may hope," I said affectionately. Why disappoint her by saying how I really felt? What happened to our family had destroyed whatever faith I might have had in a benevolent creator, and what use did I have for any other sort of God?

"Well, either way," Mother continued with a wave of her hand, "I am certain your marriage shall be blessed. And from what I know of your new husband, he'll be a good deal easier to handle than Francis was. Oh, he was a gem of a man, your father. But hard-headed as they come."

I was grateful for Mother's blessing. There were those in society who would disapprove of my decision to marry, whether to James or anyone else. Those who still clung to the antiquated notion that a widow must remain a widow forever, or at least for longer than I had. I cared nothing for their criticisms. They had no right to judge me, or the love and respect I would always have for Samuel. I was thirty-four, an heiress, and chief of Clan Mackenzie—no longer a young girl in need of permission for my freedom. Not from anyone.

"Here you are! I've been looking everywhere for you." Sporting a wide grin, James strode over to us. I was fascinated by his wondrous combination of gentleness and physical strength. Gifted with broad shoulders and powerful legs and arms, he could fell a pine faster than most of the farm laborers, yet his deep-set eyes and aquiline nose could easily make one imagine him as a painter or a poet.

"Mother was about to instruct me on how to handle you, based on her long experience with my father."

"I am certain you'll be able to work it out for yourself. In fact, you already have. But did you see your sister Frances? She was wandering about looking oddly dazed. Apologized for missing the ceremony and asked if I might inform you that she was here."

I was elated at the news that Frances had resurfaced after a long period of estrangement from the family, or at least its matriarch. "I didn't expect she would come. Please, take me to her, James." I glanced at Mother, whose pursed lips suggested that she had yet to forgive Frances for running off to Italy with a Dutch sculptor notorious for his uncouth behavior.

"She seemed so uncomfortable in the throng, I suggested she wait for you in the garden. There are fewer guests outside."

"Very well, then you can escort Mother back to the party. I'll go and find Frances. The poor dear, she must feel like everyone is gossiping about her."

"I imagine they are," Mother said drily.

I took a circuitous route to the garden, hoping to avoid being detained by well-wishers. Exiting through the rear drawing room, I spotted Frances standing alone, partially shielded by the branches of a silver birch. Even from a distance I could feel her immense sadness; perhaps it was the stoop of her shoulders, or the way she stared into space at nothing.

"Frances, darling!" Eagerly, I swept her into my arms, but she held herself rigid as though we were strangers. "I am so happy to see you."

"I'm sorry I couldn't make it earlier."

"But you are here now. That is what's important."

"I suppose Mother would prefer it if I hadn't come."

"Forget about Mother. This is my wedding, my reception, and it would not be complete without you. Come, let's sit down." I took her by the arm, steering her to a stone bench on the tree's other side. "Oh, it's good to get off my feet!"

"I met Mr. Stewart. He seems very nice."

"You shall get to know him better soon, I hope. We will be traveling to Brahan Castle the day after tomorrow. I want you to come with us."

"No, I couldn't. Really."

"Why not? I doubt that you want to stay here—with Mother."

"I'm staying with a friend outside of town, just for a few days. Augusta, Charlotte, and Helen promised to call in one afternoon. I've not seen them for ages."

"You can see them this evening. They are wandering about somewhere, as is Caroline. But I want you to return with us to Brahan Castle, Frances. It's best for you to be with Caroline and me. And James."

"Caroline is going back with you?"

"Yes, she is. Brahan Castle will always be our family home. You can reclaim your old room."

Her lower lip quivered slightly. "Do you know about all the awful things I've done since I left?"

"What I know is that, unselfishly, you nursed an ailing man back to health. And that he repaid you for your loving kindness with utter faithlessness."

She looked at me with the eyes of a wounded animal. "Perhaps it was my fault. I expected too much from him. He's a brilliant artist, you know. A genius. I think I frightened him with all my talk of marriage and wanting him to meet the family. It was too much."

"Don't make excuses for him. He used you and apparently has shown no remorse whatsoever." I reached for her hands; they were ice cold. "Forget him, Frances. Come home with me. There is much work to be done in Ross-shire. We need to spend more time with our tenants. I'm afraid they feel quite let down these days. But our family has had so many losses—" I stopped short. I had vowed to myself that I would no longer speak of our tragedies. They were in the past and must remain so.

Frances swiped at a tear sliding down her cheek. "If you're certain you want me—"

"Greetings!" Walter Scott popped out from behind the silver birch, causing Frances and me to jump nearly out of our skin. "Sorry if I startled you. I only wanted to offer my congratulations to the bride."

Though I had hoped to arrange a meeting with him during one of my earlier visits to Edinburgh, I'd not seen Walter since leaving London for India. He looked much the same, but his short-cut curls now showed a touch of grey.

"I missed seeing you earlier," I said, standing to offer him a warm greeting.

"Arrived late, I'm sorry. My terrier, Spice, suffers from asthma and is not doing well. Every now and then he has a crisis, and I simply cannot leave him until it passes."

"Nor would I have you do so," I said, recalling how Walter's letters always included references to his dogs, about whom he wrote far more frequently than he did about his five children. "But I do have a bone to pick with you, Walter."

Walter raised an eyebrow. "Yes?"

"As one of the founders of *The Quarterly Review*, I would expect your vigilance concerning the accuracy of its contents. It is not surprising that the Macdonalds would claim a superior position to that of Clan Mackenzie, historically speaking, but surely someone at the *Review* should have investigated their assertion before publishing it for all to read. I submitted a rebuttal, for which I have so far received no acknowledgment."

"I assure you, I wasn't aware," he replied, an embarrassed flush creeping over his face.

"I suspect I know which of your editors is responsible for ignoring me. The one who quite vocally supports the challenge to my chiefdom. You must know who I mean."

"Honestly, I don't always keep up with clan politics, though I should. Especially in this instance. Please accept my deepest personal apology."

Taking pity, I smiled and patted his cheek. "Come now, Walter, you don't really suppose that I would hold you personally responsible? You have far more important work than policing *The Quarterly Review*. My goodness, you are not only Scotland's most esteemed poet but now its premier novelist as well."

"You know, of course, that nothing I have written surpasses the popularity of 'The Lady of the Lake,' for which you, my dear lady, were a major inspiration."

"As you have said before, and I remain most humbled. But you will take care of that other matter, won't you? My rebuttal. Opportunities to speak on behalf of my clan are rare enough these days."

"I will see to it. You have my promise."

I suddenly realized that I had neglected Frances. But when I turned to bring her into the conversation, I discovered she had quietly departed.

"Did you see where my sister went? I meant to introduce her to you."

"She waved to someone, or so it seemed, and then took herself off."

I looked around the garden, hoping to find her engaged in conversation. If she was there, I didn't see her.

"Is that the young lady who was to have married Thorvaldsen?"

"Yes. Being brilliantly artistic herself, the poor thing fell prey to the man's reputed genius and forgot to consider his decency, or lack of it."

"A shame. By the way, I have met your new husband, Mr. James Stewart. Seems a likeable chap. Will you be moving to his Glasserton residence?"

"No, we plan to stay at Brahan Castle. I shall be pleased for him to help me sort out the rather cumbersome details of my father's estate."

"It must be a lot to manage."

I would not have been surprised if he'd heard rumors of the estate's indebtedness, but, by now, I knew enough to keep financial matters close. Creditors can easily become frightened.

"The estate's holdings are significant and rather spread out," I said lightly. "And, like everything else, economic conditions are constantly changing."

"I have thought of you often, Mary, and wondered how you were bearing up under the strain of all your family has endured. I trust this blessed occasion is but the beginning of a long period of happiness in your life. I have no doubt in your ability to overcome all adversity."

CHAPTER THIRTY-SIX
MAY 1819
BRAHAN CASTLE

"The doctor has arrived, madam." Our butler, Cameron, stood in the gallery outside my son Keith's room.

"Please, bring him here." I did not look up from the crib where my one-year-old, whom everyone had taken to calling "the little chieftain," lay with a high fever and persistent cough. His conception had been the biggest surprise of my life. Nearly ten years of marriage to Samuel had produced no children; with James, I was pregnant with our first after only four months. And, if I was not misreading the signs, a second was on the way.

"Afternoon, Mrs. Stewart-Mackenzie. Step aside, and I'll take a look at the lad." Dr. Campbell was well known in the parish for his curt manner but, more importantly, his skill in treating everything from fevers to fractured limbs.

I moved out of his way. "Do you have enough light, Doctor?"

"Yes, yes," he murmured, reaching into the crib to feel Keith's forehead, then his plump cheeks, which were rosier than usual. "How long has he felt warm?"

"A couple of days—not *this* feverish, but warmer than normal."

The baby coughed. A sharp, raspy cough that frightened me.

"How long has that been going on?" Dr. Campbell asked, checking Keith's pulse.

"It started last night."

He frowned. "Probably influenza. Anyone else in the household sick?"

"Not that I am aware." I was becoming more agitated by the second. "How serious is it?"

"Difficult to say. He needs rest and plenty of fluids. Chamomile tea, very diluted, is good. You have a wet nurse?"

"I have preferred to nurse him myself."

"Either way, he needs as much nutrition as possible. Feed him frequently, and keep him wrapped up. Away from drafts."

"Certainly." I hesitated, afraid to ask. "How long do you think it will take him to recover?"

Dr. Campbell crossed his arms over his chest. "That depends on many factors, mostly the strength of his constitution. Influenza is a serious illness, as you must be aware. Many succumb to it, and the very young are especially vulnerable. I'm sorry, but I believe it's best to be honest about such things. One must be prepared for either outcome."

"But—" I stopped, afraid of losing my composure. "I will do as you say, Doctor. When can you return to check on him?"

"In a couple of days. If anything happens in the meantime, send a messenger."

The next day, I received a letter from James. He had been away in Edinburgh for several weeks, visiting his sick brother, and knew nothing of his son's illness. His brother was no better, he said, and a measles outbreak in the city had everyone in a state of alarm. The only good news was that, while in London to see about further delaying our debt payment to the Treasury, he managed the release of five thousand pounds.

I was eager for something to take my mind off worrying about Keith and began immediately to make a list of priorities for the unexpected influx of cash. First was a new schoolhouse for the children of my tenants; the current one was too small, of poor construction, and impossible to heat adequately in the winter months. Churches in two of the parishes were sorely in need of repair. And the lack of roads on

Lewis, a serious impairment to the island's economic development, must begin to be addressed.

As for Brahan Castle, the roof needed work but otherwise it was structurally sound. James's ambitious plans for a new dining room, library, and greenhouse would have to wait.

And our debt to the Treasury? Our creditors? In his letter, James had hinted of a plan for how we could pay off everything. I had yet to hear it.

·   ·   ·

By the time James returned home from Edinburgh, Keith had recovered from his bout with influenza. The first night after his arrival, I told him that I was again expecting.

"You must start now to take better care of yourself," he said. "As long as the weather is damp, no charitable visits, and certainly no social events. I will instruct the servants to be careful about opening windows and doors, but you must have a shawl with you at all times. And wear woolen stockings to bed."

"Really, James, I know how to care for myself."

"But you mentioned occasional cramps. Have you told the doctor?"

"It's nothing. If I were worried, certainly I would talk with him."

James did not appear convinced. "Well, for now, take a glass of sherry with dinner instead of claret. And don't overdo chocolate. Some calf's foot jelly would be good for you."

"Stop it, James! You sound like an old grannie. This is not my first pregnancy, remember?" I softened my tone. "Don't you know that Scottish women are built for bearing children? When they are ready to pop out, we hardly blink."

I smiled at how I could jest in such a way, as Sarah had, after years of being convinced I was barren.

"Come now, tell me about your brother," I said. "He still is not at all improved?"

"As difficult to get along with as ever, but if you mean his health—I'm afraid he showed no improvement while I was there. I'm quite certain his end is near. Mother is also in a miserable way, and I fear she won't last much longer either. She refuses the medicine the doctor gives her. Stubbornness runs in the family, I suppose."

"What about my mother?"

"Your mother's health is fair but, of course, she has complaints. Her digestion is troublesome, and she seldom sleeps well. Misses her eldest daughters, she said. When I asked if that included Frances, her eyes watered up. She asked if I thought she'd been too hard on her."

"I trust you said she had?"

James shifted in his chair. He had never been very sympathetic to Frances's situation. "Your sister has behaved very badly, Mary. Running off with that Thorvaldsen character, living in sin … I don't blame your mother for being disappointed in her."

"Disappointed, perhaps. But turning her back on Frances is an entirely different matter. A mother should never do that to her child, no matter how they disagree."

"Well, your mother seems to have come around. She wants Caroline and Frances to stay with her in Edinburgh. Appears she is ready to smooth things over."

"Caroline? I was hoping she would stay with us."

"Stay with us? For how long?"

"I don't know. For as long as she wants to."

"And Frances?"

The tone of his questioning bothered me. Was he implying that he wished for my sisters to leave? "I would love for both to remain, but Frances needs to make her peace with Mother. Their estrangement has been difficult for her." I hesitated. "I don't know what I would have done without either of them when Keith was ill—and you away longer than you promised."

James appeared contrite, as I had intended.

"Besides that, Caroline is beloved by everyone in the parish. You say I shouldn't be out in my condition. Though I don't agree, it matters less if Caroline is here to carry on with visitations and such. We cannot ignore our duty to those who rely on us for charity and consolation."

"Very well. But it would be a shame not to honor your mother's request. One never knows when the end might come for someone her age. Or any age, for that matter."

I did not need James to remind me of the fickleness of death. "So, what is this mysterious plan you mentioned in your letter—the one you said would settle the estate's debts?"

He lowered his eyes, sipping his claret with a slight frown.

"James? Aren't you going to tell me?" I said, impatient for his response.

He looked up, cleared his throat. "I have been advised to sell the Brahan and Kintail properties. I think, after all, it's a good idea."

I sat bolt upright, disbelieving what I had heard him say. "You are suggesting the sale of my home and the Mackenzies' ancestral lands? Lands that my father and those before him sacrificed everything to protect and preserve?" I slammed my fist on the dining table. "I will not hear of it!"

"You mustn't become agitated, Mary. That is the worst thing you could do for your health—and the baby's."

"I will decide what is good for my health and what isn't," I snapped. "You know perfectly well I have been advised before to sell the very same properties. My answer was, and is, that it shall not be done. Besides, where do you propose we live if Brahan Castle were sold? Seaforth Lodge? When you last saw it, you said the entire west wing was uninhabitable."

"It is recommended that we relocate to my family's Glasserton estate and expand industries on Lewis as a continuing source of income. The island has more potential for profitability than any of the agricultural lands."

Glasserton? I was a Highland chief! I would not make my home in Wigtownshire. James should know better.

I tried to calm down, to consider whether I was being unfair. In the several years since I inherited the Seaforth estates, what had I done to resolve its debts? Merely stalled for more time, just like my father. But if Brahan and Kintail were sold, it would mean the further displacement of families who had lived and worked here for generations. Family farms would become open grazing lands for sheep. The Highlands would lose more of its history, its character. What would be left of it?

"I know you are upset, Mary. But things can't go on as they are. I have spoken about our finances to some very knowledgeable people, as you encouraged me to do. But what good are advisors if one never takes their advice?"

"There are good advisors and bad ones. The good ones do more than simply add up numbers on a page. They consider people's lives."

"That approach didn't work for your father, and it won't for us."

James was right about Father. Maybe I was more like him than I realized. But I hadn't come this far only to give up everything. "We shall do what we can to develop the Isle of Lewis, but without displacing any of our tenants. And I will not consent to selling the Brahan and Kintail properties."

"You are being quite unreasonable, Mary." He sighed, shaking his head. "If you insist, we'll hold off on Brahan and Kintail. But Lewis has to be developed. That means fishing and sheep. Tenants living on a prime location for a fishing station must relocate or become fishermen themselves. Tenants on farms and crofts where pasture is needed for sheep must move elsewhere. We can try to help them relocate on the island, but that may not always be possible." He pushed his chair back from the table. "That's all there is to it, Mary. I'm sorry, but there is no other choice."

I could not remember ever being so angry at James as I was now. Yet I understood that he was trying his best. He was a good man, not the hero that Samuel had been, but, in a different way, he was *my* hero—the one who had given me what I yearned for more than I ever knew. My darling Keith, and now another baby on the way. I hoped the next would be a girl. And that there would be more. No longer was I tormented by thoughts of Coinneach Odhar's last prophecy. While James's faith in God had not quite made me a believer, his staunch rejection of the devil's power had finally convinced me that the end of the Seaforth line had been ordained by nature, not wizardry. I was free of fear.

I owed a great deal to James. I loved him. And love sometimes requires compromise.

But, for the sake of all I held dear, this betrayal of the people of Lewis—*my* people—must be the last.

CHAPTER THIRTY-SEVEN
MARCH 1823
BRAHAN CASTLE

It was a fine March morning. I was finishing my toilette when Caroline popped her head inside my dressing room. "We have a clergy visit this afternoon, don't we?" she asked.

"Yes, at two o'clock. And then a meeting about a house for the new schoolmistress."

"I do hope she has a knowledge of Gaelic. The last one was far too concerned with English tidiness, don't you agree?"

"We shall make certain she understands the importance of tradition. But what I'm most concerned about right now is finding a suitable minister for the people of Lewis. With all the disruption in their lives over the last few years, they need someone of great strength and persuasion."

The clearances on the island, which had made way for fishing stations and sheep pastures, had been painful. But that, together with James's decision to sell his family home at Glasserton following his brother's death, had helped us to avoid bankruptcy. Temporarily.

Sometimes I marveled at the way James and I carried on, day to day, as if there were no final reckoning to come. Perhaps I had learned the lesson of my parents' lives: One can manage well enough by staying just one step ahead of the creditors.

"I have no doubt we shall find the perfect messenger of God's word," Caroline said. "I must say, Mary, it is good to hear you speaking about the importance of the ministry with such conviction."

The passion in my voice surprised me as well. James had encouraged me to establish a relationship with God; I thought of it more as a truce. But what the folk of Lewis needed and what might be lacking in me were two entirely different matters. A strict Calvinist might help to restore order in a land fraught with uncertainty and discontent.

Suddenly, Caroline clapped her hands with a gleeful smile. "When I stepped outside this morning, I could have sworn I felt a touch of spring. Since we have some time before our meetings, shall I find Frances, and the three of us can go for a ride in the pony carriage?"

"Spring cannot come soon enough for me! I'll meet the two of you downstairs in half an hour."

Frances declined to join us, being occupied with a new canvas. She had become quite the painter since her failed love affair. I often teased her, saying that some of Thorvaldsen's genius had rubbed off on her. In truth, I had always thought her immensely talented and believed her newest works were worthy of an exhibition. But Frances was not one to relish the public eye. She was happy enough as a quiet spinster creating masterpieces in the solitude of her third-floor studio.

Wrapped up in double shawls and warm bonnets, Caroline and I headed out to the stables. Old McCullough was sweeping out the stalls.

"Sorry, madam." He scratched his grey head, looking slightly sheepish. "The seat in the pony carriage split right in two, so I took it out. I'm building a new one, nicer than the other, but it won't be ready for a fortnight."

"Oh, that's a pity," Caroline said. "I had my heart set on an outing."

"See if you can't mend it a little sooner, please," I said as we left.

Caroline and I strolled towards the castle, no longer in a rush but simply relishing the fresh, cool breeze. Suddenly, I stopped. "How about the garden bench?"

"What about it?"

"We could put it in the carriage to sit on, couldn't we?"

Caroline studied the scrolled iron bench. "No, it's too heavy."

"The men can lift it. As for the ponies, they pull heavy loads all the time. And the two of us are light as feathers," I added jokingly. Caroline certainly was, but I was still carrying extra weight from my third pregnancy.

"I suppose it's worth a try."

It took only a few minutes for McCullough to harness the ponies and drive the open carriage over to the bench sitting beneath an old Spanish chestnut. Two others were found to help him lift it into the carriage, which proved an arduous task. I felt a bit guilty at how much they struggled. Afterwards, Caroline and I thanked them profusely.

Settling ourselves on the bench, I picked up the reins and off we went. Caroline was right; despite the lingering chill, signs of spring were everywhere. It had been a long, cold winter, but plants and animals alike were making up for lost time. Snowdrops, yellow daffodils, and purple crocuses dotted the gentle hillsides. Above us, a pair of golden eagles flew in ever-widening circles, in search of vulnerable prey.

"I'm so relieved that baby Caroline is feeling better now," my sister said, her eyes on the eagles' perfectly choreographed dance. "It's always frightening when a newborn falls ill. But my little namesake is quite resilient, thank God."

"As are you. Don't think I wasn't aware how poorly you were feeling yourself, but still you kept your vigil over her, day and night. And there I was, good for nothing, too weak to get out of bed. It was simply awful. I can't recall ever being so sick."

"Your body was still recovering from the strain of childbirth. Tell me, Mary—since it appears I shall never find out for myself—does it get easier the more you do it? Having babies, I mean."

"In some ways, yes. In others, no. Each time takes a little more toll on the body, but the mind becomes stronger." I glanced over at my sister, older now but beautiful as always. Among all of us, she was the only one with golden hair, and hers was the fairest complexion. "My darling, you mustn't give up on the idea of having a family. You still have time. I only wish you would look a bit harder for the right gentleman. Even if it means I must lose you."

"Why should I search, when I know I wasn't meant for it? Not everyone is."

"But you are the sweetest, most unselfish person in the world. And brilliant. What a marvelous mother you would make!"

"I'll tell you a secret. Sometimes I wish that I were Catholic so I might live out my days in a nunnery, devoting my life to charity and prayer. I doubt I would miss the rest—except for my family."

"Very well, if that's how you really feel, then let Brahan Castle be your nunnery and I your Mother Superior." I laughed. "Seriously, Caroline, you devote yourself to good works more than anyone I know. If only I could be more like you, I should be most proud of myself."

"Ah, but pride is a sin."

"Of course, you are right. Oh—I almost forgot!" Holding both reins in one hand, I reached for the small reticule on the bench between us. Opening it, I removed the strange object I had discovered only this morning, while going through the contents of an old jewelry box from my days in Barbados. "Look at this, Caroline." I handed her the Obeah charm. "It's the vertebrae from a snake. Do you know where I got it?"

She turned it over in her hand a few times. "Fascinating."

"Remember, in Barbados, when I thought I might cure Father's gout with some medicine from an Obeah-woman? She gave me that charm to ward off evil. I never showed it to anyone. In fact, I had completely forgotten that I had it. Ran across it this morning by accident. Odd, isn't it?"

"That you ran across it after all this time?"

"Well, yes. But I meant the charm itself. It's very odd, don't you think? Six tiny vertebrae, linked together. When I found it this morning, it suddenly occurred to me that each vertebra represented one of us—me and my five sisters." I grinned. "But, of course, it has no such meaning. No meaning at all. It's just a snake's skeleton. Interesting, though, isn't it?"

Caroline studied it again for a moment. "But there are only five vertebrae. Not six."

"What? I'm positive there were six. I counted them this morning. Here, let me see it." I held out my hand, and she dropped the charm into my open palm.

Suddenly, with a terrified squeal, both ponies reared up on their hind legs, whinnying and snorting.

"It's all right. It's all right," I yelled. "Calm down!"

But the ponies weren't listening to me. Panicked, they lurched forward, trying to break free from their constraints. Unable to do so, they took off at a gallop, pulling the carriage behind them with the greatest of force.

The iron bench slid backwards; still I managed to keep my grip on the reins. Clutching the side of the carriage with one hand, with the other I pulled back as hard as I could. But the ponies continued their rampage, bouncing us over rocks and stumps, mowing down anything in their path.

Then I heard a loud crack, followed by a violent jolt of the carriage. The next second, I was thrown over the side, catapulted through the air. I hit the ground face down. Though only vaguely aware of what had happened, I knew right away that my injuries were serious. Every breath I took caused severe pain, and my head felt as though I'd been struck with a sharp, heavy object.

I tried to sit up. Through the blur of blood dripping into my eyes, I saw that the ponies had succeeded in breaking loose from the carriage, which lay on the ground like a felled beast. Next to it was the iron bench.

Then I remembered Caroline.

"Caroline? Caroline! Where are you?"

A low groan came from just in front of the carriage.

"Oh my God!" I could see one of her arms next to the broken wheel. Her sleeve was bloody.

"Don't move, darling! Stay as you are." I attempted to stand but couldn't. Touching my forehead, my fingers came away red. "Caroline, I'm coming. Don't move!"

I started crawling towards where she lay, trapped beneath the carriage. Or was it the iron bench crushing my sister's slender body?

I inched forward, every movement excruciating. Still, I dragged myself closer to the carriage, closer to the bench. "Can you breathe?"

She didn't answer.

"Caroline, can you breathe?"

Another low moan was all I heard, but it was enough. She was alive.

I struggled to take a breath—the pain was staggering. Pushing myself up with my arms, I made it to my knees. Tentatively, I lifted one leg, steadied my foot on the ground and, with all my strength, attempted to stand. But with nothing to support me, my knees gave way, and I fell back.

I raised my head and peered into the distance, my vision worse than before. The ponies were far ahead, grazing near the top of a hill. If I could only walk that far ... I could ride one of them home. I could get help for Caroline.

Blinded by the sun's glare, I closed my eyes. My head pounded. I was nauseated, confused. I had the strangest sensation, as though my soul had left my body. I was looking at myself from above . . . I was dying.

But Caroline—

•   •   •

I awoke with James hovering over me. "Mary, you are home now. You're safe."

"But how—"

"Don't try to talk. I've sent for the doctor. He should be here soon. You're going to be fine."

"Caroline ..."

"She is in her room, in bed."

"Is she all right?" I murmured, amazed that I could speak at all.

"The doctor is on his way," he said again.

I must have fallen asleep as soon as the words passed his lips, because the next thing I knew, Dr. Campbell was standing over me, taking my pulse. His face was blurry, but I could sense his gloom. Was it for me, for Caroline—or both of us?

"Have you seen Caroline?"

"Ah, good to hear you speak. You took quite a spill, didn't you?"

"What about Caroline?"

He relinquished my wrist, laying it on top of the bedcovers. "Your sister is resting quietly."

"Has she spoken?"

"Yes, she can speak. We will know more in a few days."

Ignoring the pain of any movement, I grasped his arm. "Know more? What do you mean?"

"The extent of her injuries."

"But she *will* recover." It was not a question, but I wanted an answer.

"As I said, we will know more in time. Now, the important thing for you—for both of you—is to rest. And not to worry. Nature will take its course, and we will do our best to help it along."

It was useless to demand the truth. No one was willing to tell me. They didn't understand. The fear had returned. The last prophecy of Coinneach Odhar was again echoing in my head, as it used to do. But now only the final part:

She is to kill her sister.

CHAPTER THIRTY-EIGHT

I was forbidden to see Caroline. Not that I could have left my bed in any event, though I would have tried. But James and Dr. Campbell were adamant that I should not move, nor should I ask questions about Caroline's condition. The latter seemed entirely unreasonable and only served to increase my worry. What were they hiding from me? Was it possible that Caroline was dead, and they wished to spare me the news until I had recovered from the worst of my own injuries? Besides the gash across my forehead, the doctor said I had broken a fair number of ribs. I felt battered and weak; because of the opium, I was constantly in and out of consciousness. Were it not for my concern about Caroline and the children, I might not have cared. I was in that state of exhaustion that stifles the will and makes one give in to the body—even to death.

But my death only. I would not give up Caroline.

On the fifth morning following the accident, after several days and nights during which my breathing was noisy and difficult, I seemed to rally a bit. Enough to be curious about what I looked like. James denied my request for a hand mirror. I was beginning to feel that he enjoyed having absolute power over me. As soon as he left my bedchamber, I ordered Sarah to bring me the mirror.

"You won't see much. Your head is bandaged, you know."

"Just give it to me."

Reluctantly she passed me the looking glass. She was right, there wasn't much to see. My forehead was covered with a wrap-around dressing, but there was a dark-blue discoloration all around my right eye, extending down to my cheek.

"Doctor said you must have hit your head on a rock when you were thrown from the carriage," Sarah said.

I handed the mirror back to her. "I am going to ask you something, and I want an honest answer. What is going on with Caroline? No one will tell me. But Sarah—please, I must know."

She glanced over her shoulder. Seeing the door to my room was open, she went to close it before returning to my bedside. "Your sister is in a very bad way. I can't say what exactly her injuries are, but she's got a bandage like yours round her head. Those tending her say she takes little water and eats barely enough to survive."

"Who is taking care of her?" I demanded.

"Mostly Frances. She's a fine nurse, good at following doctor's orders. You might not remember, but she was here with you, too, in the beginning. But you have James and me, so Frances spends most of her time sitting with Caroline. You know, she's written to your mother in Edinburgh, telling her what happened."

What Frances had done was only right, but part of me wished that she had waited so the news would have been more encouraging. I could imagine what a frenzy my mother and sisters would be in. The morbid thoughts that would immediately come to mind. And the blame—it must be mine. But the day was so innocently beautiful, and the coming of spring made it seem as if life always triumphs over death.

"You'll let me know the moment Frances hears from them." I sighed, weary to the bone. It was frustrating how suddenly my strength would leave me. Before I could think of what else I needed to tell her, I was asleep.

• • •

After two weeks in bed, I was able to be moved to the sofa. It was a relief to be around some activity, with servants coming and going, and those responsible for my care able to look in on me without feeling they must stay. I was still in pain with each breath I took, but not as much as before. I was assured by James that Caroline was also getting better. Still, I could not see her, and I dared not attempt it on my own.

I began asking Frances for a daily report on our sister's condition. The information she provided was always sketchy and lacked the confidence I would assume if Caroline's progress were as steady as James implied. Then, on the seventeenth day, Frances let slip that the doctor had cut off Caroline's hair—all of it.

"Why was that necessary?" I demanded. "After so much time, when she is improving every day?"

Frances appeared flustered. "I don't know, but Caroline was so good about it. She was bantering with the doctor as he did it."

"That doesn't mean a thing, Frances. You know Caroline would make the best of anything, no matter how she felt."

Frances hung her head, and when she looked up again, I would have sworn she had aged ten years. "I'm sorry, Mary. I can't do this any longer—lying to you. It isn't right."

My heart froze. Was Caroline dead? "Tell me—everything."

"The doctor has bled her twice already. Today was the third time. Caroline teased about that, too—saying he wouldn't be happy until she fainted. And she almost did. Afterwards, she told him she hoped it would be the last time, because she felt so very weak. But the doctor showed her how little blood she had given up and said he must do it again."

"Oh my God. They are torturing her." I covered my face with my hands. "It's a nightmare, Frances. Our most darling Caroline—she doesn't deserve this." I dropped my hands, confronting Frances with fire in my eyes. "You must take me to her. I won't be kept away any longer."

Frances gave me one of her helpless looks. "The doctor is very much against it, Mary. For both your sakes. Please, be patient a bit longer. Things will get better, I promise."

"You promise? How can you possibly promise, after what you just told me?"

Upset, Frances turned her face away. "You are right; I can't promise. But it's best if you wait. Mother and our sisters are on their way. Together, we will be stronger. Caroline will rally. You'll see."

I had little choice but to accept what Frances said. But if what Caroline needed most was not to be disturbed, as everyone kept telling me, then why was it a good idea for them to come? Unless … unless it was to say their final goodbyes.

That evening, when James came to my bedchamber to kiss me goodnight, as he always did, he brought me his Bible.

"When you are up to it, Mary, I want you to read every day. It will give you the fortitude to deal with whatever God's will proves to be. We both have been lax in our attention to the scriptures, and that must change."

"At the moment, I prefer to put my faith in Dr. Campbell," I said, unable to control my irritation with James's meddling. He knew I was not a reader of scripture. If I felt the Bible could console me, or provide me with the answer to why this tragedy had occurred, wouldn't I have asked for it myself?

James frowned his disapproval. "I know you don't mean that, Mary. Not in the way it sounded. There is not a doctor in the world who can effect a cure without help from God. You need to remember that."

"I will remember whatever I choose." I was ashamed of how I was treating him but frustrated by my helplessness. James was becoming a tyrant, forcing his faith upon me, keeping me from my own sister. "When do you expect Mother and the others to arrive?"

He laid the Bible on my night table. "Probably the day after tomorrow."

I was surprised at how soon.

"Tomorrow I have a clergyman coming," he said quietly. "I thought Caroline would want that. And another doctor."

"Another doctor? Why?"

"I have learned of Dr. Macdonald's success in aiding the recovery of one of our tenant's sons who suffered a similar accident. I thought it could cause no harm to bring him in for a look at Caroline, just to be certain Dr. Campbell is doing all that can be done. You have no objection, do you?"

"Since when are you asking for my opinion on anything?"

"Mary …" James took my hand. "I know how difficult this has been for you. Believe me, I haven't enjoyed making decisions on your behalf, but it was necessary. Listen—" He gave my hand a gentle squeeze. "Tomorrow you shall see Caroline. Before the rest of your family arrives. All right?"

My smile was tentative. While I was elated to finally have the chance to see her, I was also afraid. What would I discover?

"Now get some rest." He extinguished the oil lamp and tiptoed from the room, as though he were putting an infant to bed.

I awoke half a dozen times during the night, troubling dreams and images running through my mind. Exhausted, I would fall back asleep only to wake again from a fresh nightmare. When the first rays of sun peeked through a gap in the velvet curtains, all I could think of was seeing Caroline. What I would say to her. How I would keep from crying.

It was late morning by the time James helped me down the long gallery to Caroline's room. Standing outside the closed door, I took a deep breath, something that still caused me pain. Already I felt faint at the prospect of seeing the damage I had done to my most beloved sister. If ever I needed to pray, it was now—and so I did.

James opened the door, walked me inside, and assisted me into the chair beside her bed. Caroline had seen us enter, and her face brightened with a smile.

"Mary, you look a mess," she teased. She obviously spoke only with great effort, and my heart sank. Looking at her, she was a ghost of her former self. Pale, emaciated, and drained of life's energy. I could easily believe Frances's account of how little blood Dr. Campbell had got out of her the last time he tried. As for visible signs of injury, all I could see was a wicked gash across her forehead, which was healing at about the same rate as mine, and the discoloration that went with it. The rest of her body was covered by quilts, offering no clue as to the condition of her torso and limbs.

So absorbed was I in assessing her appearance that, at first, I failed to notice the man in rolled-up shirtsleeves and no jacket, standing on the opposite side of the bed. Whatever he was doing there, he had stopped to observe me.

"Mrs. Stewart-Mackenzie, this is Dr. Macdonald," James said. "I mentioned to you that I wished to hear his opinion on your sister's condition and treatment thus far."

"Yes, I am anxious to hear it as well. But—" I hesitated, glancing at Caroline. Her eyes had drifted closed. "If you gentlemen would give my sister and me a few minutes alone …"

"Of course." Dr. Macdonald spoke before James could consider a different answer. The two men went out, closing the door behind them. I leaned in, touching Caroline's hand.

"Darling? Are you still awake?"

Her eyelids opened slowly, as though even so small a movement was a trial.

"I wanted to come before now, but they wouldn't let me. I kept asking about you, and no one would tell me anything. But now—" I swallowed, but the lump in my throat refused to budge. "Finally, we are together. Oh, Caroline—can you ever forgive me for my stupidity? The garden bench—it was a terrible idea. But I never thought—"

"Mary—" The sudden firmness in her voice made it seem as though someone else had spoken, not the frail shell of a woman before my eyes. "It isn't your fault. Don't you see?"

I had known she would never lay the blame on me, no matter the truth of it. But I wished she would. I did not want her to make excuses for my failure to protect her.

"Haven't I always longed for heaven?" she said. "I've seen a glimpse of it now, and it's beautiful."

"No, you are mistaken." I could not allow her to think this way. It would mean the end of her. "Whatever you saw was only meant to give you hope. The doctor says you will recover, but it's going to take time."

I was lying. Neither doctor had ever spoken to me of her recovery. Not yet. But I could not let her believe that she was dying. If I had learned anything from my time in Barbados, it was the power of belief. I had witnessed it in India, too. And here, in the Highlands. Everywhere it was the same: When a person believes in something with their entire being, it can easily become a self-fulfilling prophecy.

But worse yet is to believe without even being aware of it.

"Did you hear me, Caroline? I said that you are *not* going to die. Heaven will have to wait for my darling sister. The rest of us still need her. Have they told you that Mother is on her way to help nurse you until you can be on your own again?"

"Yes, Frances told me. And the rest of them, too."

"Everyone wants to help."

A slight smile played at the corners of Caroline's cracked lips. "I am grateful," she said. "I only hope they get here soon. There isn't much time."

My blood turned to ice. "You haven't been listening to me, darling. You must stop thinking like that. The most important thing now is to believe."

"But I do believe, Mary. That's why I am happy. God wants me with him. I am truly blessed."

There was a tap at the door, and Mother entered the room, hurrying as best she could to Caroline's bedside. She must have just arrived and had not even stopped to remove her cloak.

"We started packing the moment we received Frances's letter." Mother kissed Caroline's bandaged forehead before turning to look at me. "I have been so worried about you both."

"We are on the mend," I replied, glancing at Augusta, Charlotte, and Helen hovering in the doorway, as though afraid to venture inside. "All of you, come in. You needn't be shy."

"We're not shy," Augusta retorted. "But James advised that Caroline might be sleeping. That's what she does most of the time, he said."

"Caroline is wide awake. And she's been looking forward to your visit. Haven't you, dear?" I said, trying to appear as normal as possible. Though soon enough they would see that I was still unable to walk on my own.

"Thank you for coming," Caroline murmured.

"You don't need to thank us," Augusta said. "We could not have lived with ourselves if we had missed the chance to see you."

I threw her a warning look, which she did not appear to understand.

"There will be plenty of opportunities for all of us to be together," I said, "but it's wonderful to have everyone here. The weather is turning lovely, and we've much to talk about."

"Can Caroline get out of bed?" Helen asked. Charlotte gave her a sharp jab in the ribs.

"Not for a few days yet," I replied.

Mother, who had been tenderly stroking Caroline's cheek, suggested that her daughters might wish to freshen up a bit. I readily agreed, saying I must lie down for a while. Mother should have some time alone with Caroline.

James must have been waiting just outside, because he appeared within seconds of my declaration. As soon as my sisters had left, and after urging Mother to make herself comfortable, he helped me from the chair. Acting as my crutch, he steered me out of the room and down the gallery, towards my bedchamber.

"Is Dr. Macdonald still here?" I asked. "I want to speak with him."

"I'm afraid he's gone."

"But what did he say about Caroline?"

"He believes Dr. Campbell has done everything possible for her."

I halted in the middle of the gallery. "And what does that mean? She will continue to improve under his care?"

"He didn't say exactly that."

"Then what *did* he say?" I understood that James was trying to spare me, but I would no longer stand for him skirting around the truth.

"I inquired if there was any hope. And he answered, 'There is always hope.'"

I almost asked if he wasn't confusing the doctor with the clergyman; but, of course, he wasn't. Dr. Macdonald was simply being honest: He didn't know whether Caroline would live or die.

No one did.

CHAPTER THIRTY-NINE

I woke up in a feverish sweat. My room was dark, no sliver of morning sun between the drawn curtains. I did not know how long I had been asleep, only what had awakened me. A nightmare more wrenching than any I'd ever had.

Caroline was dead.

It felt so real. I had gone to her room to visit her. But when I entered, I saw that her canopy bed had been replaced by a closed casket, draped with a cloth of white silk. I approached it noiselessly, as though I were afraid of waking her. Standing beside the coffin, I ran my hand over the smooth white cloth, noticing that everywhere I touched instantly turned blood-red. I looked at my hand; it was perfectly clean and white. And then I heard Caroline's voice from inside the coffin. "You won't ever find the reason until you stop looking for it."

Now I lay awake, thinking about what she meant. But it was not Caroline speaking. It was my inner voice, telling me how foolish I was to believe I could find a way around Coinneach Odhar's curse. Ignore it, decry it, fight it. None of it had worked. And now, if Caroline was dead …

I struggled to sit up and swing my legs over the side of the bed. Every part of me hurt, but pain was the least of my concerns. I held on to the edge of the night table as I stood, waiting a few moments to be certain I was steady on my feet. I was not supposed to walk on my own, but I didn't care.

Taking tiny steps, one by one, I reached the door and opened it. The gallery was without light, but I could navigate the path to her room even with my eyes closed. Using the wall for support, I inched my way towards the bedchamber where Caroline had lain for weeks. And yet it seemed so much longer since I smiled at her beneath the early spring sky, the two of us closer than ever. Sisters. The best of friends.

My eyes welled up with tears, and I stopped to wipe them with my free hand.

Arriving at her door, I turned the handle and pushed. The door creaked, announcing my presence. There was no other sound; it seemed that Caroline had not awakened.

A lamp had been left burning low, I supposed so she would not awake in the night to blinding darkness. With tottering baby-steps, I crossed to the bed and grabbed hold of the carved wooden post at its head. Caroline's eyes were closed. A slight smile lifted the corners of her sweet lips. Perhaps she was dreaming of happier times, of the joys that awaited her once this living nightmare was past.

But I had to be certain.

Carefully, I pulled down the quilts that were tucked under her chin, revealing just enough of her nightdress to confirm the steady rise and fall of her chest. Thank God! She was alive.

"Is she all right?"

Startled, I twisted around and would have lost my balance if not for the bedpost. "Augusta! What are you doing up at this hour?"

"I should ask the same of you. I thought you weren't allowed to walk without help, but it seems you are better off than we were led to believe."

I could not miss the prickly edge to her tone. "I shouldn't be up, it's true. But I wanted to check on Caroline."

"So do I." She came to stand next to me. In the soft lamplight, her reddish curls cascading down her back, she looked like a Rembrandt painting. I had never fully appreciated how very lovely she was as a woman in her thirties. "I had the most awful dream," she said in a whisper, staring down at our sister, who still hadn't moved.

"I did, too. But thankfully, it was just a dream."

Augusta turned to me. "Caroline is going to die."

The anger in me rose up like a fiery dragon. "How dare you say such a thing. And *here*, standing right next to her bed! What if she were to hear you?"

"She knows it herself, Mary. In fact, everyone knows it—except perhaps the one responsible for it."

Her poison arrow hit its mark. "You should not speak if you are unaware of the facts," was all I could think of to say. It was a lame rebuttal. In my heart, I knew she was right.

"Perhaps there are things I don't know," she said with a touch of contrition. She reached down to stroke Caroline's cheek, the worst thing she could have done. Our sister awoke with a jolt.

"Oh!" Caroline saw us, and appeared relieved. "Is it morning?"

"Not yet," I said. "Augusta and I wanted to make sure you were sleeping soundly. Looks like you were—until we woke you. I'm sorry, darling."

"Don't be sorry."

"Go back to sleep. We'll see you in the morning," I said, making sure the quilts I had displaced were pulled tight again. The gesture made me think for a moment of my children. How neglected they must feel, their mother unable to care for them with the closeness that we so loved. But I would have many years more with them. Would I with my darling Caroline?

Augusta and I needn't have worried about having interrupted her slumber. Already her eyes were closed, and she was breathing in the soft way of sleepers.

"Would you mind helping me back to bed?" I asked Augusta.

"Of course not." She gazed lovingly at Caroline, peaceful as an angel. "Every time I look at her, I fear it will be the last. I dreamt that she died in my arms. And I have the strongest feeling she will—today."

Caroline's eyelids opened. "You must call for the clergyman. Now, please."

I wished I could slap Augusta across the face. But what good would it do? She had no understanding of what she'd done. "No, sweetheart. Augusta was only speaking of a dream she'd had. It wasn't real. You must go back to sleep. We'll talk in the morning."

"Please … call him now."

"I'll go and find James." Augusta said.

"No, you won't." I laid a hand on her arm. "Caroline is only reacting to what you said. You've frightened her."

She yanked her arm away. "You are not going to pin the blame of whatever happens to Caroline on me, when everybody knows the truth. It was you, Mary. It's always been you." She started towards the door. "I'm finding James and telling him to send for the clergyman, as Caroline wishes."

"Augusta—" I called for her to stop, but she did not.

Caroline's hand reached out from beneath the covers. "Mary, I tried …"

Her breathing was labored, her hand losing its grip. How could I have let things get so out of hand with Augusta? All it had done was to upset Caroline, something she could ill afford.

"Please, forget about Augusta. Our quarrel had nothing to do with you. It was just one of those foolish spats between sisters."

There was no response. Not a word. Not a breath.

At first, I could not believe that my bright little bird had flown away, without a last song or a final flutter of wings. In the dead of night, when she loved the sunrise most of all. I had always thought, if there is a God, Caroline must be his most perfect creation.

But now I was more certain than ever. There was no God. Or He would have saved her.

CHAPTER FORTY

"A re you sure you don't want to be downstairs with the others?" James said, sitting on the edge of my bed. I was curled up under several quilts, my back to him.

"They don't want me there."

"Of course they do. Why would you say such a thing?"

"You must know what they are thinking."

"If you mean Augusta—"

I rolled over. "She's been going on to everyone about how Caroline's death is all my fault. But I can't blame her; I feel the same."

James was silent for a moment. "Apparently, your sister attributes all the tragedies that have befallen your family to the Brahan Seer's curse. Augusta does not understand the ways of God, though your mother is trying to talk sense into her."

I stared at James, tempted to throw everything in his face. Without realizing, I'd allowed him to convince me that faith could defeat the powers of evil. If not my own faith, then his. I had let down my guard.

"And if it *was* the Seer's curse that took Caroline? Wouldn't that make *me* his agent of evil?"

"Mary! Do not ever let me hear you utter such blasphemy again."

"But how can I think otherwise? After all that has happened? What else would you call it but the work of the devil?"

James seemed truly horrified by my words, and why shouldn't he be? His wife and the mother of his children, an agent of the devil—unwitting or not? But instead of recoiling from me, he gathered me into his arms.

"Mary, you mustn't do this to yourself. I don't believe that Coinneach Odhar had the gift of Second Sight, but if he did—" James hesitated, even the possibility difficult for him to acknowledge "—but if he did, his last prophecy is spent. The curse on the Seaforth line has run its course. The future is what we shall make it—you and I, together." He raised my chin with his finger. "Listen to me, Mary. You have said it yourself, many times. The wellbeing of twelve thousand souls is in our hands, people who have little choice but to trust us to look after them."

"And how are we to do that? We can't even look after ourselves. Sometimes I think the easier way would be to leave it all behind. Let the creditors have everything! Start again somewhere else."

"That is not Mary Stewart-Mackenzie speaking! Not the Mary I know. You can't have forgotten." He kissed my cheek. "You are chief of Clan Mackenzie."

Such a lofty title, perhaps with little meaning anymore. A symbol of a rapidly fading past. But I should not need James prodding me to defend what remained of my clan's proud legacy.

There was much in our history to be revered. Much in our Highland traditions worth saving.

I looked at James, so serious and sincere, appreciating him perhaps as never before. My husband was not a Mackenzie by birth, but he had taken my name as a show of faith. And he believed in me. Even now.

"You realize, don't you, that I shall carry the stigma of the Seer's prophecy for as long as I live. And my darling Caroline—the best and purest of us . . ." My voice caught. "I shall always feel responsible for her death."

"We all mourn her loss, and will forever. But the best way you can honor Caroline's memory is by continuing to devote yourself to the people of Ross-shire. That's what you are called to do, Mary."

I remembered for a moment how I used to envy those with the power to make a difference in the world. I would think to myself *If only I could change even one life for the better.* I hoped, by now, I had. But there were so many others, people desperate for help. For someone simply to care. People right here in Ross-shire, my home.

I sat up in bed, pain ripping my insides. I could endure it. All of it. For Caroline. For the others taken from me, and the ones who still remained. My family. My clan.

And no future chief of the Mackenzies shall bear rule at Brahan or in Kintail.

So says the last prophecy of Coinneach Odhar.

I almost had to smile.

He was wrong.

EPILOGUE
NOVEMBER 1862
FORTROSE, ROSS-SHIRE,
SCOTLAND

The procession headed for the graveyard of the ancient Fortrose Cathedral was one of the largest the Highlands had ever seen, more than one hundred and fifty carriages and many thousands of mourners on foot. Mary Elizabeth Frederica Stewart-Mackenzie, once known as Lady Hood, had passed at the age of seventy-nine in her ancestral home, Brahan Castle. She had borne six children, three girls and three boys. Two sons had predeceased her, as had her husband James and, almost fifty years earlier, her first husband Sir Samuel Hood.

Among her mourners were persons of wealth and renown, but most were simpler folk. Some as children had romped alongside her across the moors, for the innocence of youth takes little note of rank and circumstance. And when, later, she returned home—bereaved of father and brothers and husband—they knew her as their chief, proud as any before her.

But all things come to an end, as did the Seaforth line, the noble family's estates, and now, the lady of the last prophecy.

"Such a devout woman." An elderly mourner, her plain woolen cloak scant protection from the damp and chill, wiped a tear from her eye as she plodded along the road to the cathedral's burying ground. "A true saint, she was."

The young woman walking beside her looked puzzled. "How can you say that, when she sold the land out from under her clansmen and their families? I tell you, I wouldn't be here except for you asking me to, Grannie. My Jaimie's family won't ever recover what they lost 'cause o' her."

"Miss Mary couldn't help what happened. She wasn't the start of it, and she held out longer than most. When you get to be my age, dearie, you'll understand. Nothin' ever stays the same, no matter how we want it."

"Maybe so. But what about her sister? The one she killed, just like the Seer said she would."

"An awful accident, it was. They say Miss Mary spent the rest of her life atoning for it. Plenty of good work she did. Look how many have come out to wish her eternal peace! They won't forget her kindness."

"There's other folk don't like that she brought all those preachers here, with their fiery talk and stern warnings. And she wasn't even a believer herself. You never heard that?"

"I dinna listen to gossip. I've got my own eyes to see with."

"You ever see her at church?"

"Most likely I did."

"When was the last time?"

"Stop badgering me, girl!" the old woman growled. "You know my memory isny what it used to be."

She trudged along with her head bent, thinking. Perhaps praying. Suddenly she stopped, grabbing her granddaughter's arm.

"Whatever happened to her father, her brothers, her sister—it was God's will, plain and simple. God's will."

She drew in closer, her voice a whisper now. "But, dearie, don't you ever forget there's evil in this world. And where it's gunna strike next, only the devil knows."

AUTHOR'S NOTE

The story of Mary Elizabeth Frederica Mackenzie takes place primarily in the Regency era, a time when society's roles for women were strict and narrowly defined. Mary appears to have often skirted the worst of these constraints. In my research on her life, I discovered varying assessments of her character, described as everything from "saintly" to "scandalous," but most commentators, past and present, acknowledged her adventurousness. One modern historian suggested that Mary may have been the "first feminist," a claim that would be difficult to prove. But according to an entry in her India travel journal—a copy of which I obtained through the National Registry of Scotland—she was more than slightly miffed when the young Rajah of Mysore greeted her by saying he was almost as glad to see her as if her husband had come, too. And, of course, there is her claim to the chiefdom of Clan Mackenzie following her father's death, a claim widely disputed.

Mary's political and moral views on slavery and other aspects of British colonialism were not explicitly stated in her journal or any personal correspondence I was able to access through the Registry. However, her father's campaign against the brutality shown towards enslaved Africans in Barbados, where he served as Governor from 1801–1806, is well documented. Additionally, Mary's brother William, a Member of Parliament until his untimely death in 1814, is on record advocating an immediate end to the slave trade. One could reasonably assume that these attitudes were likely to be shared by Mary.

On the broader issue of British colonialism in India, while on her 1813 journey to the Kingdom of Mysore, she noted these reflections in her journal: "In walking over these deserted mansions of the Sceptered dead, I contemplated an awful instance of human vicissitudes. These so lately the scenes of the pleasures and the magnificence of a great Prince have now passed into the hands of a Company of merchants in a remote island, whose very existence is hardly understood by the natives of India ... Now his wives, children, and all his family ... are prisoners and captives, without prospect of release."

Mary was not a crusader or activist, being very much entrenched in the social order of her day. But it is recorded by many who knew her, or knew of her, that Mary possessed a kind heart. I believe it more than likely that her scruples were informed at a relatively young age by the harsh realities she observed in colonial Barbados, and her later exposure to the plight of native peoples in India seems to have evoked at least sympathy, if not regret.

Mary was undeniably ahead of her time. There were those who criticized her freewheeling manner, especially her friendships with prominent men—some of whom may, or may not, have been lovers. I did not delve into all these relationships, but touched upon her friendships with Henry Russell and Sir Walter Scott; the latter's admiration for Mary (by all accounts purely platonic) is apparent in his description of her as having "the heart of a chieftainess, through and through."

There are a great many gaps in our knowledge about Mary. As a writer of historical fiction, I'm not bothered by the missing pieces of the puzzle. In fact, I welcome them. To me it's as important to explore speculative aspects of a character as factual. Nevertheless, I have tried, as much as possible, to respect the truth of what is known of Mary Mackenzie and to fairly intuit the rest. In my Acknowledgments, I name a variety of resources that were important in establishing a framework for the development of Mary's character as well as that of her father and mother, husbands, and siblings.

The legend of the Brahan Seer, also known as Coinneach Odhar, was what first drew me to Mary's story. I learned of the Seer early in 2023 from a remarkable woman, Jude McKenzie, an organizer of Celtic festivals in the United States. Until then, I was unaware of this controversial figure, who some regard as the Celtic version of Nostradamus. It should be noted that the Seer's prophecies were handed down by oral tradition until historian Alexander Mackenzie collected and documented them in his book, published in 1877, *The Prophecies of the Brahan Seer*. In conveying the precise content of the last prophecy—the ruin of the Seaforth line, the return of the white-hooded lassie to inherit her father's crumbling estate, and the subsequent "killing" of her sister—I relied upon Alexander Mackenzie's wording, even though his book was written well after the events of my story occurred. The authenticity of the numerous prophecies attributed to the Seer has been refuted by most serious scholars. Nevertheless, questions remain and continue to tantalize would-be believers.

I was astounded that, as far as I could determine, no one has previously published a historical novel about the fascinating life of Mary Elizabeth Frederica Mackenzie or attempted to understand the impact the Seer's prophecy must have had on her personal outlook and religious faith. As I discovered more about Mary, I found her to be the sort of hero I love. Bold yet kind, philosophically inclined, and devoted to family and duty. I loved every minute of researching and writing her story. *The Seaforth Heiress, Lady of the Last Prophecy* is the second novel (following *Sisters of Castle Leod*) in the series Historic Women of the Highlands.

ACKNOWLEDGMENTS

There are many resources without which the writing of this book would have been impossible. Among the most important were the historical documents accessed through the National Registry of Scotland, which included personal correspondence to and from Mary Elizabeth Frederica Mackenzie and many pages of entries in her India travel journal. These materials were invaluable in providing insight into Mary's life and that of her family, including their conflicting emotions and family squabbles following Caroline's death as predicted by the Brahan Seer.

I am indebted to the meticulous historical research on the life of Lord Seaforth (Francis Humberston Mackenzie, Mary's father) in the comprehensive work *Lord Seaforth: Highland Landowner, Caribbean Governor* by Finlay McKichan (Edinburgh University Press, 2018). My understanding of Britain's colonial conquests and practices in India was informed greatly by William Dalrymple's book *White Mughals: Love and Betrayal in Eighteenth-Century India* (William Collins, an imprint of Harper Collins Publishers Ltd., Harper Perennial 2004 edition), in which the tragic story of Henry Russell's love affair with a high-ranking Muslim woman was first revealed. I discovered a wealth of information about Mary in a little book by Alastair McIntosh, now out of print, *Island Spirituality: Spiritual Values of Lewis and Harris* (The Islands Book Trust, 2013).

My research on the practices of Obeah was aided by the impressive studies of Jerome S. Handler, author of "Slave Medicine and Obeah in Barbados, Circa 1650 to 1834" (*New West Indian Guide*, 2000, www.jstor.org). On similar subjects, a book by Londa Schiebinger, *Secret Cures of Slaves: People, Plants, and Medicine in the Eighteenth-Century Atlantic World* (Stanford University Press, 2017), provided many interesting facts. *Slave Society in the City* by Pedro L.V. Welch (first published by Ian Randle Publishers, 2003) painted a realistic picture of the lives of enslaved Africans in Bridgetown, Barbados during the British colonial period. *Life in India: Or, Madras, the*

Neilgherries, and Calcutta by John Welsh Dulles (Hardpress, 2017) offered helpful information on the landscape of Madras during the time of Mary's residence in Admiralty House. *Highland Second-Sight,* edited by Norman Macrae (AlbaCraft Publishing, 2017), introduced me to the complete prophecies of the Brahan Seer, as did *The Prophecies of the Brahan Seer* by the noted scholar Alexander Mackenzie (web edition, Global Grey, 2023). Additionally, the website of the Clan Mackenzie Initiative (clanmackenzie.org) provided wide-ranging articles on many aspects of Mackenzie history, including a balanced discussion of the arguments for and against the existence of the Brahan Seer.

I appreciate the other sources, too numerous to list, from which miscellaneous facts relevant to my characters and settings were readily available.

My thanks to the entire crew at Black Rose Writing, especially Reagan Rothe whose publishing savvy is legendary among his growing stable of authors. Thanks as well to my editors in the United Kingdom, Eleanor Leese, whose analysis of my manuscript was eye-opening, and Sarah Dronfield, whose ever-vigilant eye for errors of all sorts helps me sleep at night.

Finally, unending gratitude to my husband Bob for supporting me in what I love to do. His patience in the face of neglect has grown in proportion to our love, and both, by now, are enormous.

READING GROUP GUIDE

1. As *The Seaforth Heiress* opens, Mary Mackenzie is already aware of the Brahan Seer's prophecy about the coming ruin of her family and the possibility of her own role in its fulfillment. Yet she is determined not to believe in the "gift of seeing" or other forms of magic. Does her visit to an African Obeah-doctor on the island of Barbados suggest that she is more open to the possibility of magic, or supernatural powers, than she wishes to admit? What significance does the Obeah charm have to Mary's story?

2. What do you think is Mary's primary motivation for marrying Sir Samuel Hood? Is it love? Admiration? The promise of adventure? An opportunity to leave Barbados? Desire for a stimulating life in London? Family life and children? Something else?

3. Do you feel that Mary challenges the status quo of her time? Would you say that, relative to most women of her era, she is a "feminist"? Is her criticism of British colonialism deeply felt, or do her convictions have limits?

4. Which of these men in Mary's life do you think was most important to her later development as a woman of strong character? Her father, Lord Seaforth? Her first husband, Sir Samuel Hood? Her second husband, James Alexander Stewart?

5. Mary and her entire family to some extent live under the shadow of the Seer's curse. In your life, have you ever had a strong sense of a specific fate, something inevitable and beyond your control, that has caused you fear or worry?

6. What event in the story do you feel is the first "turning point" in Mary's attitude towards the Brahan Seer's prophecy? How does her attitude change throughout the book?

7. Should landowners such as Lord Seaforth and, later, Mary and James be held accountable for the disruption caused by the Highland clearances? Or were these landowners, as much as their tenants, victims of inevitable forces of economic and social change?

8. What was the root of Mary's battle with religious faith? If there were multiple causes, what were they?

9. Was Augusta's insistence on blaming Mary for Caroline's death consistent with how she is portrayed earlier in the story? How?

10. In the Epilogue, on the occasion of Mary's funeral procession, we learn that she was greatly beloved for her kindness and good works. Does this signify a change in her character following Caroline's death, or had she always been devoted to her tenants and her clan? Do you believe in good works as an atonement for sin?

ABOUT THE AUTHOR

Elizabeth Hutchison Bernard is the author of bestselling historical novels. Her 2023 release *Sisters of Castle Leod* is Book 1 of the series *Historic Women of the Highlands*. The novel, inspired by true events, is an Amazon Kindle #1 Bestseller (Historical Biographical Fiction, Historical Literary Fiction), winner of the 2023 Maxy Award for Historical and Adventure Fiction, and an Editors' Choice of the Historical Novel Society. *The Seaforth Heiress: Lady of the Last Prophecy* is Book 2 in the series. Elizabeth's biographical novel *Temptation Rag* (2018) is hailed by Publishers Weekly as a "resonant novel... about the birth and demise of ragtime... in which romance and creative passions abound." Her historical suspense-thriller *The Beauty Doctor* (2017, 2024), finalist for the Eric Hoffer Book Award, is a gripping, fast-paced mystery set in New York City during the Edwardian era. Elizabeth currently lives in Arizona. Learn more about her books at www.EHBernard.com.

OTHER TITLES BY
ELIZABETH HUTCHISON BERNARD

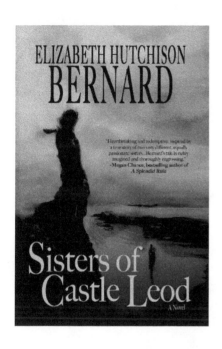

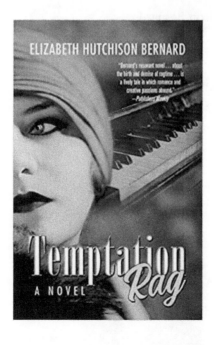

YOUR OPINION COUNTS

Word-of-mouth is crucial for any author to succeed. If you enjoyed *The Seaforth Heiress*, please leave a review online—anywhere you are able. Even just a sentence or two makes all the difference and would be very much appreciated.

Thanks!
Elizabeth Hutchison Bernard

We hope you enjoyed reading this title from:

BLACK ROSE
writing™

www.blackrosewriting.com

Subscribe to our mailing list – *The Rosevine* – and receive **FREE** books, daily deals, and stay current with news about upcoming releases and our hottest authors.
Scan the QR code below to sign up.

Already a subscriber? Please accept a sincere thank you for being a fan of Black Rose Writing authors.

View other Black Rose Writing titles at
www.blackrosewriting.com/books and use promo code **PRINT** to receive a **20% discount** when purchasing.

Printed in the USA
CPSIA information can be obtained
at www.ICGtesting.com
LVHW040330290924
792368LV00001B/2